FOUNDED ON BLOOD AND MAGIC

FOUNDED ON BLOOD AND MAGIC

THE HOUSE OF WARD BOOK ONE

A.R. ABBOTT

Lost Warren Books

First paperback edition July 2025

ISBN 978-1-967520-0008

Published by Lost Warren Books LLC.

www.arabbott.com

ALSO BY A.R. ABBOTT

Bonded by Friendship and Fate: The House of Ward Book Two

Strengthened by Love and Fire: The House of Ward Book Three

Challenged by Tradition and Desire: The House of Ward
Book Four

For Shari, my Alpha.

1

KATE

My life was a mess, and not the kind of mess that you could easily handle with a paper towel—more like the kind where you're stuck in a low-paying job, no longer reaching for your dreams, feeling like a freak, and can lose an entire shoe on the floor of your apartment sort of mess. At least I could claim this disaster as my own. No one had broken in while I was at work and tossed my stuff around or thrown my ambition in the trash. That was all me.

The muscles in my jaw ached from clenching my teeth in frustration as I scanned the floor, trying to find my shoe. I opened my mouth and rotated my lower jaw, trying to relieve the tension. At the same time, my eyes stumbled over piles of clothing, craft projects in various stages of completion, and all the colorful disorder that filled my apartment. It was no use. My frustration was building, and I was running out of time.

Despite my best efforts, Sara would stand around waiting for me for the millionth time. And I'd tried so hard. I arranged my schedule with a co-worker to have the evening off. I wore my fancy accessories to work to avoid fussing with the details. I even laid out my outfit—sans shoes—to ensure I wouldn't experience decision paralysis that might prevent me from catching my bus on time.

But the world conspired against me.

My boss at the art supply store showed up just before I clocked out. He had a bad attitude and a list as long as my arm of tasks he wanted me to complete before leaving. I should have said no and just walked out. I should have shielded myself from his oily mood. I should have reminded him that I was leaving early, but I didn't. I hurried through his list and rushed out the door half an hour behind schedule, his dark emotions trailing out behind me.

I was forced to walk several blocks out of my way to get home because of construction, and when I finally reached my street, I noticed my landlord's truck parked out front. Being a week behind on the rent, I ducked behind a neighbor's car and waited. I wasn't in the mood to beg or make excuses, and I knew his frustration would only add fuel to my already growing emotional fire. It was almost ten minutes before I could safely emerge and shut myself inside with barely enough time to change.

The many delays left me ping-ponging around my studio apartment, searching for my lost ballerina flat. I stopped where I stood and closed my eyes, trying to picture where it might be.

I could wear the heels instead. But they would be hell on my feet. However, the heels would look better with my dress. No, I had to stop this train of thought. It wasn't helpful. I needed to keep looking.

The dress was the only nice one I owned. It was made of a fluttery material that tried to be silk but wasn't. It had cap sleeves, a deep V in front, and fell from a high waist to a point well above my knee. The hemline made me slightly self-conscious, but showcased my legs nicely and would admittedly look ten times better with heels.

I realized I still stood with my eyes closed and my mouth open, frozen in a swirl of thought and emotions. Talk about a freak. Taking a deep breath, I closed my mouth and tried to steady my mind. I inhaled calm and exhaled the turmoil of the last hour. Feeling more stable, I opened my eyes and returned to searching.

My apartment was more studio than apartment, and I finally found the missing flat under a stack of half-finished canvases. I glanced at the clock on the wall; it was already six-thirty. How had so much time gone by? I told Sara I would meet her at seven. Even if I left at that moment, I wouldn't arrive until nearly seven-thirty. I swallowed my frustration, grabbed my coat and black shoulder bag, and headed for the door. At the last moment, I turned back, snatched the pair of dusty heels from beside the clothing rack, and added them to my stuffed bag.

I was already going to walk in late; I might as well look good doing it.

The bus stop was three blocks from the apartment, and I made it in record time. I arrived just as the bus did and plopped down into a seat by one of the windows. While I caught my breath, I watched the brightly colored lights of the businesses and cars flash by as we headed south toward Seattle.

The sun set early in October in the Pacific Northwest, so it was already dark, providing a perfect black backdrop for such a light show. I glanced down and saw I had a strangle-hold on my poor bag. My muscles were still tense from my hurried flight to catch the bus. The people around me shifted uncomfortably, so I focused on relaxing and turned my attention back to the soothing lights. The dancing flashes of color calmed my nerves as the bus rocked my body, and I loosened my grip.

Although the lightscape was beautiful, I would have preferred to be home, settling in for a night of bad TV and sweatpants. But I'd invited Sara, and I couldn't cancel. Not that Sara would necessarily mind, but I would have felt like a coward. We were meeting at the old Downtown Theater on Madison for an art exhibition. But it wasn't just any exhibition. The artist was a girl I'd beat out for first place at our senior art show in high school.

It had been a bit of a shock when I'd received the invitation. I was happy for Jocelyn and loved a good art show, but it reminded me of everything I hadn't accomplished since leaving school. How had so much time passed that she could be in the position to hang her own show? Then I remembered that it had been eight years since graduation.

Jocelyn and I were friendly, if not quite friends, in high school. We shared many classes, including all the same art classes. After graduating, we both went off to art schools, but that was where our similarities ended. Now, I, the art school dropout, rode downtown on a crowded city bus in my Target dress after an eight-hour retail shift to attend Jocelyn's art exhibition.

This had not been the plan.

My bag shifted in my lap as the bus took a turn, and I remembered that I needed to dig out my cell and text Sara. She would wait, but only for so long. I didn't want her to think I'd stood her up, not after she'd driven all that way. Plus, if I had to walk in alone, I'd probably chicken out.

I attempted to thumb open the phone, but all I got was my face staring back at me in the reflection off the dark screen. By forgetting to plug it in when I'd gotten home, I'd turned it into a very expensive paperweight—not that there'd been much time to charge it. I let out a long sigh. The evening was not improving. *Sara, don't give up on me*, I prayed.

My anxiety and frustration were building again. I needed to remain calm and be in a better frame of mind by the time I reached the theater. There was no reason to ruin the evening for everyone around me. I focused on the woman sitting across the aisle and a few rows up. She was an island unto herself. She radiated the calm, green confidence of growing things. I could feel her mood seeping in to replace my own. I started to relax. The tightness in my throat eased, and my shoulders loosened, falling back against the seat. This was better. As I closed my eyes, I let my head rest on the cool window beside me.

I'd always been able to feel the emotions of those around me. As a child, I'd mentioned it to my mother, who quickly dismissed it and told me not to talk about such things. As a teenager, I'd learned she was right. People become uncomfortable if you even hint at woo-woo topics, like feeling other people's feelings. Therefore, I didn't discuss it, even with my closest friends, even with Sara.

But just because I didn't discuss it didn't mean it didn't impact my daily life. Crowded places felt overwhelming when you could sense the swirling emotions of those around you. Relationships were challenging when you knew exactly how the other person felt, regardless of what they said out loud. Sometimes I could block it out, but often it was tough to distinguish my feelings from those of the people in my life. Was I angry, or were those feelings from the customers? Was I falling in love, or was that my current boyfriend's emotion? Was I disappointed, or was that my professor? It all felt very confusing. Most of the time, I kept to myself. I went to work, had one best friend, chatted with my mom and brother on the phone, and that was all I needed.

The bus hit a bump, and my head banged against the window, jolting me from my light sleep. I glanced out the window just in time to see the front of the theater whiz by. I looked up too late to catch my stop, but not too late to spot a familiar figure waiting outside: Sara, with her short, dark curly hair and a worried expression on her face.

Damn.

I pulled the cord and hoped Sara wouldn't be too mad.

I hopped off at the next stop, just one block from my intended destination, and started jogging back toward the theater. My long, dark hair whipped in the breeze behind me, and the old trench coat I wore flapped around my legs. I turned the corner and struggled to see through the crowd on the sidewalk in front of the theater. But as I got closer, I spotted Sara in the distance, still waiting outside. She wore black velvet slacks, low-heeled boots, and a black wool coat over her favorite shiny silver blouse. It was practical yet very stylish, just like Sara. I felt relief upon seeing her, but also annoyance with myself for making her wait.

"I'm so sorry," I called, still half a block away. "I tried. I really did." I stopped in front of Sara and reached out, placing a steady hand on her shoulder, then bent down to remove one of my shoes. When I made contact, her emotions stood out in stark detail. Relief washed over me. She wasn't mad at all; she was worried, which made me feel guilty, and now she was confused. But the confusion eased as I reached into my bag and pulled out a high heel, slipping it onto my bare foot.

Sara listened to my apology while I quickly changed my shoes.

"It's no problem. I'm glad you made it," she said with a warm, genuine smile. "Let's go check it out."

She was trying to be encouraging, and I smiled. That was exactly why I asked her to come. I felt unsteady, and not just from the three-inch heels. Sara was my support, my backup. It had been that way since high school. She was one of the few people I knew who said exactly what they felt. And when she couldn't respond without hurting someone's feelings, she remained silent. Some of our friends in school found her strange, but for me, it was a relief to be near her. I reached over and squeezed her hand.

"Thank you for waiting," I said.

Sara wrapped her arm around me, and I tilted my head, leaning into a half-hug as we walked toward the ornate double doors. By the time we entered the bustling outer lobby, I was already feeling steadier.

We dropped off our outerwear at the coat check and plucked glasses of champagne from a tray held by a circulating waiter. I pushed aside the swell of emotion as we joined the crowd and entered the main atrium, which served as the gallery for the evening. I stopped, gasping in awe. It was stunning. Golden columns encircled the two-story space, supporting the stained-glass ceiling and a second-story balcony that ran around the entirety of the expansive room.

Two large staircases framed either side of the doors into the main theater, which accessed the balcony. The walls were painted white, but the sculptured molding and intricately carved decoration made up for the lack of color, not that the space lacked color that evening.

At regular intervals, paintings of various sizes bursting with color hung on the walls. Soon, the space's architecture faded, and all I saw was the art. Over two dozen pieces adorned the main floor and the balcony above. People blocked my view of anything but the closest piece, so I drifted toward it. It was a figure with exaggerated proportions, twisted in on itself. The body was filled with colors and textures, each unique yet all in perfect harmony. As I stared at it, I felt both awe at the beauty of the work and a sense of woeful inadequacy. This is what had slipped away from me as I'd gone about my day-to-day over the last eight years.

"Is it good?" Sara asked from over my shoulder.

Her question pulled me from my reverie. I took a deep breath and sighed. "Yeah. It's good," I said, leaning closer to examine the edges of Jocelyn's overlapping materials. "I wanted to be able to hate on it, but Jocelyn's talented." I paused before adding, "I would be proud if these were mine." And I meant it. They were fantastic. The level of skill and creativity was impressive. I could see some of her earlier work in the art before me now, but she'd clearly matured and developed as an artist since I last saw her work.

"You're being such a grownup. You're taking all the fun out of it," Sara teased. "I was ready to hate it if you needed me to." She squeezed my shoulder, sending a thrill of happiness through me.

I turned my head and mouthed, *"Thank you,"* before moving on to admire the next piece.

We made our way down the first wall. My enjoyment of the art was only heightened by the feelings of impressed wonder and admiration from the others staring at the paintings. I let those emotions wash over me. They were almost as good as the art itself. More than anything, I longed to create something that evoked such feelings in people, or evoked anything really.

When Sara and I ran out of art, we climbed the steps to

the balcony to view the paintings on display there. Halfway up, we noticed Jocelyn surrounded by a group of people engaged in animated conversation.

Sara tugged my arm. "Let's go say hi." I noticed a question in her eyes as she spoke. She was giving me an opportunity to back out if it felt overwhelming.

"Yes, we should," I said, offering Sara a reassuring smile.

As we approached, Jocelyn spotted us and broke into a wide grin. She excused herself from the conversation and stepped forward to greet us. She was just as I remembered her: tall with long red hair, high cheekbones, and kind brown eyes. She gave each of us a hug and thanked us for coming. She was nervous but proud.

"Your work is beautiful. You've always been talented, but these pieces are extraordinary," I said, meaning every word. "And it looks like I'm not the only one who thinks so. I noticed that more than a few of them have already sold." I smiled at Jocelyn.

"Thank you," Jocelyn said, leaning in conspiratorially. "I was so worried. This place is much fancier than anything I'm used to. Frankly, I'm just glad people showed up, and I'm blown away by the fact that they are actually buying my pieces." She leaned back and mimicked wiping sweat from her brow. It was easy to feel happy for her when she so clearly meant what she said and truly deserved the praise.

"How long will it be up?" Sara asked.

"Just for tonight, and then what's left will go to a small gallery a few blocks from here for the rest of this month. It's been a lot of work, and I know there's more to come, but I'm just trying to enjoy this for now." Jocelyn smiled warmly.

"You should. You deserved it," I said, reaching out to touch her arm in reassurance.

Jocelyn thanked us once more for coming, and we

drifted away, letting her be swallowed by the crowd again, all eager to connect with the evening's star and share in a piece of her success.

I watched as someone handed her a glass of champagne and offered a toast. The bitterness I expected to feel wasn't there. Jocelyn's success was not my failure, I realized. It was an example of where I could have been, and where I could still be. Just because I hadn't figured things out yet didn't mean I never would. Maybe it was time for me to do that. Figure things out.

"Are you doing okay?" Sara asked as we finished our circuit of the balcony and descended the stairs.

"Yeah, I'm surprised myself, but I'm doing great. I'm glad we came. It was good to see Jocelyn, and the art is amazing. It's inspiring," I said, smiling at my best friend. She might not know about my secret ability, but she knew me better than anyone and understood how much I longed for what Jocelyn worked so hard for.

Sara smiled back, but her expression soon changed as she glanced around the room. Her mood shifted from its usual cheerful demeanor to one of cautious alarm.

"Hey, are you okay?" I asked, not sure what just happened. When she didn't respond, I tried again. "Sara, are you okay? What's wrong?" I asked, shifting to get into her line of sight.

"What? I'm sorry, I didn't catch that," she replied, blinking in confusion.

"I asked what was wrong."

"Oh, nothing. I'm fine," she said. She gave me a half-smile and rubbed the back of her arms, making her wooden bracelets clack together. She seemed better, confused, but better. "I just have this weird feeling. Maybe I'm tired."

I nodded. "It's getting late, and I'm ready to crash for the night, too. I have work in the morning. How about you?"

"Oh, yeah. You know me; every day's a workday when your mom's the boss," she said, winking as her mood brightened again.

"Yeah, but you love working with your family," I said.

"Yeah, I do," Sara said, her expression softening. "Hey, speaking of which, my mom and aunt were just asking where you've been and why they don't see more of you. You should visit sometime. I've been working on some plans to expand the shop. I'd love to talk them over with you, and I'm dying to complain more about my lack of a love life," she added with a snort. "Let's plan a girls' night sometime soon. You could come over. I could pick you up after work."

"Yes! I really need that. I could use a break, and I want to hear all about what you've got going on. I've been a terrible friend lately. Well...maybe I always have," I said, nudging her with my elbow.

She smiled back. "Good. Let's go. Do you want a ride home?" she asked as we grabbed our coats and headed to the door.

"Thank you, but no. The bus stop is right here. You go. When I get home, I'll charge my phone and text you. Let's plan a night together soon."

We agreed, hugged goodbye, and parted ways outside the theater.

Overall, it had been a lovely night. Better than I had hoped.

I hurried to catch the bus. As I boarded and sat down, I reflected on my feelings about the evening. I expected to feel jealousy and the familiar self-loathing I often experienced when I thought about all I had not accomplished. Not *yet* accomplished, I corrected myself. But I didn't feel that way. I wanted to find Jocelyn's success unfair or undeserved, but it wasn't. Jocelyn was just the same as she'd been in school—kind, modest, and hard-working.

Instead of feeling discouraged or overwhelmed by the exhaustion of the passengers around me, I felt motivated. I had a renewed drive to create and to see what I could accomplish if I put in the effort. I resolved to make more time for painting and to spend more time drawing instead of sitting in front of the TV or scrolling through Instagram on my phone.

I would do better. Be better. And while I was at it, the rest of my life could use some organizing, too. The apartment was beyond messy. Staying in touch with Sara and her family had become a struggle. My mom still hadn't gotten the call—or the visit—she deserved. A surprising urge welled up: to move forward, to finally do something just for me, to live up to all that potential my mother always saw. I drew a deep breath and let it out slowly. Nearby, a few people straightened in their seats, some of their weariness lifting. I smiled to myself.

Before I knew it, I was back in my neighborhood and at the stop three blocks from home. I stepped out onto an empty sidewalk, devoid of any emotion besides my own. Most of the businesses were closed for the night, and there wasn't another person in sight.

With no one's emotions to guard against, I relaxed and let my thoughts and hopes for the future fill me up. I was moving on. I was finally ready to grow up, to become what I was always meant to be. The quiet excitement of my thoughts lulled me into inattentiveness as I stepped off the curb and onto the road, and I looked up just in time to see the headlights of the car that plowed into me a heartbeat later.

And then, I saw and felt no more.

2

JAMES

Descending the grand staircase of the manor house, I stepped into the foyer and listened carefully. There were no sounds except those made by the servants on the first floor. I moved across the expanse of marble, my leather shoes whispering against the tile, when I suddenly froze.

I could hear the rhythmic breathing of my sire's dogs on the other side of the doors to the front parlor. My sire, Alexander, was undoubtedly with them. Holding my breath, I quickened my pace. I was fairly certain he was occupied, but I didn't want to risk running into him. I wasn't in a hurry, but if I moved quickly, I could slip away without being delayed.

It wasn't that I didn't want to speak to my sire. He was the head of our House, and I was a loyal member. Lately, however, I'd felt increasing pressure from Alexander and didn't want to be reminded of my unfulfilled duties. I had plans that night that didn't involve Alexander's demands or listening to him drone on about his dream of resurrecting the good old days.

I accepted my coat from one of the many staff members,

placing a finger to my lips to keep her silent, and walked soundlessly toward the front exit. I hadn't made it halfway there when the parlor's large wooden pocket doors were pushed aside, and Alexander appeared in the doorway.

He was of normal height, around five-ten, with long dark hair that cascaded in waves to his shoulders, a closely trimmed beard, and gray eyes. He was imposing, not due to his size—he had an average, lean build—no, it was Alexander's demeanor and the intensity of his gaze. They signaled to others that he was in control of any space he occupied. And no matter how many times I saw him, I was always impressed. Sometimes annoyed, but always impressed.

Alexander pushed the doors wider, allowing his two Visilas to squeeze by, and stood dabbing at his mouth with a crisp white handkerchief, a satisfied smile on his face. Even from where I stood, I could see the red spots on the linen and smell the blood lingering in the air.

I stopped, stifled a sigh, and bowed slightly in his direction as the dogs circled me. The large copper-colored hunting dogs were an annoyance and one of Alexander's ways of tormenting me. They got along with everyone else in the House but seemed to have a particular hatred for me. I kept my eye on the two red fiends that continued to walk around my legs, sniffing. *Was that blood on one of their snouts?*

"You're leaving? Where are you going this evening, James?" my sire asked in his smooth, cultured voice.

My attention snapped back to him as I straightened, trying not to flinch away from the hot canine breath against my left hand. They tended to bite me—not that it caused any lasting damage, but it hurt like a bitch—and I didn't dare defend myself against them. I shuddered to think what my sire would do if I harmed a hair on their pampered heads.

"Sire, I have errands in the city," I said. "I must also stop by the hospital tonight," I added as an afterthought. Slowly, I withdrew my hand from the dog's reach, but didn't move.

"Ah, yes," Alexander nodded, pretending not to notice my discomfort. "Your hobby. Well, I hope you have a pleasant evening. But you will remember what we discussed, right? I want this House full again, James," Alexander declared, making a grand sweeping gesture with his arm. It was a little over the top, but it was very Alexander. "It's been far too long. I need new candidates. You will keep an eye out, won't you?"

"Of course," I said, groaning inwardly and momentarily forgetting about the dogs. "I'll be looking this very evening." I paused to consider. "However, it's a complicated matter and may take some time," I added.

"Ridiculous," Alexander said dismissively. "Before all this modern bookkeeping, you simply grabbed the next attractive thing to run by. I don't understand why it needs to be so difficult." His tone was petulant, making him sound more like a spoiled child than the leader of a once-powerful House.

"I'm sure that would be much easier, Sire. Nevertheless, I will be on the lookout. Is there anything I need to take with me on my way out?" I asked, gesturing toward the parlor. My sudden movement caused the dog to my left to flatten its head and let out a low growl as it fixed its golden stare on me. Prompted by his brother, the other hellhound began barking from where it lurked behind me.

"Oh, no." Alexander waved his handkerchief. "That's kind of you to offer, but it was just a snack. I'll have one of the humans handle it."

"As you wish," I said, but made no move to leave.

Alexander sighed and finally acknowledged the two

menacing beasts. "Agyar, Karom, enough," he said lazily. Instantly, both dogs turned tail and trotted to his side. He bent down, scratched one on the head, and then lifted its chin to wipe its snout with the handkerchief. I shuddered and turned away.

Closing the front door behind me, I walked toward my car. I felt the bite of my keys in the palm of my hand and realized I was clenching my fist as well as my jaw. It wasn't the dogs that bothered me; I accepted the monsters Alexander called pets long ago, but I was annoyed by this obsession with adding to our household. Did he even bother to stop and think how much more work it would be for me?

There were four of us in the House, including Alexander. Miguel was never around, preferring to fuck off to points unknown rather than spending time at home—I couldn't blame him. The other was Josephine. She was practically catatonic and hardly ever left her room. While this made it easier for me to care for her, I was still responsible for looking after everyone's needs. Fortunately, I was never asked to tend to the beasts; Alexander never allowed anyone to handle them or see to their well-being.

I was the youngest in the House by far. The older our kind got, the lazier they seemed to become. As a result, I ended up with all the shit jobs none of the others wanted. Alexander spent his nights lounging at home or visiting the extravagant homes of the other elders, while I ran around supporting his lifestyle. The hospital was hardly my hobby. Working there, even part-time, provided our House with access to essential physical and technical resources.

Beings as old as Alexander didn't grasp how complicated modern life was, or how much effort it required to keep everything in order, everyone fed, and the humans unaware of it all.

Gone were the days of raiding villages under the guise of mysterious plagues, leaving bodies lying in the streets. Access to the morgue, the hospital's blood supply, and the nearby cemetery were all benefits of my little "hobby." Everything would be much easier if Alexander would evolve and utilize the Council-sanctioned services now available. It would also help if he adhered to the Council's numerous prohibitions, but I wasn't holding my breath.

There was an upside to this servitude, however. I rested my hands on the steering wheel of my expensive convertible, something I could never have afforded in my previous life. What I really wanted was more time to enjoy the perks of the life I'd chosen.

I considered Alexander's request. It might mean more work in the short term, but it could be nice to have someone younger around to take on the bulk of the scut work. I only wished it were as easy as picking someone off the street. I dreaded the paperwork that a new household member would bring. No matter how much Alexander flaunted the laws, there was no escaping the necessity of registering a new vampire with the Council.

I looked down at my clothes. I wore dark grey slacks, a black cashmere sweater, a wool overcoat, and black leather loafers. I was dressed for a night out at the more exclusive clubs in the city, not for a trip to the hospital. But I kept a bag in my car for just such occasions. And although I needed to put in some work to keep my human job, I refused to be completely derailed. I deserved a little diversion first. I drove onto the highway and headed for the city's club district.

Hours later, I entered the hospital through my usual set of doors near the morgue, but then wandered through the corridors following a scent I couldn't get out of my head. I went to where the smell was strongest: the emergency department.

This wasn't my department; there was no reason to be there, but I couldn't be anywhere else. So I waited and kept out of sight.

I stayed close while they worked on the woman, a victim of a hit-and-run. Eventually, she was moved upstairs to the ICU, and I followed. As the night wore on, it seemed Alexander would get his way, and sooner than I hoped. The night took a turn, presenting me with an opportunity I couldn't pass up.

Sneaking upstairs in my scrubs in the middle of the night was easy. Convincing Alexander to come north was more challenging. And getting him into the room without anyone asking too many questions was even more difficult.

But there we both were, just hours after I caught her scent.

I watched the woman lying in the bed for any external sign of the transformation I hoped her body would undergo. She was in bad shape by the time she arrived at the hospital, suffering from multiple broken bones, head trauma, and internal bleeding. She roused enough to drink from Alexander, but it was never guaranteed.

I looked at Alexander, who was rolling down the sleeve of his button-down shirt. He'd shed the doctor's coat I smuggled him in with. It lay crumpled on the floor at the foot of the bed. He wore a vest and tailored slacks. His suit jacket and coat were draped over a nearby chair, folded with care.

"I've done all I can," he said, sounding bored by the whole thing, but I knew better.

Alexander glanced around the dimly lit room. "I don't like this place. It's filthy and full of disease." He sniffed and turned his head toward me, his eyes darkening. "This is not what I meant when I said *candidate*. Consider this a favor, but do not ask me to return here."

"Understood, Sire," I replied, averting my gaze. "I appreciate your presence nonetheless."

I knew I was fortunate that Alexander answered my call. I also understood there would be repercussions. This wasn't typically how things were handled in the modern world. But Alexander was old-fashioned. He wouldn't fuss much over the morality of what we'd done—acting without someone's consent. If everything worked out, we would all get what we wanted. Alexander would have a larger family, and I would have fulfilled my duties while gaining an ally. At least, that's what I told myself. Deep down, I realized there was more. Something drew me to this woman in a way I couldn't explain.

I glanced at Alexander; he stared at the woman with an unreadable expression.

I'd never seen my sire turn anyone, not since my own making. But I watched him feed many times, and this time was different. It was a risk to call Alexander. I knew how the woman affected me when I first caught the scent of her blood and altered my evening plans. It was no surprise that Alexander reacted to her as well.

When Alexander bit into the woman to drain what was in her veins, his nostrils flared, and he gripped her in a way that seemed extreme even for him. In the end, I practically peeled Alexander away from her throat before her heart gave out. He mumbled something about the taste of her blood, which was a mixture of various blood sources after the transfusions she received. I had to admit she still smelled wonderful, even after losing most of her blood before reaching the hospital.

"I suppose we can't take her with us tonight? She would be missed, wouldn't she?" Alexander asked.

"Yes, Sire. I can arrange for someone to take you home," I said. "You don't have to wait. I'll let you know if the transformation has taken hold."

"No. I'll wait to see for myself, and then you can take me home. She won't wake up for another full day, if she wakes up at all. And I want you to bring her directly to me if she survives," he said, an edge to his voice.

I flinched and looked toward Alexander. Redressed, he sat on the padded bench beneath the window. He was utterly still. Not a muscle twitched. He remained frozen, staring at the woman in a way only a statue or a very old vampire could. Even for me, it was unsettling, and I turned back to check for changes in the woman's condition. Crossing my arms, I stepped closer.

Even in her current state, she was breathtaking. Her straight, dark hair pooled around her face, beautiful even through the bruising. She had long, dark lashes, high cheekbones, full lips, and a pointed chin. I imagined her smiling up at me, and my own lips turned up in response. Realizing my distraction, I shook my head to clear it and continued my examination.

She wasn't breathing, but that was not a concern. I could no longer hear her heartbeat, but that, too, was no indication of her health. I leaned closer and took a deep breath, attempting to catch her scent again. It was there but overshadowed by the smell of my sire's blood that now permeated her body. Her limbs twitched slightly, and I nodded, satisfied. Her bones were reknitting. It was working. A thrill of hope surged within me, but I pushed it down, schooling my expression. I watched as the fresh bruising faded from the side of her face, and her skin began to take on a healthier hue. Yes, it had begun. I let out a sigh and then glanced back at Alexander.

He stood just behind me.

I jumped in surprise. Despite my heightened senses, Alexander's ability to sneak up on me was a reminder of just how much older my sire was.

"We're done. Let's be away," he said as he turned to leave.

I straightened up and retrieved Alexander's belongings. Before leaving, I reattached the monitors that would summon the on-call nurses and doctors. They might notice some changes in her body. Her legs were straighter, and her face had less bruising. However, they wouldn't be able to ignore the absence of a heartbeat or breathing, and her subtle movements would be undetectable to the busy staff. They would do their best, but she would likely be declared dead and taken to the morgue, where she would be safely tucked away for the day. I made sure to leave detailed instructions in her file before summoning Alexander. She would be undisturbed. I hoped.

Alexander and I were out the door and halfway down the hall before the first alarm blared. I glanced back, feeling a pang of worry and loss at leaving her behind, but I knew this was the best and cleanest way to handle things. I reassured myself that I would be back before she woke up. Hearing the rush of footsteps coming our way, I hurried after Alexander before anyone could notice.

3

SARA

I walked to where my car was parked, feeling confused. I should have felt good. Kate had finally shown up and actually enjoyed herself. She took Jocelyn's success in stride and was in a good place. I thought the art show was great. I knew little about art, but the paintings were vibrant and fun, and the theater was impressive. I should have felt relieved as I got in my car and started for home. But I didn't.

Something was off, and it had me on edge. It started just before we left. The hair on the back of my neck stood up, and I felt prickles running up and down my arms. I pulled out my phone and texted my mom. She replied right away; she and my aunt were okay. I sent another message to Kate, asking her to text when she got home safely.

I let out a sigh. I understood a feeling that intense often meant trouble, but if I wasn't sure where it came from, there was nothing I could do about it. I started the car but remained hyper-alert as I merged onto the highway and headed home.

The evening passed without incident. Everything was normal, and everyone appeared to be fine. Before bed, I checked my phone, but I still hadn't received a text from Kate. I sent her a goodnight text, hoping for a response letting me know she got home okay and plugged in her phone. Nothing.

I woke up early the next morning to the sound of my cell buzzing. I'd slept fitfully, like I'd been awaiting the call. When I saw the name on the caller ID, my stomach dropped, and my chest tightened. It was Kate's mom, Melanie. Not only did she rarely call me, but she never called in the early hours before dawn. I struggled to keep the panic at bay as energy surged within me, searching for an outlet. I lifted the phone to my ear.

I answered with a shaky *"Hello"* and heard the anxiety lacing my voice. The line was silent, and then Kate's mom began to speak. As her words tumbled out of the small speaker, I knew my life had changed forever. When her voice faded away, I took a deep breath and swallowed hard. I cleared my throat, feeling a wave of anguish threatening to overwhelm me as the energy within me continued to build. "I'll be right there," I croaked before I was consumed by the emotion that ran through me. I pulled my phone away and glanced at the blank screen through my tears. The phone was dead.

I glanced up. My mom stood in my doorway, still in her nightgown and wrapped in a shawl. She'd sensed something was wrong with me. How could she not? She gazed at me with a question in her eyes. I merely shook my head and said, "Kate." It was all I could manage, and then I was wrapped in my mother's arms.

She held onto me for several minutes before I could speak. I shared what Melanie told me about the car accident, and that Kate was gone.

"I knew it. I knew something was wrong," I said, tears

streaming down my face. "I should have driven her. I should have done something. I knew Momma. I just knew." I clung to her strong arms.

"Shush now," my mother said in the firm yet soothing voice of my childhood. "That's enough. This wasn't your fault, sweet girl." She rocked me like when I was young, but it did little to ease the pain.

She offered to drive me down, and I gratefully accepted. I needed my mother's comfort and support. And, despite my mother's insistence, I had only one thought as we drove south: this was my fault.

I knew something bad would happen. I should have insisted that Kate take the ride I'd offered. Why hadn't I pushed harder? I knew better than to ignore my feelings. I had been taught to trust my gut. Why hadn't I acted? Maybe I hoped that if I didn't acknowledge it, the bad thing wouldn't happen, but that's not how life worked.

By the time we arrived at the hospital, I was cried out with grief and guilt. I found Melanie in the lobby waiting for me. We hugged, and I whispered how sorry I was, but I couldn't meet her gaze. My mom was right behind me and stepped in to offer her condolences while I pulled back. I waited until Melanie was ready, and then she took us both to the elevator bank and down to a waiting attendant.

My mom asked me if I wanted her to come along, but I shook my head and tried to smile before following Kate's mother down the hall. The attendant disappeared through a door to the left, but Melanie stood outside, waiting. I stepped up beside her. She reached for my hand, but I put my arm around her instead; it was safer that way.

There was movement through the glass panel in the door, and I caught sight of a sheet-draped gurney being wheeled in. Fresh tears pricked my swollen eyes. Kate's mom ducked her head, appearing so small and frail, not the capable woman I remembered from when I was younger. She wept silently, her grey-blonde hair hiding most of her face, but I could see tears dripping from her chin.

The attendant signaled us to come inside. I stepped carefully, placing one foot in front of the other, yet I couldn't feel the floor under my feet as we entered the small room in the hospital's basement.

The staff member positioned themself at the head of the gurney and lifted the edge of the sheet, pulling it down to reveal my best friend's face. Kate's mother let out a heart-wrenching wail, and I pulled her closer. I looked at Kate lying there. She appeared peaceful, as if she were asleep.

She felt peaceful too; her energy was relaxed.

With a start, I realized I could feel Kate as if she were still in the room. That shouldn't be possible.

My heart raced, and I dropped the arm around Melanie, stepping closer. I'd been around several dead people in my life. Both my grandparents and my father passed away, and I helped with their funeral rites. I knew how it felt to be in the presence of the departed. They felt like nothing. The energy left the body, leaving only the shell behind. But this was different. Kate was here, and I could feel her just like I could feel her mother and the man from the hospital standing beside me.

I stared down at Kate's face, examining her features. I glanced up at the attendant in green, who stepped aside. He dropped his gaze to the floor, allowing me some privacy.

I reached out and touched the back of my hand to Kate's cheek. Her skin was cold, too cold.

My heart sank.

I didn't know what I expected. I knew she was dead; I just didn't want to believe it.

I sighed. Maybe it took some time for a person's energy to leave the body. Did that mean Kate was still here for now? I wondered if she could hear me. I leaned down closer to her ear.

"I'm so sorry, Katie. I'm so very sorry," I whispered before straightening up and stepping back.

I waited as Kate's mom said goodbye and then walked her to the door. I glanced back one more time, hoping to see some change, but nothing was different.

Kate lay there just as before, still dead.

I knew I was supposed to leave now, but I couldn't shake the feeling that I was leaving my best friend alone, leaving her behind. Everything felt so...so wrong.

I was silent during the ride home. My mom remained quiet, allowing me space. I appreciated this; I needed to think and process. I still had trouble believing what happened.

"Mom?" I said after a while.

"Yes, Dear."

"Can you sense a person's energy? Their force, when they're nearby? I never thought to ask." I twisted in my seat and glanced at her profile as she answered.

"No, that's not one of my gifts," she said, offering me a tight smile. "Why do you ask?"

"Oh, it's nothing. I just... I thought I could still sense Kate. When I saw her at the hospital, I mean."

"Hmm. I don't know. Maybe she was still there. Maybe she was sticking around to say farewell. Maybe she was still on her way to the other side," my mom said. This time, her smile was genuine, and I noticed the gentle lines around her eyes when she glanced my way. "I wouldn't worry about it, Love."

"Yeah, I'm sure you're right," I said, leaning my head

back against the seat. "I'm so tired. I don't really know what I'm feeling right now anyway."

She reached over and squeezed my hand. I was glad she'd come. Her warm energy felt steady and calming.

I leaned my head back and closed my eyes. I should get some rest. The shop would be closed tomorrow—later today, I corrected myself. I could sleep all day, if I let myself, but there was still a lot to do, and I didn't want to fall behind. I let myself drift off, but it was anything but restful.

I dreamed I was back in the small room at the hospital. I smelled the disinfectant and felt the cool basement air against the bare skin of my face and hands. I was alone this time—just me and the sheet-draped gurney against one wall.

My tennis shoes squeaked loudly as I crossed the space and reached out to pull the sheet down. As it slipped past my friend's dark hair, across her smooth, pale forehead, and finally exposed the features of her face, I gasped.

Kate's eyes were open. She tilted her head toward me and tugged her blue-tinged lips into a sad smile. "Sara?" she asked. And she sounded just as I remembered. She lowered her brows, and her smile faded. "I'm scared," she said, her voice trembling.

I shook my head and stepped back from the gurney.

"Sara? Sara?" Kate cried and reached out a hand as I turned and bolted for the door.

4

KATE

There was something I was supposed to do.

Something important I needed to remember.

I was supposed to go somewhere, but I couldn't recall where.

I grasped frantically for the thought, but then everything faded to black and slipped out of reach.

The next time I was aware, there was only pain.

Pain, unlike anything I'd ever experienced. It felt like an insurmountable barrier. A massive wall I couldn't see around. An overwhelming noise I couldn't hear over. It surrounded me and filled me, pinning me in place. Only faint signals slipped through for me to notice. Bright lights in my eyes, voices yelling, hands touching me, and pain, pain, pain.

When the darkness came again, I went willingly, and it was a blessing.

I wanted to stay in that dark place where I felt safe, where I was comfortable. But I couldn't. Something shook me, making my insides feel like they were filled with broken glass, cutting and poking. Someone spoke to me. The voice sounded kind and soothing yet insistent. A face looked down at me—dark hair, green, worried eyes. "Not long now. Just hold on a bit longer. Stay with me." I felt worried but hopeful.

I tried to take comfort in his words and follow his advice, but I was so tired. I would rest for just a little while.

Machines beeped, and people spoke.

"This is not what we discussed."

"But you are merciful. Please, Sire."

A man's face, with grey eyes and a dark beard, hovered above me. He leaned down like he would to kiss me.

How strange, I thought.

Something rough brushed against my cheek, stirring a jumble of emotions, and there was more pain.

I closed my eyes again.

The next time I surfaced, my thoughts were clearer, but my body felt distant. Something soft pressed firmly against my face, covering my lips. I could barely feel it; I was so numb. My mouth filled with liquid, warm and velvety on my tongue. It carried with it strong feelings of wonder and desire, but I couldn't swallow.

I was choking.

Panic ripped through me. With the little strength I had left, I managed to constrict my throat and swallowed what threatened to drown me.

A warm sensation flowed down my throat and radiated outward, filling my body. And then the pain struck with full force.

My nerves were as alert as my mind, and I screamed out in agony as the signals from my severely broken body registered in sharp detail.

My screams were muffled by the flesh still pressing against my open mouth. I swallowed again, unable to breathe, as my mouth was flooded once more. This time, as the warm feeling spread through my body, the pain began to fade. I moaned in relief and clutched the source of my salvation, drawing in great mouthfuls, savoring the intoxicating flavor and fragrance it brought with it, swallowing greedily. The pain completely washed away, replaced by a sense of well-being, strength, and overwhelming exhaustion. Did these feelings belong to me? Did they belong to the stranger I clung to? I didn't care. I closed my eyes and drifted into a dreamless sleep.

I breathed in slowly, drawing air through my nose, and cringed. *God, something smelled terrible.* Growing up in a semi-rural area, I'd encountered enough roadkill to recognize the scent of death.

Where was I?

I reached out with my other sense but couldn't feel anyone nearby. I was alone.

I cracked one eyelid open, but all I found was darkness. In addition to the smell and absence of light, the first thing I noticed was that I was no longer in pain.

That was a good start.

But something was wrong, and nothing made sense. It was pitch black, and I lay on something hard. I could feel a feathering touch against my lashes and cheeks, so I reached up to brush whatever it was off my face, and my hand struck something just above me. My eyes flicked open wide, and alarm raced through my body.

I reached out with both hands, still unable to see anything. I was covered in a sheet of fabric. I grabbed handfuls of cloth with both hands and pulled it down, revealing my face. The air felt wrong, and the smell was overpowering. I waved my hands around, trying to comprehend where I was. There was a wall to one side and nothing on the other. I raised my hands and found metal less than a foot above me. My panic surged, and I instinctively jerked my knees up, hitting the metal with a muffled thunk that sounded strange to my ears.

Dread filled my body as realization hit, and I opened my mouth, releasing a half-sob, half-panicked scream. My hands shot to the door I knew was just behind my head. There was no latch or release on this side. Why would there be? I took a quick breath and tried again.

"Heeeeelp," I managed.

The sound was still off, but now I understood why, and it was horrifying. I called out again—once, twice, and a third time—before I devolved into incoherent sobs while banging on the metal door with both hands.

Panic choked me, and I couldn't catch my breath. How had this happened? How could I be here? It felt like a nightmare straight out of a movie.

Just when I thought I couldn't take any more, the panel behind me opened, and light flooded the drawer where I lay. I scrambled backward and almost fell onto the floor when a hand landed on my back, steadying me, and the hard metal I rested on was pulled out into a brightly lit room.

"Hey. Whoa there. You're okay. Hey. Hey," the man attached to the hand said as I jumped off the metal bed and slammed into the nearest tiled wall, panting.

My mind recoiled from the reality of my situation. I don't know how someone starts to process waking up in a morgue drawer. I stood frozen, completely naked, with my hands pressed against the warm tile behind me.

The man looked young, probably around my age. He

had short, dark hair and a medium build. He wore hospital scrubs and a concerned expression on his handsome face. He walked closer with his hands raised. "You're okay," he repeated. "I'm not going to hurt you." He seemed completely unsurprised to see me; in fact, he looked relieved. *What the hell?*

"What the fuck is going on?" I demanded. The profanity was unusual for me, but it felt like the best way to get to the bottom of what was happening and express my current mood.

The man halted, his gaze roaming over my body. He glanced away and turned quickly, grabbing for the sheet that hung halfway out of the hellhole I just climbed from.

"I don't want that," I shrieked when he held it out, pressing myself closer to the wall.

"Oh. Of course. Sorry," he said, looking down at the fabric.

He tossed it aside and walked over to a cabinet against the far wall. Taking out a folded cloth, he offered it to me.

I snatched it from him, opened it up, wrapped it around myself, and waited.

The man looked at me with wide green eyes. It was his eyes that triggered the memory.

"I've seen you before," I said.

He nodded. "Yes, you have. That's good. Let's start with what you remember," he said, leveling his gaze at me.

"What do I remember?" I asked, incredulous. "I remember waking up in there." I pointed to the gaping hole in the wall of stainless steel doors. "Why was I in there? And who the hell are you?" I was practically shouting now.

The man raised his hands once more. "My name is James," he said. "I know it must have been a shock, and I'm sorry. It was the safest place for you—"

"Safe?" I interrupted. "From what?"

He exhaled deeply. "Let me start from the beginning," he said.

But instead of speaking, he turned around, grabbed a stool from a workstation, and rolled it toward me. I shook my head and pressed my back more firmly against the wall.

"Have it your way," he said, taking another for himself.

Once seated, he rested his hands on his thighs and took another deep breath.

"You were in an accident," he said, stirring another memory.

I got off the bus.

I stepped off the curb...lights.

I glanced up at him and nodded.

He cleared his throat. "You were brought to the hospital, and the doctors and nurses did their very best, but—"

"Whoa, hold on a second," I interrupted once more. "Are you telling me I'm dead?" My voice was so strained I barely recognized it.

"No. No," he continued. "Not really. At least I don't think so."

"You don't think so?"

"You were changed," he said matter-of-factly.

"Changed? Changed into what?" I looked down at myself. Aside from panic, I didn't feel much different. And I didn't look any different. Something was wrong, though. Ever since I awoke, the world felt...off.

"Well, a process was started to transform you into one of us. It was the only way to heal the extensive damage caused by the accident. Had you been awake, you would've needed to give permission, as it was..." he trailed off, tilting his head from side to side.

"This still doesn't make any sense. What process?

Change me into what?" I asked, not understanding what he was trying to tell me.

"A vampire," he said.

I studied his face. Surely, I heard him wrong, or he was joking. Yet this seemed a bit extreme for a joke, and he looked utterly serious.

I studied his emotions. Like most people, he experienced a range of emotions simultaneously. He was nervous and somewhat frustrated, but he truly believed what he said; of that, I was certain.

He must be crazy, I decided.

I tried to think. I recalled the accident, or at least the events leading up to it. After that, everything became unclear.

Then, I remembered the pain. It was intense. As I thought about it, my knees threatened to buckle. I held the sheet wrapped around me with one hand, with the other I reached out toward the stool James brought over. Lying my palm flat on the seat, I breathed slowly through my nose.

James didn't move. He just waited.

I sat on the stool and looked at him. "I remember a few things," I said.

He shifted in his seat, worry flaring within him, but stayed silent. His gaze remained fixed on mine.

"I remember being in terrible pain."

I extended my arm and examined it. There were no marks or signs of injury anywhere on my body that I could see. Just one more thing that didn't make any sense.

"How long have I been here?" I asked.

"You arrived at the hospital last night—less than twenty-four hours ago," he said honestly.

Less than twenty-four hours? I shook my head.

"I should be a mess," I said, clutching the sheet more

firmly. "But you really don't expect me to believe that I'm a vampire? That you're a vampire? Vampires don't exist."

He smiled. "We do, and you're not a vampire yet," he said. "You've started the process, but it isn't complete. You'll need to feed and rest."

"You are seriously deluded," I said, rising from the stool.

I wasn't sure what he was trying to achieve, but I wouldn't sit in a room with someone who believed what this man claimed. Sure, I couldn't explain what happened. I couldn't reconcile my memories with my current state, but I didn't buy what this guy was selling.

There was only one door in the room, and I moved toward it, still clutching the sheet to my chest to hold it in place. I suspected I didn't appear very dignified, but my dignity was the least of my concerns.

James blocked my way. "Kathrine, please. You have to come with me. I need to take you somewhere safe where we can discuss this. I'm here to help you."

I hesitated when he said my name, but quickly recovered. I continued moving forward, putting an exam table between us. I rushed toward the door only to collide directly with James, who was somehow in front of me. It felt like running into a brick wall. I bounced off his chest and fell, sprawling onto the floor.

I blinked up at him, surprised. Scooting back, I pulled the sheet over my exposed skin.

"You can't keep me here," I said, embarrassment warring with anger.

"I'm not trying to keep you here, but you can't just run off into the night. You need help." He was genuinely worried.

"I don't need anything from you," I said. "I just need to

go home and sort this all out," I mumbled, getting to my feet.

James stood blocking my way. Then he nodded. "Very well. I won't keep you. Believe it or not, I'm on your side."

He stepped away from the door, and I didn't wait for him to change his mind. I pushed into the dimly lit hallway. There was no one around. The glow of an exit sign at the far end of the hall caught my eye, so I headed toward it.

My stomach clenched with fear as I walked faster. The urge to escape surged within me, and I sprinted toward the door, my bare feet slapping against the linoleum floor. I passed a row of elevators on my way, but kept going. I didn't want to emerge into the hospital lobby wearing nothing but a sheet. Before I pressed the bar of the emergency exit door, I glanced back down the hall. James wasn't following me. I exhaled and felt my anxiety ease just a bit.

Through the door, I found a flight of steps and climbed to ground level. There, another emergency exit dumped me into the hospital's back parking lot. The air outside felt damp and warm, which was odd for the time of year and added to the sense of wrongness I'd felt since waking up.

It took me a moment to get my bearings. I glanced around the mostly empty lot and noticed a cemetery across the street. I recognized the old, low stone wall. I was less than a mile from home.

Climbing over the rough stone with ease, I cut through the cemetery. The sheet I wore flapped in the breeze as I ran, but I didn't care. Getting home was all that mattered. That thought drove me forward, and I ran as if being chased, even though I looked back several times and saw no one.

I exited the cemetery onto the sidewalk, my bare feet colliding with the pavement. This part of town was quiet and dark at this hour. Running full throttle, I passed two people on my way, and while I'm sure they stared, I didn't pay attention.

I made it to my front door faster than should have been possible. My purse was who knows where, and my keys were with it. Luckily, I'd hidden a spare under a pot near the trash cans on the side of the building. I let myself into the studio, closing and bolting the door behind me.

Once inside, my body collapsed, my bare bottom landing on the tile floor. I sat with my back against the door. Wrapping the thin fabric of the sheet around myself, I hugged my knees to my chest. I was home. I was safe. It was over.

5

———

JAMES

Pausing, I decided to give Katherine a few minutes' head start. I'm not sure what I expected, but I wasn't prepared for her not to believe me. My own transformation was the only experience I had to go on, and I'd been fully aware of what was happening at the time. I should have considered how to approach her better. I should've planned it out. I should've arrived before she woke up.

After dropping Alexander at the manor house the night before, I'd returned north and driven by the woman's apartment. I wanted to see what I was dealing with. Did she have roommates, family, pets, potential complications, or any reasons she might want to hold onto her human life?

I hadn't gone inside, but I didn't need to. I could tell what I needed to know just by looking in the windows. It was sad—a cramped, messy studio with a late rent notice stuck to the door. She had nobody and nothing of value.

After that, I went to my apartment near the hospital. The one I used when I didn't have time to go back to the manor before dawn or when I needed some space. It was as close as I could get, and I'd hoped to be back in time.

In my mind, I was there before she awoke, and everything went smoothly. She was grateful to be saved and excited about her new life. But that's not how it went at all. And now I was forced to chase her down and try to convince her she was a vampire before bringing her back to the manor and Alexander.

I went to the hospital's garage and unlocked my Boxster. It wasn't the Portofino I loved so much, but it would do. I wasn't sure where she was headed, but her apartment was a reasonable guess. If she weren't there, I'd have to backtrack and follow her scent on foot.

I pulled up outside her building. Light shone through the cheap, thin curtains covering the windows of her unit, and I could see her silhouette. I sighed in relief. That was one less complication to handle.

The sidewalk leading up to the front door was covered in wet leaves and debris. The yard—if you could even call it that—was merely a collection of weeds and moss, overshadowed by a squat, twisted tree. The place contained at least four units, but it seemed no one cared for the grounds or the building itself. Perhaps if you invested a lot of money into the place, it could be charming, but in its current state, it was simply depressing.

I knocked on the door and waited.

I heard her footsteps as she approached. "Who is it?" she called.

"It's James," I said, keeping my voice low. She could hear me perfectly well.

The door cracked open, held in place by a strong chain. She peered out at me.

"How did you know where I lived? Did you follow me?" she asked, sounding both scared and angry.

"Your driver's license," I said, raising her shoulder bag so she could see it through the gap in the door.

She sighed, stepped back, closed the door, and removed the chain. As she opened the door, she moved forward, blocking the way. She wore gray sweats and a rumpled T-shirt. Her long, dark hair was tied back in a ponytail. And although there was an annoyed look on her face, there was worry, too.

"I feel strange," she said, her voice small.

I nodded slowly. "Yeah, I remember," I said gently. "Things feel too hot, too cold, the lights are too bright, and noises are too loud? Your skin is too sensitive, and you feel dizzy when you move about?"

She blinked at me and then nodded. After a beat, she stepped aside to let me pass.

She shut the door, and I handed her the purse. "There were some clothes, too, but they were in pretty bad shape," I said, using the last of my breath. When I inhaled again, I froze.

There it was. That scent that first drew me to her. It was stronger here in her apartment, where she spent so much time. I inhaled deeply, savoring the fragrance. It was the vanilla of old paper, honeysuckle, and warm rain all mixed together. I shook my head, trying to clear my thoughts, and realized she was speaking to me.

"Hello? Are you okay?"

"Um, yeah. I think so," I said, hoping it was true. The scent of her surrounded me, intoxicating me. It was unlike anything I'd ever experienced. "Where was I?"

"My clothes," she said.

"Yes, I'm sorry; they were a total loss."

"It's okay," she said, eyeing me warily.

"May I sit so we can talk things through?" I asked, but

looking around, I realized there were very few seating options.

"Oh, sorry," she said, hurrying to flip the duvet over the unmade futon before clearing a stack of notebooks off a nearby dining chair.

I selected the chair, while she sat across from me at the end of the futon. Her posture was rigid, and she held her arms tightly to her body. She looked like someone who had been called into a disciplinary meeting.

"Sorry for the mess," she said.

I dismissed the comment with a wave. "I'm sure you didn't expect company."

"No, I didn't."

"And you believe me now? About what's happening to you?" I asked. Her scent still made my head swim, but the longer I stayed, the easier it was to focus.

"Not entirely," she said. "But I will admit that something is happening." She reached up and touched a finger to the gums above one of her canine teeth.

"They're sore?" I guessed.

She nodded, and her lip began to tremble. I was relieved she couldn't see the blood-red tears welling in her eyes. While it would make my point, it would likely upset her even more. I reached into my coat and retrieved a dark-colored handkerchief, holding it out to her. She accepted it and dabbed at her eyes.

"This can't be real," she said, sniffing.

"I know it's a shock," I said. "Would you like more proof? Other than the changes you're starting to experience?"

She leveled a wide-eyed gaze at me and nodded stiffly.

Leaning closer, I opened my mouth and let my fangs descend. It wasn't hard to coax them out with her heady scent all around me. She was mouthwatering, and I knew my eyes had dilated, turning from green to black.

To her credit, she didn't flinch. She remained motionless and nodded again.

I sat back, closing my mouth and willing my fangs to retract. It was more difficult than it should have been. I waited until I thought I could manage speech again. "I'm sure you have questions," I finally said.

"Okay." She pressed her palms against her thighs and took a deep breath. "Let's start with what happened to me when I got to the hospital and how this happened," she said, indicating her body, unharmed and undergoing its current state of transformation.

"You were brought in after a car accident. You arrived in pretty bad shape—multiple broken bones, including two broken legs, a fractured skull, and several internal injuries. The doctors and nurses managed to stabilize you, but just barely. At some point during the night, your condition worsened, and it became clear to me that you wouldn't survive."

"Were you one of my doctors?"

"No, I'm not a doctor, but I occasionally work at the hospital and saw you come in. I monitored your condition throughout the evening. When you were past the point of no return, I..." I paused.

Despite my initial reasons for coming, I didn't want to tell her what I did. I didn't want to reveal how I called and begged Alexander to come and change her. I didn't want to mention Alexander at all. Just the thought of him stopped me in my tracks.

I swallowed hard and tried not to imagine what it would be like when Alexander got hold of this woman. He'd barely been able to control himself when her veins had been diluted with the blood of others. If she maintained this enticing scent after her full transition, Alexander wouldn't be able to resist her. He would consume her. At the very least, she would become his pet, his plaything. No, I decided right then that I wouldn't let that happen to her.

I shook my head. "There was nothing else I, or anyone else, could do for you. It was the only way," I said.

"And, you changed me. Into a…" She narrowed her eyes but didn't finish the sentence.

I smiled tightly and nodded again. "A vampire."

I saw a shiver run down her body, but she didn't say anything, so I kept going.

"I reconnected your monitors and then left. Of course, I would have preferred to take you with me, but if you turned up missing, they would have searched. As it was, you were declared dead. You would have seemed that way to the doctors, regardless of how hard they worked to revive you, and you were taken to the morgue.

"I apologize for not arriving earlier. I intended to have you out of the drawer before you woke up. I realize you weren't expecting this, but all things considered, it's a good way to explain your exit," I said.

"My exit? What are you talking about?"

"From human society. An accident is perfect. It's much harder to remain in the same general area if humans are searching for you. But don't worry. We'll figure it out," I assured her.

She shook her head. "I don't want to exit human society. I have a life, you know?" she said, lowering her eyebrows and giving me a fierce glare.

I surveyed the disaster of an apartment. "You can't stay here. You can't hold onto your human life. It's not possible. I have a place for you to go where you'll be properly taken care of and safe." I didn't have a plan, but I did have an apartment. It was a starting point—a safe place to stash her while I figured out what to do next.

"But I don't want that. I want to stay here." She no longer sat hunched in on herself, but leaned forward, motioning with her hands in frustration. "I don't want to give up my family and friends. Is there any way to change me back? Undo it?"

I scoffed. "The only way to undo it is through death. Real death, the kind you can't come back from. The kind you faced last night in the ICU. You don't want that, do you?" I asked.

"No, I don't," she said, her tone petulant.

I was becoming impatient. This conversation was pointless. She'd received a wonderful gift, and now she was trying to return it.

"But I still don't see why everything has to change," she said.

"You don't?" I asked, letting the irritation show in my voice. "I'm guessing you have a job and friends who would expect to see you walking around in the sunlight, which you can no longer do, not without ending up as a pile of ash." I glanced at the thin curtains over the windows. "I bet it gets pretty bright in here during the day, and you won't want to spend those hours locked in your tiny bathroom. You'll also want to eat—probably not your neighbors. And even if you could solve all those problems on your own, you still wouldn't have a choice. You're part of something much larger now—larger than you and me. It's not as simple as deciding to opt out. Unless the exit you seek is death. That's the only way."

She remained silent for a long time. "Am I dead?" she asked again, her voice barely a whisper.

I sighed. "It's complicated," I said, softening my tone. I

knew it was a lot to take in. "But if it helps, I've never considered myself dead. We move, we think; our hearts still beat—albeit slowly—and we must eat," I continued. "Speaking of which, are you hungry? You'll need to eat before you can complete the transition."

Her eyebrows lifted. "No, I'm fine," she said. She touched her tongue to one of her canines, and I suspected the idea of eating made them ache again.

"Come with me," I said. "I promise this will get easier, but you can't stay here. It's too dangerous."

"And then what?" she asked.

"Then you begin your new life as a vampire."

"I don't know what that means," she said.

I grinned at her. "Let me show you."

She didn't seem convinced. Even worse, she looked miserable. I stood up from the chair and crouched in front of her, bringing her large brown eyes in line with mine.

"I'm sorry, Kathrine. I'm sorry this is happening to you. I understand it's a lot to handle. I don't mean to rush you, but this is for the best. I believe you'll find it's a wonderful life you've been given."

"Kate," she said. "Please call me Kate." She tilted her head and tried to smile.

"Kate," I repeated and smiled back.

She nodded, and I stepped back to give her some space.

"You can bring a few things," I said. "But nothing that anyone will miss."

Her head snapped up. The smile was gone. "Miss?"

"Yeah. When someone comes to pack this all up, if your luggage and clothes are missing, people will start asking questions. Anything you need can be replaced."

She looked even more miserable—if that was possible.

I didn't want to start things out with her so upset. I

sighed once more. "Take whatever you like. I guess I could always stage a robbery."

"No. It would only upset my mom more," she said, letting out a choked sob.

It was clearly going to take more than a suitcase full of belongings to comfort her. I walked closer but hesitated. Before I could change my mind, I took that final step and put an arm around her. She didn't pull away.

She shook gently as she cried. I wasn't surprised she was overcome with emotion. It felt nice to be able to offer her comfort. And, I admitted to myself, it felt good to touch her. She leaned against my shoulder in a way that made me feel needed, not just for what I could do for someone else, but for who I was. I hadn't experienced that in a long time.

Her closeness made me feel bold. I leaned in and pressed my cheek against the top of her dark head. I breathed in, and surprisingly, the scent from her wasn't as strong as it was around the apartment. I mostly smelled Alexander, but it was still there—that special something that belonged only to her. Something irresistible was hidden beneath the powerful scent of Alexander's blood. I closed my eyes, savoring the proximity and her weight pressing against me.

And then it was over. She pulled herself upright, out of my embrace, and wiped her eyes with my handkerchief. I felt flustered and a bit guilty about where my thoughts were headed. She dabbed at her face, and I took a moment to compose myself. She glanced up and smiled weakly at me.

"Okay," she said. "Let's go."

6

KATE

Closing the bathroom door, I changed into my jeans and favorite sweater. It took me several minutes of staring into the mirror and assuring myself that it would be okay before I could join James in the main room.

My hands trembled as I packed my sketchbook, some toiletries, and a photo of my mom and brother into my bag. I shoved a change of clothes on top. The bag overflowed, but it would suffice. I was fairly certain no one would notice these items were missing.

I looked at my shaking hands. I was in shock. A part of my brain recognized how absurd this all was, yet I found I couldn't make any decisions for myself at that moment.

I wasn't convinced James was right about leaving my life behind, but I needed his help. Soon after I returned home, I knew something was wrong, and he understood exactly what I was going through. *But a vampire? Seriously?* I decided to go with him for the time being. It felt like my best shot at figuring out what was happening and what I needed to do about it.

"What about my purse?" I asked James, carrying the now bulging bag on my shoulder.

"Don't worry about it," he said. "I made sure it wasn't listed with your belongings. The cops will think it was stolen during the accident."

"Does that really happen?" I asked.

"All the time," he said with a shrug.

"People suck," I murmured as I gazed around my apartment for the final time. Then a realization struck me.

"Wait. What about me? What about my body? Won't anyone notice that I'm gone?"

James tilted his head and smiled at me. "You have such little faith," he said. "I know what I'm doing. According to the records, you've been scheduled for cremation, and your ashes will be delivered to the funeral home next week."

"But won't they need a body for that? Cremation, I mean."

"I can always get a body if I need one," he said. He sounded annoyed, but his mood was more tired.

I wasn't sure I wanted to think too much about that statement. But I couldn't believe he was so relaxed about it all. I was still reeling from everything that happened, feeling numb and on the verge of a total breakdown. However, James remained very calm. Maybe it was a vampire thing—being accustomed to discussions about bodies—or maybe it was just his nature. Regardless, he was trying to do what he believed was right.

After I finished packing, I grabbed my hooded jacket, and James followed me outside, pointing to a car parked next to the curb. I wasn't a car person, but it looked very fancy. It was way nicer than anything I'd seen in person, let alone ridden in.

"This is your car?" I asked.

"One of them," he said. "I can get you your own if you want." He flashed me a smile and slipped into the driver's seat.

I shook my head and climbed into the passenger side. I felt completely out of place, but the smell of leather wrapped around me like a cozy blanket, and I snuggled into the upholstery and closed my eyes. It was all so overwhelming, and the movement made me feel sick.

Thankfully, he didn't take me far. Just a few minutes later, we entered the parking garage of a large residential building. It was less than a mile from my old place, I noted. James led the way across the concrete garage to the elevator. We stepped inside the modern stainless steel lift, and he pressed the button for the third floor.

As the elevator rose, my nausea grew stronger. It was a relief when we arrived at the correct floor and the door slid open. A short walk down a dimly lit, carpeted hallway brought us to the apartment. James located the right key, unlocked the door, and held it open for me. As I stepped inside, my jaw dropped. I momentarily forgot about my queasy stomach as I took in the apartment. It was a major upgrade from my studio.

The design and decor were modern. The walls were mostly brick, while the flooring was buffed concrete. There was exposed ductwork, black-painted metal beams overhead, and concrete columns supporting the upper floor. The main area was open, combining the kitchen, living room, and study into one space. The furniture was minimalistic, with dark grey fabrics, black metal accents, and a touch of brown leather for variety.

"It's not much, but you should be comfortable here," James said as I walked over to one of the windows overlooking the park. I ran my fingers along a metal track at the edge of the frame.

"It has some features that the other units in the building don't have. There are lightproof shutters that can be lowered over all the windows," he said with a grin. "You can sleep in an actual bed today and feel safe and comfortable at the same time."

I smiled at him, feeling embarrassed for some reason. "Do you live here?" I asked.

"Sometimes," he said.

I could sense he was proud of the place but guarded and apprehensive about something.

"It's convenient when I work at the hospital, but it's not my only residence," he said. "I'll be sleeping somewhere else today since there's only one bed." He cleared his throat and then led me to the kitchen area.

Maybe he was married or had a lover; it didn't matter to me. Back in my apartment, I sensed a fleeting impression of attraction that didn't come from me. Perhaps he was feeling guilty.

"Anyway, the fridge is fully stocked," he said, opening a stainless steel door to reveal shelves lined with plastic bags but no food. He pulled out an IV bag filled with a deep red substance that my senses told me could only be one thing—blood.

My nostrils flared as my body instinctively reacted to the smell of the bag's contents. When I realized what I was doing, I cringed. *Gross.*

"I thought you might want to eat right away. I remember how hungry I felt in the beginning," he said.

Eat? When he asked me if I was hungry earlier, I'd been thinking about food, not...

"Typically, a sire would present a new vampire with a

human and open a vein for the first feed, but this seemed more practical. Since this is all new to you, I thought it might also be more comfortable," he said.

I shook my head. The thought of drinking blood from a bag was bad enough, not to mention picturing drinking it from someone else. Yet, even though I knew I should be disgusted, I couldn't take my eyes off the bag he held. The liquid rolled around inside, its movement captivating.

"I don't think I'm ready for that yet," I said, finally tearing my gaze away, though my stomach twisted with hunger.

"Kate, you need to drink to complete the transition. I told you. You're not in the clear yet, medically. You have to feed," he said, watching me closely. He sounded kind, but there was a hint of irritation in his voice.

I knew he didn't want to argue again, but I wasn't ready to give in. I shook my head once more and stepped back from the kitchen, my legs colliding with the sofa behind me.

"Can we discuss this first?" I asked. "I still have so many questions and..." I trailed off.

He raised his eyebrows but returned the bag to the fridge. It was easier to concentrate with it out of sight. Placing his hands on the granite countertop separating us, he studied me closely.

"Fine. Go ahead and ask your questions," he said. "But it won't change what needs to be done."

I turned around and sat on the grey couch. James huffed out a sigh and walked to a modern black and chrome chair nearby. I placed my hands in my lap, squeezing them together, trying to figure out how to begin. How do you convince someone who is sure they are right? Finally, I looked up.

James lounged comfortably in his chair, one leg crossed

over the other, watching me. He was so relaxed, and it annoyed me. My life was crashing down around me. I was losing everything I knew. My body ached, my skin crawled, and my head pounded. And it was all his fault.

But I was also alive, and that was his doing as well.

It was all very confusing.

I cleared my throat. My tongue felt thick, and my mouth was dry. "So, what happens when I drink and complete the transition?" I asked.

"Just that," he said. "You will fully become a vampire. The pain you must be feeling by now will ease. Your senses will be further enhanced. Your teeth will work like a true vampire's. You'll be faster, stronger, and more durable."

"And what will happen if I don't drink?" I asked, looking down.

He laughed, but didn't sound amused. "You'll die," he stated. "You've been healed by consuming...my blood. However, your transition depends on an infusion of human blood. It's incomplete without it."

"How long do I have to decide?" I asked, my eyes darting to his face.

"Decide? What the hell are you talking about?" he said, leaning forward, his voice rising. "What's there to decide? You said you don't want to die. This is how you keep that from happening."

"I know what I said, but are you really sure? I mean, have you ever known anyone who didn't drink? Maybe I'll go back to being human."

"No," he admitted. "I haven't. This is a unique circumstance. There are usually safeguards in place, but we didn't have time for that."

I nodded. He was still telling the truth, but he was hiding something as well. Maybe there was a way out; he just hadn't thought to look for one before. I decided to change the subject for the moment. "You mentioned earlier that I was part of something bigger than both of us. What did you mean?"

He took a deep breath and leaned back. "As a vampire, you are bound to your sire, but there is also an entire bureaucracy with its own rules you must adhere to."

I snorted. "A vampire bureaucracy? You're kidding?"

"Nope. It's the twenty-first century; we've all had to adapt. We call it the Council. They determine what the rules are and enforce them."

"What kind of rules?" I asked

"There are too many to list," he said, running a hand through his dark hair. This line of questioning was no easier for him than the last. "It's mostly what you'd expect. Don't let the humans know about us. Pay your taxes. Try not to kill. That kind of thing."

"*Try not to kill?*" At least that made me feel better. But rather than discussing killing and death, I focused on something else he mentioned. "Taxes...?"

"Yeah, it's a government," he said with a shrug. "All governments need funds. But you don't have to worry about that. I'll handle it and any paperwork you need."

"So, are you my sire? The one who transformed me?" I asked.

"Yes," he said, seriously. There it was. He was definitely hiding something. I wondered if I was the first vampire he ever created.

"Every vampire belongs to a House. Unaffiliated vampires are not tolerated. This ensures that everyone behaves and is accountable to someone else. You will be part of my House. As I mentioned, I will ensure you have the necessary documentation. No one should bother you."

"How many vampires are there?"

"There are about four hundred in this region," he said. "I'm not sure how many there are worldwide, but it's a lot."

"How is it that I've never met one before?"

"You probably wouldn't realize if you had. We tend to stick to certain areas. Some businesses cater to us specifically. I'll take you downtown sometime, but not until you're stable. We don't want you slaughtering innocent humans as soon as you step out of the car."

I swallowed hard, trying to dispel the images that came to mind. "Will it be that bad?" I asked.

"Not for long. And not as long as you're well-fed. But don't worry. I won't let you slip up. Just do what I say, and you'll be alright. I promise." He smiled kindly at me, and I could feel the goodwill that accompanied the gesture.

I smiled back, but it didn't make me feel any better. None of this was comforting.

"Hey, listen, I have to go," he said, standing up.

His sudden change in mood gave me whiplash.

I stood up as well, but my legs felt shaky. "What? Now?" I asked. "I still... I mean, what will I do?" I didn't necessarily want to spend more time with this stranger, but the thought of being left alone made me uneasy.

"Don't worry. You'll be safe here," he said reassuringly.

He turned to me as he reached the door and paused. "I left my number on the fridge. Your cell is in your bag, but don't contact anyone except me. No one can know you're still alive. If they find out, there will be consequences," he said, his eyes growing dark.

His voice had an edge, but it was the emotion rolling off him that made me grow cold. He was deadly serious, and at that moment, I did not doubt that he was capable of real violence.

But then he turned around and continued as if nothing had happened. The mood vanished, and he resumed feeling annoyed and rushed. "Don't leave the apartment. I'll be back as soon as I can tomorrow night," he said. "I'll have my housekeeper stop by during the day, so lock the bedroom door before bedtime. She knows not to go in, but just in case. Make a list and leave it on the counter if you need anything. She can get whatever you want. Oh, and make sure to be in the bedroom with the window covers closed before sunrise." He stressed this last point by pausing and looking at me again, but there was no trace of the earlier shadow. Like it never happened.

I stood frozen as he opened the door. "You okay?" he asked, frowning. He looked down at his watch. "I guess I could stay a bit longer, but I do have to get going soon." At that point, he was more annoyed than concerned, and despite my earlier misgivings, I just wanted him to leave.

I shook my head. "It's okay," I said. "I'll be fine."

He looked at me for a moment longer before nodding. "Good. And eat something, please," he said, waving as he closed the door behind him.

Then he was gone, and I was alone.

I stood there in disbelief, confused about what had happened. He was sending me very strange signals. One minute, he was sympathetic; the next, hostile. Perhaps this was normal for a vampire, but he was the most challenging person I'd ever tried to read. His emotions were chaotic and intensely strong. And he was my only ally in this situation. I didn't know whether to laugh or cry.

Feeling rather lost, I wandered through the open front room and into the bedroom. Sandwiched between two small side tables was a large king-sized bed done up simply in gray linens. A long yellow bolster hugged a headboard lined with pillows, and a dark throw draped off one end. A tufted bench stretched along the foot of the bed, impressionistic paintings adorned two walls, and a wardrobe stood in one corner. It looked straight out of a magazine compared to what I was used to. The room had one window, and an open door revealed a white-tiled bathroom beyond.

I returned to the main room and grabbed my bag. I placed it on the bench and began searching through it. I decided to unpack, but arranging my few belongings among James's clothes and toiletries felt awkward. I felt like an intruder in his personal space. I discovered an empty drawer at the bottom of the wardrobe and placed my items inside. Glancing down, the drawer still looked pathetically empty.

Closing the drawer on the remnants of my life, I returned to the living room and sank heavily onto the sofa. Now that there wasn't anyone else's emotions to process, my mind reeled with all the new information. Some of what James said made sense, but it felt so wrong, too. I suspected he didn't have all the answers, and he certainly didn't tell me everything.

I reflected on what he said about the Council. I hadn't chosen this; why should I be bound by new rules? Most importantly, I didn't want to lose the people I loved. I didn't know James and didn't want to be a vampire. There had to be a way out.

I felt agitated and confused. I got up and walked to one of the windows overlooking the dark city, which wasn't dark after all. There were points of light glowing as far as I could see. The lamp posts throughout the park cast a soft, golden light on the trees. The branches swayed in the breeze, making the light dance beautifully. I sighed, beginning to feel the exhaustion from the past twenty-four hours. It was hard to believe that I slept all day.

My phone was still dead, but I guessed it would be several hours until dawn. I decided to locate the controls for the windows, just in case. I found remotes stashed around the apartment, each of which operated all the windows. I lowered the covers one by one, blocking out the view below while ensuring my safety. When the last one clicked fully into place, I carefully returned the remote to the side table. I decided to get ready for bed early, relishing the thought of being in an actual bed instead of on a futon. If I were stuck here, I could at least enjoy some of the perks.

I passed the kitchen on my way to the bedroom, purposely not looking at the fridge. I was hungry—very hungry—but I wasn't about to drink what James had stocked away. I wasn't so sure he knew what would happen to me if I didn't drink. I spotted a pad and a pen on the counter, and left a note for the housekeeper before turning for the bedroom.

I decided to take advantage of the shower and was rewarded for my choice. The water pressure was incredible, and the hot water felt soothing on my sore body. I had to work to find the right temperature. It seemed the water in the apartment was either scalding hot, or my body was more sensitive to temperature changes. As I adjusted to the warmth, I gradually turned the temperature up higher and higher. By the end of my shower, it was as hot as it could get, and the bathroom was filled with steam.

When I opened the bathroom door to clear some of the fog, I was shocked at the cold air that rushed in. Whatever was happening to my body had my senses completely out of whack. After a few minutes, I felt better, and by the time I was dry, I felt much better.

Wrapping myself in a robe, I pulled back the bed covers and climbed in. The sheets felt incredibly soft and had a pleasant scent. The aroma of clean linen clung to the pillow beneath my cheek. I took a deep breath and nestled deeper into the plush mattress. Staying here wouldn't be so bad, I thought. It would be like a vacation in a nice Airbnb while I figured things out. I tried to reassure myself that this was all just temporary. I would find a way to get back to my life somehow; I just didn't know how yet.

7

JAMES

Looking over my collection of sports cars in the garage, I chose the Porsche we arrived in. It still smelled like her—well, her and Alexander. I inhaled deeply as I settled into the driver's seat. But as I drew in her fading scent, the reality of what I was doing hit me hard in the stomach.

What was I thinking? Was I really doing this? Was I prepared to hide Kate from Alexander? Because that's what I would have to do if I didn't go back into the apartment, collect her immediately, and take her to him. That was what was expected of me. I knew my thoughts were insane, but I couldn't force myself to do anything different. I couldn't take her to him.

I'd left my apartment at sunset, hoping to find Kate alive and ready to meet her true sire. That was the plan. But everything changed when I stepped into her studio and remembered what drew me to her in the first place. She was special; there was no other way to put it. She was too good for Alexander. Despite his polished manners and nice clothes, he was a brute, an elder with little regard for life, human or vampire. No, I would keep her as far from him as possible. I wasn't sure how yet, but I would protect her.

Inhaling once more, I paused. I couldn't go to Alexander like this, reeking so strongly of her. He would assume I'd come into contact with her body, but I didn't want the scent to remind him of what happened during her making. No, her attempted-making, I reminded myself. I needed to get the story straight in my mind if I was going to convince him. He was too good at reading me.

I took my bag, stepped out of the Porsche, and opened the door of the Lexus next to it. I stripped off the scrubs I still wore, tossing them aside, and dressed in the clothes I wore the night before. They were a bit wrinkled, but that was fine. There was no trace of Kate on them at all. At the last moment, I reconsidered bringing the bag. It had been in the car with Kate, and I wasn't sure if the worn leather would retain her scent. I opted not to risk it and returned the bag to the Porsche.

On my way back to the Lexus, I glanced down the row of cars belonging to me. Alexander knew about most of them; he wasn't stingy with his wealth and didn't care how I spent his money, and there was more in his accounts than anyone could ever spend. But, I took special pride in the ones he didn't know about. I enjoyed having this apartment and these cars all to myself. It was a subtle rebellion, but one I relished. My gaze fell on the Portofino at the end of the row, snug beneath a black cover. It was my current favorite, but it would have to stay here for now. I sighed. How much further was I from living the life I craved? It was time to sort this out, and the first step was talking to Alexander.

So I drove south to lie to my maker.

Instead of solving my problems by bringing Alexander a new vampire, I'd multiplied them. I rolled down the windows and let the cold wind whip through my hair. I wanted to get as much of her scent off me as possible before arriving at the manor. I tried to think of what I would say. I figured I had about an hour to sort it all out, but before I knew it, I was pulling through the manor's wrought iron gates.

I parked in the driveway and straightened myself as much as I could before stepping out into full view of the house. I could never tell if Alexander would be in a watchful mood or if I would find him absorbed in a book or some other form of distraction. I wanted to appear as composed as possible.

By the time I reached the top of the porch steps, the massive wooden doors stood open. Someone was watching. One of the human housemaids greeted me politely as I entered. Handing over my coat, I realized we were no longer alone. I was unsurprised when I spotted Alexander waiting at the foot of the central staircase. He was relaxed and looked bored, as if he'd been there for hours rather than appearing just seconds before.

I spared a moment to look around for the dogs. They were blessedly absent.

"Sire," I said, inclining my head.

"You're alone," he observed. His voice was steady but carried a sharp edge, and not a muscle in his body moved.

I swallowed and averted my gaze. "Yes, Sire," I said as I stepped forward. I was surprised to hear my voice remained steady, though I quaked inside. "I regret to inform you that the woman did not survive the transformation."

He was quiet for so long that I looked up to make sure he still listened. It wasn't unusual for him to let his mind wander during a conversation if he wasn't engaged, but I was confident this topic mattered to him. I met Alexander's gaze, and his cold grey eyes pierced into me with such intensity that I drew a sharp breath. I lowered my eyes back to the floor. My pulse raced, and my muscles tensed. I was in trouble.

"Sire, there was nothing I could do. I am truly sorry," I said, hurriedly tripping over my words. I was about to continue when his hand grabbed my lower jaw, silencing me.

I hadn't sensed him move at all. I froze, waiting to see what he would do with me.

He tilted my head up and held me with his gaze. "Quiet," he whispered through clenched teeth. "This is your fault. I told you she was too far gone. I warned you that a body as broken as hers would never recover. But you insisted."

He paused, his face going blank. Leaning closer, he drew in a long breath, his nostrils flaring. I couldn't look away. I saw his lip peel back and his fangs descend. My God, they looked monstrously long up close. I held my breath. There was no point in struggling or trying to run. He was so much more powerful, so much faster than I was. How did I ever think I could hide anything from him?

"What did you do with her?" he asked, and I couldn't interpret his tone.

Did he know? Should I come clean and tell him the truth? What would he do to me if he found out later? I waited for him to loosen his grip before I could speak. "Cremated, Sire," I managed to say. *What the fuck was I doing?*

Shuddering, he let me go completely. He stepped back; the expression on his face was one of grief and loss.

I sagged with relief. He believed me. He believed she was dead. And he was...sad?

I hadn't considered how this might impact him beyond his reaction to me. Was he saddened that one of his children didn't survive, or had he been as captivated as I'd become? Either way, it made me feel even more protective of Kate.

I stood taller, my determination solidifying. I could make this happen. I waited for him to say something.

"Find someone else. This time, bring them to me. Don't count on any more favors," he said, and I winced at the sharpness in his words. "If you can," he continued, his tone softer now, almost pleading. "Find someone like her. You were on the right track. She was…"

"Yes, Sire," I said when he didn't continue. "I understand and will put my full effort into it." I paused, a thought occurring to me. "I will stay downtown until I find what you're looking for. I will dedicate myself to this task."

This would give me what I needed: a break from my duties, time to help Kate adjust, and time to figure out my next steps. And who knew, maybe I would find another? Perhaps I could give Alexander what he wanted and keep Kate all to myself.

I just needed time.

Alexander nodded. "Very well. It's good to see you taking your responsibilities seriously for once," he said, moving toward the stairs. He climbed the softly carpeted steps slowly, running his hand along the wooden banister as he went. He moved with deliberate care. He would know as soon as I turned away. He wanted an audience, and I knew better than to think I'd been dismissed.

At the top of the steps, he turned to face me again, gazing down at me from beneath his long, dark lashes. I could still see the fire burning in his grey eyes. "Don't disappoint me again, James," he said, and then he vanished.

I stood there for a while, ensuring he was truly done with me or perhaps just waiting for the feeling to return to my legs so I could move without falling. I witnessed the aftermath of Alexander's rage before. I understood what he was capable of.

When I first joined Alexander, just before he turned me, there was another vampire in the House besides Miguel and Josephine. His name was Henry. He befriended me and brought me to Alexander. Henry was the one who first told me about this life and all I could gain from joining the House. He helped me learn everything I needed to know about the day-to-day running of a large estate and how to care for our elders. He showed me how to survive in this world. Henry also taught me the most important lesson of all: never cross Alexander.

Ten years after I was turned, Henry challenged Alexander for emancipation. He'd had enough. He wanted out and petitioned the Council for the right to form his own House. Alexander found out and reacted poorly. Miguel was allowed to travel for years at a time, and Josephine was permitted to lock herself away in her rooms, but you didn't leave Alexander. You didn't ever reject him.

I came home from the clubs early one morning to find pieces of Henry scattered all over the foyer and parlor. The floor was slick with his blood, and the walls were coated in gore. I found Alexander sitting in a chair by the fireplace, gazing into the flames. He, too, was covered in my brother's blood. It was dried on his face and flaking off the backs of his bare hands. His clothes were drenched, and the blood seeped into the chair and rug where he lounged.

He didn't look at me when I entered. He didn't acknowledge my presence at all. I learned later that the staff was forbidden from touching anything until we'd all taken a good look. The message was clear. I'd never gone against him, at least not directly, until now.

I shook myself out of the memory. I needed to think. I'd

bought myself some time, but there were other matters to address. It would be foolish to ignore the Council in all this. I might be able to hide Kate from my sire, but I would also need to ensure her safety from them. I didn't know if we would stay in the area. Leaving the West Coast altogether might be safer, but that would take time. I had to prepare for the possibility that she would encounter other vampires. Even Seattle vampires.

There was no chance of her running into Alexander on the streets, but she would need paperwork to be out and about. Unregistered vamps were not tolerated. Luckily, I knew the right people to get her what she needed without going through official channels. It just had to look official if anyone challenged her. No one would run a check on her if she were out with me, and I had no plans to let her out of my sight.

Going to my office, I took Alexander's seal out of the wall safe. I also grabbed some cash and my registration paper-work. With my ID, the forger should be able to doctor up everything that Kate needed. Packing it all into a backpack, I quickly left the manor. I didn't want to risk running into Alexander again.

I drove to the city's vampire district and parked on the street. I also kept an apartment in the city, which mostly served as a place to entertain other vampires or the occa-sional human. I typically didn't stay there during the day, but it would be more convenient for my needs. There were things to do and people to meet before dawn, and there was no way I would go back to the manor until I had a plan and found Alexander a suitable distraction. Someone to sink his teeth into besides me.

8

———

SARA

Hunched over the desk in the back of my family's shop, I squinted at the computer screen. It had been a tough couple of days. Every time I closed my eyes, I found myself stuck in a version of the same nightmare where Kate wasn't dead, but she wasn't alive either. Exhaustion only intensified the sense of unease I felt about Kate's death. I thought diving back into work would be best for me, but I'd been staring at the same line on the screen for the past half hour while thinking about Kate.

I expected to be devastated by my friend's death. But instead of being overwhelmed with grief, I found myself caught up in the mystery of what I felt at the hospital. Ultimately, I think my mind refused to accept that Kate was gone. It would likely take some time, I reminded myself. It was so unexpected, such a shock. No wonder I questioned how this could be real.

Kate's mom chose cremation but hadn't set a date for the funeral yet. It had been less than two days, after all. I was confident that by the time the service arrived, I would be ready to face what happened. And hopefully, the night-mares would stop, and I would get some sleep.

I sighed and rested my head on my arms at the desk. I was supposed to be finishing the last of the online orders while my aunt Lucia manned the front of the shop, but my mind wouldn't settle. Most of our income came from internet orders that shipped out daily. We mainly sold herbal supplies and supplements. I handled the online traffic while my mom and aunt rotated dealing with customers and managing inventory.

The store itself was small, measuring approximately twenty by forty feet. It had natural wooden floors, vintage wooden tables and dining hutches for display, and small windows that let in just enough light to see by without damaging the inventory. There were never more than one or two customers at a time, which made it feel more like an office than a store.

My mother was at home, tending to the greenhouse, which was her domain. She grew much of what we sold and provided the ingredients for most of what my aunt cooked up and bottled for the shop. The items we made, bought wholesale, and imported from around the world supplied our wider community. We shipped to locations worldwide and were known for the quality and authenticity of our goods and ingredients.

I lifted my head and rubbed my eyes. I didn't dare to sleep in the shop, not so close to my aunt. What if I made noise or showed some sign of my troubled sleep? She'd worry if she knew I had nightmares about Kate; it was a bad sign. I placed my fingers on the porcelain keys of my custom keyboard and forced myself to review the most recent order. It was pretty standard: an herb sampler, two Tonics of Clar-ity, and half a dozen candles. I printed the invoice and shipping stickers, then went to check on my aunt before heading to the post office with the day's shipments.

My aunt Lucia sat alone in the main room, leafing through a brightly colored travel magazine filled with images of blue seas, green forests, and pink sunsets over exotic locations.

"Where are you going this time?" I asked. My aunt had taken several trips over the years, but none recently. She was always dreaming of distant places, though, and I knew she would travel full-time if she could.

"Ugh, nowhere. Not right now, at least. I would love to go somewhere warm this winter, though," she said, continuing to thumb through the pages.

The chime over the door sounded, surprising us both. I glanced over to see a familiar figure. His large form blocked out most of the late afternoon light as he ducked through the doorway. His thick brown hair was tousled from the wind, and the cold air had brightened his tanned cheeks.

"Good afternoon," Silas said, his smile wrinkling the skin around his honey-colored eyes.

I took a deep breath and smiled back at him. I didn't expect to see him that afternoon, and his presence was a pleasant surprise. "Hi," I said, noticing my voice sounded slightly strained. My aunt shot me a look, but then also greeted Silas.

"I just stopped by to check if you needed anything taken to the post office," he said. "I was on my way, and I thought..." He shrugged, keeping his yellow gaze fixed on me.

My aunt made a sound in the back of her throat and then turned back to her magazine, one eyebrow raised.

"Oh, yeah. Thanks. Just give me a minute," I said, hurrying to the back room. I emerged with an armful of brown shipping boxes, and Silas rushed to take them from me. "I've got a few more," I said. "If you don't mind."

"Not at all," he said, and we carried the load out to the parking lot. I thanked him as he loaded the boxes.

He paused before getting into his truck. "I'm sorry," he said. "About your friend. I wish I'd gotten a chance to meet her." He kept his eyes on the ground, and I was grateful as I felt my eyes start to water.

It took me a minute to find the right words. I constantly thought about her and her death, but hearing it spoken out loud still took my breath away. "Thank you," I finally managed. "She would have liked you."

I smiled, but my face felt too tight, and my eyes still prickled. Silas nodded and turned away. It was probably the longest conversation we ever shared. I knew he liked me; he wouldn't keep stopping by if he didn't, and I was crazy about him, but neither of us quite knew what to do about it. If anything, I knew his people would be just as unimpressed with our feelings for each other as mine were. I lifted a hand in farewell and sighed as he drove off.

When I returned to the shop, my aunt was still reading the magazine, but her expression indicated that she was thinking about something else. I let the door close harder than necessary, and my aunt stiffened.

"He shouldn't come around here so often," Lucia said, sniffing. "And you shouldn't be encouraging him."

I pursed my lips and looked at my aunt, but didn't say anything. We'd been having this discussion for a while now —well, not a real discussion since that would require two people talking. But my aunt and mother both made their feelings clear on the matter. I knew they meant well. I understood they were trying to protect me and my place in our town. However, they were also trying to safeguard their reputations, which made me feel sad and frustrated.

"You never had an issue with Kate," I said a tad too sharply. "She wasn't part of our community either, but it never seemed to matter."

"That's different, and you know it," my aunt said. "Kate never looked at you the way that boy does." She sounded so much like my mother that my breath caught, and I felt my cheeks grow hot.

My aunt took a deep breath but didn't look up. "Besides, Kate's gone now, so it doesn't matter." She spoke so softly, her voice tinged with sadness.

Kate had been my best friend since high school, but I sometimes forgot how much time she spent with my mom and aunt. I knew they were hurting too, and I felt guilty for my comment, ashamed that I hadn't stopped to consider how she might be feeling.

My aunt decided our talk was over. She set aside her magazine and began shutting down for the day. I joined in, and we both worked quietly. Soon, the small store was tightly closed and put to bed, and we headed to our cars.

I drove back down the highway toward our small town. It was dark, but I knew the way and easily navigated the twisting and turning road. The trees grew denser as the road narrowed, and the rock walls rose sharply on either side. The Toyota grumbled slightly when the incline became too steep, but I trusted the car. It was an older model, more machine than computer, which suited someone like me just fine.

After a few minutes, I slowed down and crossed the bridge over the river to the town I called home. Nearly one hundred people lived there, nestled on the mountainside. Many families had lived there for generations. My grandparents moved there in the seventies, coming from the South, searching for a quieter place to raise their girls. The settlement was perfect for them, filled with people just like themselves, and an ideal location to open a store that catered to the local needs.

I grew up in a larger town but moved back after high school. My mother and I moved in with Lucia to help run the business. It was initially my grandparents' business, with my aunt taking over as they grew older. Now, the three of us ran it together and lived under the same roof. This arrangement worked well, but it left me feeling lonely for peers my age. I was one of the only twenty-somethings in the valley.

Not many younger people stayed anymore; most moved to larger towns or cities. Silas and his family lived in a similar town on the other side of the Pass. Our town and shop were out of his way, and my aunt and I both knew it. It added to the strain when he "happened to stop by," but I was glad he did. Even though we didn't talk much, it felt nice to have someone who understood what it was like for me living out in the middle of nowhere as a young person, and I valued the moments we spent together.

I pulled into the gravel driveway and parked beside the three-story house. My grandparents built it when my mother and aunt were very young. It was a mix of Victorian and Craftsman styles. It had a large wraparound porch and a shingled roof with a weather vane shaped like a crow on the highest point.

I walked in through the door that led to the kitchen. My aunt Lucia beat me home and chatted with my mom, who was cooking at the stove. Watching them together, it was clear they were sisters despite their different personalities. My aunt was a tall woman with short, curly, grey-brown hair that she wore in a mass above her ears. As usual, she was dressed in long, flowing linen slacks and a loose, matching top in green. My mother wore a similar outfit in brown with a large apron, and although she was shorter and plumper than her older sister, she mirrored her posture and expression, hands on hips, head tilted to the side, eyebrows raised.

They stopped their conversation and turned to me as I entered, their faces becoming unnaturally blank. They were discussing me. I wasn't certain if it was about Silas, Kate, or something entirely unrelated, but I didn't have the energy for whatever it was.

"Hi, Mom," I said, shrugging off my coat and hanging up my keys. Maybe if I kept my back to her, I could dodge the conversation.

"Hello. How was work?" she asked.

I turned around to see her pick up a spoon to stir the pot she tended. "It was okay," I sighed. "I'm just tired."

My mom set down her spoon and wiped her hands on the skirt of her apron. She looked at me, her gaze soft and her eyes filled with concern. "I know, dear. I'm so sorry. Maybe you should take some time off. It might be good for you. You need time to process, time to grieve."

"I'm fine. I really am," I said, though I only half meant it. "I think it's best if I avoid the subject for a bit, actually. I've been spending too much time processing it. It's all I've been able to think about since it happened."

"That's normal. But think about it," she said. "And if there's anything I can do, anything you need…"

"I'll ask. I promise," I said, glancing at my aunt, who leaned against the counter beside my mother, watching me. "And I'm sorry for you both, too. I know you loved Kate."

They exchanged sad smiles, and I felt my eyes welling

up again. "Hey, I'm going to my room to lie down," I said, turning toward the back stairs to hide my face.

"Come down later if you get hungry," my mom called after me.

I mumbled something vaguely affirmative but continued up the steps to my room. Once safely inside, I shut the door and fell onto the bed, letting my body rest where it landed on the soft mattress. It felt good just lying there, collapsed where I was. I seriously considered falling asleep, but I was still fully dressed, including my shoes, so I allowed myself only a few minutes of wallowing before I summoned the energy to get up and get ready for bed properly.

As I brushed my teeth, washed my face, and changed into something more appropriate, I reflected on what my mom said. Maybe I did need some time off, some time to rest and process what happened. I thought of Kate and tried to imagine her at the art show where I last saw her happy and alive. But all I could picture was her on that gurney in the hospital. I squeezed my eyes shut.

She was my best friend. I spent countless days with her doing all sorts of things; why couldn't I picture her that way? Why couldn't I imagine her like she used to be? Why was my mind determined to show me the worst moment we'd spent together?

I got into bed and tucked myself under the covers. I was so tired, yet at the same time, I dreaded sleep and the nightmares I knew would come. I didn't know what to do or how I would find what I needed. I didn't know how I would convince myself that she was really gone. I clearly needed some closure.

Just as I closed my eyes, I heard my phone buzz on the table beside the bed. I reached for it in the dark, my hand knowing exactly where it was. There was a message from Kate's mom.

For a moment, my heart leaped. I don't know what I expected. I knew she wasn't texting to tell me it was all one big mistake and that Kate was back, but I was still hopeful when I opened the app to read her message.

Her message was brief. She asked for my help with packing up Kate's apartment. I bit the inside of my cheek as tears threatened, and my throat tightened. I felt so foolish. I'd hoped for something different—what, I don't know. Something to make sense of what I felt. But this was good. I texted Melanie back, and we arranged a time to meet.

I set my phone back on the table and closed my eyes. As I began to drift off, I felt less worried about my dreams. Maybe this would be the last time I saw Kate in my sleep. Perhaps after helping Melanie, I could think of Kate without feeling like I'd failed her.

9

KATE

It was all darkness when I awoke again. Panic rose within me, and my breathing quickened in response. I slowly raised my hands, fearing I would find a metal drawer above me, but there was nothing—only black space. The air in the room smelled fresh. The fog of sleep faded, and the soft mattress beneath me registered in my mind. I wasn't trapped. I was in a bed. I was okay. Or was I?

I reached over and groped blindly for the lamp. Switching it on, I winced and turned my face away from the bright light. Blinking, I pushed myself up to a sitting position. It took more effort than it should have. Every muscle in my body ached. I felt like I'd come down with the flu. I was also starving, which didn't surprise me. I hadn't eaten in over two days. I'd sipped water from the faucet the night before, but my throat was beyond dry, and my tongue stuck to the roof of my mouth.

Getting out of bed, I went into the bathroom and took a few more sips from the tap, but I still felt no better. Splashing cold water on my face helped, but then I caught sight of myself in the mirror. I was thinner. A lot thinner. I leaned in closer to get a good look at my face. I pulled the robe apart and stared down at my stomach and legs. Normally, I had a healthy build—just the right balance of muscle and fat to be strong but still have some nice curves. Now, I was nearly supermodel thin. It felt so strange, like looking at someone else's body. How long had I slept?

I stumbled back into the bedroom and retrieved my phone from beside the bed. It was fully charged and showed that only a few hours had passed since my arrival. How had this happened? How had I lost so much weight in just one day?

But I knew.

I wasn't sure whether vampires were magical or merely biological creatures. Yet, whether by biology or magic, a vampire helped my body heal from the trauma of my accident, and it had probably taken an immense amount of energy. I just needed to eat. I needed calories. Wrapping the robe back around me, I tied the belt tightly and went searching for food.

I unlocked the bedroom door and peered out. The lamps were on, but the shutters remained closed over the windows. I didn't sense anyone else in the apartment, yet it felt like someone had been there while I slept. I went to the kitchen to find the requested items neatly arranged on the countertop. There was instant coffee—no coffee maker—, bagels, bananas, and almonds. I assumed the milk, orange juice, and cream cheese were in the fridge, but I wasn't ready to open that door yet. The housekeeper also left paper plates, bowls, coffee cups, and plastic cutlery. I figured I was the first human guest James ever hosted.

For all the things the kitchen lacked, it did have a microwave, and I had a hot cup of coffee sitting on the counter in just a few minutes. I stared down at it, frowning.

Usually, I added a generous splash of milk to my daily coffee. But milk would mean opening the fridge and confronting what else was in there. I sighed. I didn't know why I felt so hesitant. I'd seen it the night before. It was no big deal, I reassured myself as I gripped the shiny silver handle and gave it a yank.

Despite my pep talk, I still braced myself before looking inside. It was empty. I sighed with relief. Nothing was in the fridge except for the things I'd requested. I took a long, steadying breath, pulled the items out, and placed them on the counter.

I loaded up the bagel, poured myself some orange juice, and doused my coffee with milk, just the way I liked it. Carrying my breakfast to the side of the kitchen island, I sat on one of the tall bar stools. I looked down at the food I prepared for myself. It was completely unappetizing. And not just because the coffee was instant, which I knew was a crime. Nothing looked or smelled good at all. But I was hungry, so I picked up the cup of coffee and took a sip.

It was revolting. I clenched my teeth to keep from spitting it across the pristine marble island. I choked down the hot liquid and set the cup aside. There was no way it should taste that bad. Even instant coffee ought to taste like coffee, but this was something entirely different. I leaned forward and sniffed the cup. It smelled how it should. I picked up the bagel and brought it to my nose. It smelled like a bagel with cream cheese. I took a bite.

It was terrible, even worse than the coffee—if that was possible. Still, I forced myself to chew and swallow. I knew I was starving, and I needed to eat; this was the only food I had. Yet, I suspected the food wasn't the issue. My taste buds were off. That was all. Before I could overthink it, I took several more big bites and finished half the bagel, washing it down with some extremely bitter orange juice.

I pushed myself back from the counter and stood. I needed a minute. I felt awful. The food sat in my stomach like a rock, and instead of subsiding, my hunger got worse, and I felt nauseated. I needed to walk. I needed air.

I was sure it was night, but I had a moment of anxiety when I pushed the button to raise the shutters. As they retracted, light streamed in from the windows. But it was just the soft yellow glow from the streetlights below. I could hear the wind rustling the trees outside, and I longed to feel the cool breeze against my face. The air in the apartment felt stuffy and hot, and the pain in my stomach gnawed at me. I approached the nearest window and examined the frame, but I couldn't find any latch or release. I tugged on the bottom of the sash, but it didn't budge. I needed to get out.

I dressed in the same clothes I had worn the day before and sat on the sofa, pulling on my shoes, when I heard the keys in the front door. James stepped into the apartment, shutting the door behind him, and froze. He was no longer wearing scrubs. This time, he wore his leather jacket over a black sweater, grey slacks, and dark boots.

I felt both relieved and anxious to see him. I was beginning to get genuinely worried. My body was experiencing something I had no context for, and I hoped he could help. Yet, at the same time, I wasn't certain I wanted the solution he was likely to propose.

"Kate," he breathed. "Oh, God." He dashed to my side so quickly that I thought I would be sick from the motion.

"What happened?" he asked. "Have you fed?"

I didn't think the weight loss was that extreme, and his alarm frightened me.

"I tried," I said, leaning back slightly to create space. He crouched so close I could feel his breath on my face. "I ate some breakfast, but it only made things worse."

His brow furrowed, then he lifted his chin, sniffing the air.

"Wait. What did you eat?" he asked, his voice rising and his worry shifting to incredulity.

I gestured toward the kitchen and my partially eaten breakfast.

James glanced at my plate, wrinkling his nose like I'd left roadkill on his lovely countertop. He sighed and turned back to me.

"Kate, you can't eat that stuff anymore. Honestly, I'm surprised you could get any of it down," he said. His voice was soft, but I could sense his frustration. "I left you what you needed."

He walked into the kitchen and stopped when he saw the groceries. "You didn't leave the apartment, did you?"

He was curious but not mad.

"No," I said. "I left a note, like you said. It was all here when I woke up."

James opened the fridge and then closed it again.

"Did you move the blood?" he asked.

"It wasn't me," I said, raising my hands for emphasis.

He nodded and walked to a door I'd assumed was a coat closet. It opened onto a hallway, and James disappeared from view. He returned a moment later, carrying several bags of dark red blood.

"The housekeeper moved them to the fridge in the laundry, probably to make you more comfortable. I'm sure she thought you were a human."

"I am a human," I said, though I couldn't take my eyes

off the bags in his hands. My mouth began to water, and I swallowed hard.

"No. You aren't," he said, sounding irritated. "You were. And now you're starving because you haven't completed your transition. We discussed this." He spread the bags out on the counter. "Do you want it in a cup or directly from the bag? I can heat it for you if you prefer."

He was annoyed and a bit angry, too. I could tell he didn't want to have this discussion again.

I shook my head and tore my gaze from the bloody offering. "I just need to get some air," I said. "My stomach is upset, and I think a walk would help me."

I stood up and took my coat from the back of the chair beside the sofa, avoiding his gaze.

Before I noticed him move, I felt his hand on my shoulder, his fingers digging into my skin. The suddenness of it made me jump.

"The only thing that will make you feel better is going to the bathroom, getting rid of that disgusting mess in your stomach, and feeding properly," he said, his anger intensifying. "Your digestive system no longer functions like most of your organs. Once you transition, your heart will start beating again, but you'll never be able to eat human food. Ever."

My response caught in my throat. I stood there gazing up into his stormy green eyes.

"...again," I said so softly that I almost mouthed the word. I placed my hand on my chest and waited.

Nothing.

I felt nothing.

How had I not realized that my heart was no longer beating? I gazed down at my hand resting on my chest. I drew in a ragged breath and then another.

I felt the hand on my shoulder relax. I turned to look at James, and whatever he saw in my eyes moved him to wrap his arms around me and pull me close.

"It's okay," he said, his tone soft and soothing. "You're going to be okay." He rubbed my back, and I could feel the knobs of my spine beneath his fingers.

I shuddered and pulled back. "I just want to return to how things were," I said. "I don't want to be...what you are." I finished weakly.

He nodded, placing a firm arm around me, and nudged me toward the kitchen. I took several reluctant steps but paused before we reached the counter. I leaned back and glanced to the side, trying to avoid what lay there. I couldn't deny that I was drawn to the liquid in those bags. It felt right, and that terrified me.

I shifted my body and turned toward James. "I think I need to use the restroom," I said.

He nodded again. "Yeah, that will help. Clear your stomach, and we'll get you fixed up."

As I pulled back, I looked up at James. I could feel that his anger had cooled, and I was glad. But, as I gazed into his eyes, I sensed a new emotion blooming within him: desire.

My body stiffened, and he lowered his arm. I turned and fled for the bedroom, shutting the door behind me. I felt more at ease with the door closed between us. However, there was still the issue of my stomach. I went to the bathroom, locked the door, and turned on the water. I didn't want to be disturbed or overheard.

I had no experience making myself sick, but it didn't take much coaxing for my stomach to give up what I forced down. Afterward, I felt better. I was still hungry, but my stomach didn't ache like before. I rinsed my mouth and stood with my arms braced on the sink, looking in the mirror.

What was I going to do? I didn't want this. I didn't want to be a vampire. I didn't want the life James offered. I didn't want James. I couldn't lose everything and everyone I loved. I thought of my mom and little brother, as well as Sara and her family. I wondered what they must be going through, thinking I was dead. My bottom lip quivered, and I felt tears welling in my eyes. I watched my reflection as blood-red drops spilled down my cheeks, staining my skin. *What the hell?*

I turned the water back on and scrubbed my face, horrified. No food, no heartbeat, alone except for a mercurial vampire—and now I cried blood. This couldn't be my life. I wouldn't let it be. A glance in the mirror confirmed my face was clean before I stepped out of the bathroom.

James waited patiently in the kitchen, one elbow resting on the counter, the blood still on display.

"I'm not ready," I said. "Tomorrow. We'll do this tomorrow."

10
_____

JAMES

ocking the apartment door behind me, I shook my head. I didn't know whether to be angry or impressed with Kate. She was clearly suffering. I could smell the hunger on her and noticed how she reacted to the blood I'd offered. Her rapid weight loss made me nervous. However, I was confident that before dawn, she would give in and suck down most of what I'd left in the apartment.

I considered force-feeding her. Especially in her weakened state, it would be easy to overpower her and get the job done. But there was no harm in allowing her an extra day. It would be simpler if she arrived at this decision herself. She was right; she wasn't given the choice to become a vampire, so at least she could think of this step as a decision she made independently. Ultimately, biology would win out. I straightened my jacket and headed for the garage.

I still couldn't believe that she'd eaten human food. I know it had only been a couple of days since she had been living off of that stuff, but I had no idea how she could stand the smell, let alone the taste of it anymore. Just thinking about it made me feel nauseated.

She was right; I didn't know what would happen if she didn't feed. But it was clear she wasn't headed in a good direction. She couldn't hope to survive if she didn't transition soon. Yeah, it was only a matter of time. It was either that or true death. I was certain.

I thought about what to do with the rest of my night. I'd hoped to spend the evening with Kate. But I couldn't just wait around and watch her struggle to resist feeding. I had to admit that dealing with Kate had become increasingly irksome. Playing the concerned sire had grown tedious, and I looked forward to the next step.

The more I thought about it, the better I could picture a place for her in my life. I wanted a companion, someone just for me. Like one of my cars, the thought of having something of my own that Alexander didn't know about was exhilarating. Keeping up the charade for a few more days wouldn't kill me. I was eager for her to decide and become the vampire I knew she could be. I wanted someone to have fun with, someone who would improve my life, not complicate it. I would be the dutiful ward of Alexander while at the manor, but in the city, I would have Kate. The idea made my heart race and my blood surge in my veins.

There was still the small matter of finding new House members for Alexander, and I didn't see why I couldn't handle that as well. It would reduce my burdens at the manor and give me more time in the city where I wanted to be. More time to enjoy my nice things. Yet instead of the usual images I envisioned when thinking of the life I desired —the cars, the apartments, the stylish clothes—I found myself thinking of Kate.

With my mind made up, I set off for the city, specifically to the areas often visited by creatures like me. Creatures like me and humans who desired to become like me. Most vampire-owned businesses employed humans, either as staff or food, or sometimes both. No human entered our world without signing a contract—one that was nearly impossible to escape. Whether they stumbled into our world by chance, were brought in by someone they knew, or sought us out based on rumors, once they were inside, they were trapped. Death was typically the only way out. But there was a never-ending supply of humans eager to sign on because there was always a chance to become one of us. It would be the best place to search for what Alexander was looking for.

The main issue, and the reason I hadn't taken that route already, was that most willing humans were loathsome. They were overly eager, simpering romantics. I'd never found their company bearable, let alone appealing. I'd never seen any of them as particularly worthy of anything but being a meal. However, in the past, it was about choosing a housemate —someone I could tolerate being around and work alongside. Now I had Kate. I didn't need someone worthy; I just needed someone to take my place. Someone to distract Alexander so I could live my life the way I wanted, like Miguel did. I thought of Josephine in her room, still, unmoving, and I shuddered. I needed to escape. I needed to find a way to free myself from Alexander, or I would end up like her someday—if he let me live.

An hour later, I sat at a table in one of my favorite clubs with a few familiar vampires. Their company helped with my mood. We chatted and sipped warm blood from wine glasses as I watched the crowd swirling around us.

There were plenty of humans present. Most were either working or paired with a vampire for the evening, but a couple of tables were occupied by humans alone. I laughed at something one of my companions said, but kept my eyes on the available humans. They looked so pathetic, dressed in their best club attire, waiting to be chosen as a vampire's plaything for the night. I sighed. This was pointless. All I wanted was to go back to Kate.

I jumped when one of the vampires, Callie, gripped my arm. I looked up to find her staring at me with concern on her pretty face.

"Are you Ok?" she asked.

"I'm fine," I said, brushing off her concern. "I just have some business to take care of."

She smirked and raised a perfectly sculpted eyebrow, glancing in the direction I'd been staring.

"You better get to it, then," she said with a wink.

I sighed, rose from the table, and bid my companions good night.

I made my way to the nearest table of humans. Six pairs of eyes looked up eagerly at me as I approached. I scanned the table, trying to decide which of these creatures I could tolerate spending the evening with, when one caught my attention.

She was young and slender, with dark hair and brown eyes. Her creamy complexion and flushed cheeks betrayed her anticipation as she waited to see if she would be the one chosen.

I crooked a finger at her, and she jumped up so quickly she knocked against the table, spilling her drink.

"It's your lucky night," I said to her as I offered my hand and gave her one of my best smiles.

She beamed at me, and I struggled to keep my smile in place. She was lovely, but she wasn't Kate.

The woman's cheap clothing and cheaper perfume grated on me as I guided her across the dance floor toward the exit. She pulled on my arm when she noticed where we were going.

I patted her hand that was tucked into my arm. "Don't worry, my dear. I just want to talk with you somewhere more private," I said above the music and din of voices.

She swallowed hard but nodded. Her eyes were wide with worry, and she gripped my arm more tightly as we stepped out into the night and left her friends behind.

I took her to my city loft. It was just a few blocks from the club, and we talked as we walked that short distance. Her name was Sophia. She trained as a pastry chef and worked at a hotel before she entered our world. She currently cooked for one of the larger Houses, feeding the human staff and catering parties when the House hosted non-vampire guests, which was rare. She felt disappointed that she didn't get to flex her skills more often. She mentioned she was looking for a change.

She was perfect.

When we reached the loft, I offered her a drink, and she arranged herself on the sofa while I poured her wine. I handed her the glass and snagged a folder off the coffee table. I'd come prepared. I would do this properly. Before I took her to Alexander, she would sign all necessary waivers and agreements. There was no guarantee that Alexander would accept her, but it would absolve the House of any responsibility, no matter his decision.

I watched her as I laid the proposal and a significant amount of paperwork before her. She sat with her neglected drink in hand, her mouth slightly agape.

"Sophia, do you understand what I'm offering?" I asked.

She nodded slowly, setting her drink down on the table in front of her. She closed her mouth and bit her bottom lip. "When do I meet him?" she asked breathlessly.

I could hear her heart pounding behind her chest, and the smell of her blood intensified. I took a deep breath but felt only disappointment. It was just blood. No hint of the heady scent that flowed in Kate's veins, not that I'd expected anything different. Would Alexander be disappointed, too? Probably.

"Later tonight," I said, glancing down at my Rolex. There were still several hours left before dawn. I looked back at Sophia on the couch in her pleather skirt and black lace top. "We should get you cleaned up first and changed into something else," I added.

She nodded again. "Yeah, of course. Whatever you say." She breathed easier now that the initial shock was wearing off.

"First, I need you to sign these documents," I said. "Anywhere you see a yellow flag." I pointed to the markers placed throughout the stack of papers. There were quite a few of them.

She licked her lips and reached for the pen I held out.

As she signed, I went to a wardrobe in the corner and rifled through the clothing I had on hand. Unlike the apartment where Kate stayed, I primarily used this place for entertaining and stocked it with anything I might need for a night in or out with a companion. I liked whoever was on my arm to match my style, which sometimes meant dressing them myself.

I shoved aside a leather bustier and several other less decent outfits and reached for a cream-colored silk sheath that looked about the right size. Alexander's style was elevated but old-fashioned. The dress would be perfect. I hung it on the back of the bathroom door and laid out a variety of soaps and perfumes for Sophia to choose from.

Sophia was finishing the last of the signatures when I

rejoined her. Her dark head was bent over, and her hair fell in front of her face. I paused, imagining Kate sitting there, eagerly agreeing to join me in this life, happy to accept the incredible gift she'd been offered.

Sophia sensed me beside her and looked up, breaking the spell. I gave her a tight smile, took the pen, and gathered the papers from the table. Tucking them back into the folder, I felt a sense of relief. Alexander might not accept her, but my job was to find candidates, and I'd done just that. Ultimately, the evening wasn't as unpleasant as I'd anticipated. I'd delayed this for far too long, but now I was motivated. As troublesome as it was, it would be worth it if it freed up my time later.

Sophia stood, and I motioned her toward the bathroom. "Everything you need is ready for you," I said.

But instead of going to the bathroom, she walked toward me with a small smile. "I don't know how to thank you," she said. "I've been dreaming of this. Hoping for this."

She drew closer and placed her hands on my chest, looking up at me through her dark lashes. The scent of her perfume made my nose itch, so I stopped breathing as she leaned closer. I considered pushing her away and urging her toward the bathroom, but we did have plenty of time. And I did want to be on good terms with a potential new housemate.

I slipped an arm around her waist, drew her against me, and kissed her. Her mouth was warm and soft. I ran a hand through her silky, dark hair, cupping the back of her head, and deepened the kiss. She parted her lips willingly, and I plunged my tongue inside. She was sweet and tasted of mint. I drew Sophia closer to me, feeling the heat of her body against mine.

Gripping her with both arms, I lifted her from the

ground. She let out a squeal of surprise but held on tight, wrapping her legs around my waist as I walked her backward to the sofa.

I braced a hand against the back of the couch and lowered us both down, settling between her thighs. The pleather skirt ended up around her waist, and I pressed myself against her as I stroked her mouth with my tongue.

She reached forward, pulling down her lace top and black bra, exposing her breasts. I took the cue and kissed my way down the column of her neck and across her chest. I sucked a nipple into my mouth, and she let out a soft moan, arching her back in encouragement.

As I flicked over her taut nipple, I slid a hand between our bodies. Her skin was soft and supple, and when I reached her core, I discovered she wasn't wearing anything under the horrid skirt. I found her wet and ready for me.

I released her breast and pulled back to undo my pants, freeing myself. She was slick and hot, and it took no time at all to find a rhythm that had us both breathing hard, as I held on to her hips.

I thrust faster, our bodies slapping against each other. Reaching forward, I gripped the arm of the sofa above her head for leverage and continued pounding. She placed her hands back on my chest, and I felt the sting of her nails as she dug in, drawing blood. I glanced down at her face and the heated smile on her lips.

I captured her mouth again and kissed her hard. As I began to orgasm, the waves of pleasure breaking over me, I pulled back from her mouth, and she tilted her head to the side, offering her neck. I didn't refuse.

I thrust one last time and then lay still inside her as I drank. I stroked her long, dark hair, so much like Kate's. Closing my eyes, I dared not breathe, happy with my fantasy. I thought of everything I had to look forward to. I imagined Kate's body underneath me, my cock buried inside her. I wanted desperately to be with her, touching and tasting her.

Kate would come around, and then we would be together forever, just like this. She was mine, only for me. It would be perfect, I thought, as I felt the strength of Sophia's blood filling me up. I swallowed again, waiting for another blissful mouthful that didn't come.

I flicked my eyes open and pulled back, glancing down. Sophia's body lay limp in my arms. I listened, but there was no sound, no beating of her heart. *Fuck.*

I released her, and she lay unmoving, her sightless eyes staring up at the ceiling. *At least she won't bleed all over the couch*, I thought. I groaned, and I glanced down at Sophia's corpse. Her dark hair splayed across the sofa, looking like Kate's. At least I knew what I would do with her body.

I pushed myself off her. I was back where I started, but now, with the rancid taste of drugstore perfume lingering on my lips. I wiped my mouth with the back of my sleeve, pulled my cell out of my pocket, and called my contact at the crematory.

The night wasn't a total waste.

11

KATE

When I awoke the following night, I knew exactly where I was. There was no panic and no momentary disorientation. I'd crawled into bed long before sunrise, unable to summon enough energy for anything other than lying in bed and contemplating what tonight would bring.

I felt my eyes prick, and a sob rose in my throat, but I swallowed it back down. I pictured my blood-smeared face in the mirror from the night before. I would not allow myself to cry.

I inhaled deeply, and the now-familiar scent of the apartment filled my nostrils, but the effort left my lungs aching. I lay still. Everything hurt. I was so incredibly tired. I closed my eyes, but there was no returning to sleep. Sighing, I turned on the light and squeezed my eyes shut as a headache slammed through my skull.

It took me two tries to sit fully upright. I pushed back the covers and swung my legs over the side of the bed. I sat for a minute, waiting for my eyes to adjust. I'd slept in the robe I borrowed from the bathroom and blinked, staring at my bare legs where the robe parted. I hardly recognized them. I reached out to touch the top of one thigh, where the muscle had wasted away, and gasped. My hand didn't look like my own; my fingers were knobby, and the bones and tendons protruded through the skin on the back of my hand.

I stood in a rush to get to the bathroom mirror and nearly fell to the floor. I was weak and dizzy. Gripping the dresser near the bed, I waited until the black spots cleared from my vision. Slowly, I made my way to the bathroom and turned on the light.

The reflection that greeted me was horrifying. Dark purple shadows like bruises encircled each of my sunken eyes. My cheekbones were as sharp as razors; my cheeks were hollowed out. Jutting collarbones peeked out from beneath the bathrobe. I took a shuddering breath and nodded at my reflection. It was time.

I took my leggings out of the drawer I'd claimed and managed to pull them on, along with my favorite dark grey sweater, without looking too closely at my ravaged body. I twisted my hair into a messy bun, covered my bony feet with warm, thick socks, and padded out to the main room.

The blood bags I left on the counter had disappeared. No doubt the housekeeper took them away. I was thankful. I suspected I might still be hungry, but the pain in the rest of my body now masked the gnawing hunger, or perhaps my body had given up. The thought didn't bother me like it should.

My tennis shoes were neatly lined up by the front door. My feet slid in with plenty of room. I pulled the laces as tight as I could and tied them securely. My jacket hung on a hook. I slipped it on and zipped it up to my chin. Aware of my appearance, I decided I didn't want to attract attention and pulled the hood over my head.

I paused and leaned against the door. Getting dressed

took a considerable amount of energy. I shook my head. I needed to get moving. If James returned soon, I knew he would try to stop me, and I needed to get out. The night air called to me, and I wanted to see the fall colors one last time.

Yanking the door open, I shuffled carefully into the hall and pulled it shut behind me. With one hand on the wall, I hobbled to the elevator, stepped on, and pressed the button for the ground floor.

When the doors opened, the noise and light from the lobby were shocking. Even the softly playing music in the lobby was overwhelming. I suspected the lighting was dimmer than I was used to, but my eyes stung from the reflection off the white marble floor.

I slipped my hands into my pockets and tried to walk normally, keeping my head down and hidden beneath my hood. With each step, it became easier to move. By the time I reached the automatic doors leading outside, I felt steadier. No one seemed to notice as I stepped out into the night.

The cool evening air felt wonderful against my skin, and I paused, turning my face into the gentle breeze. It was completely dark, with the streetlights positioned above me, and my eyes thanked me for escaping the harsh electric light of the lobby. I was right to leave. This was better.

Then, I caught the scent.

My emotions had been so overwhelming that I hadn't noticed the people walking around me as I stood there. One person bumped into me with their elbow and quickly apologized as they passed.

I was startled at first. I was so focused on leaving the lobby that I hadn't considered the people present. Now, as some of the aches and pains began to fade and the scent of those nearby filled the air, I felt a surge of fear. I realized with horror that I could smell their blood.

I hadn't been thinking when I decided to leave. It was a stupid choice; I should have considered the danger I might pose to others. I waited for the urge to attack, pounce, or... something. But nothing happened. The smell enticed me in a way that made me squirm inside, but I was tired. I barely had the energy to walk, let alone tackle someone and try to bite them. I shivered, not from the cold, which didn't bother me, but from the thought of seeing myself as a monster capable of such a thing.

I peered around, past the people walking by, and recognized the busy street one block over. Quickly orienting myself, I chose the darker side street that ran parallel to the main road and headed west. As I put one foot in front of the other, I kept one eye on the sidewalk in front of me, careful not to trip while looking out for James. No one so much as glanced in my direction.

The combination of businesses and apartments transitioned into solely residential buildings, and the hum of traffic faded behind me as I continued. When I was several blocks away, I felt safe enough and settled into a steady pace, trying to enjoy the tranquility of the tree-lined street and the sensation of the pavement beneath the rubber soles of my shoes. My joints felt loose, the pain nearly disappeared, and walking became easier.

The homes in this area of town were similar: two-story Craftsman bungalows with front-facing living room and dining room windows that looked out over small front yards. Several of these homes were lit up, revealing people going about their evening routines.

In one window, two children sat at one end of a table, appearing to do homework, while two older adults walked back and forth, setting dishes on the other end. In another window, a couple sat on a sofa watching TV, their heads bent toward each other. Across the street, two people sat together, sharing a meal, with one laughing at something the other said. And I was on the outside.

I wasn't part of that kind of life anymore. My reflection in the mirror was proof enough of that. There was no going back or undoing what had been done. I wouldn't sit down to enjoy a meal with my family again. I would no longer be welcome in my friends' homes. I was apart, separate. But before this life was truly over, I wanted to return home one more time.

Seeing my family would have been my first choice, but my mom and brother were too far away. I didn't think I could make it that far. However, my apartment was within reach. I was nearly halfway there, and as I got closer, I recognized several landmarks, and soon every house and tree were familiar.

I passed the spot where I'd seen a neighbor rescue a baby squirrel from the middle of the road, and the house that caught fire one Christmas but had since been beautifully renovated. I turned the corner where a monstrous hydrangea erupted in soft green blooms each year, and the fence sagged into the yard next door. And up ahead, just out of sight, was my home.

I trudged onward, my pace slowing as my legs grew heavier, and each step became a struggle. As I drew closer to my apartment, I noticed that the view of the front door was blocked by a truck parked out front—the type you would rent for moving or hauling something large. I crossed to the other side of the street, hidden by the cloak of night and the deeper shadows cast by the aged trees separating each driveway.

Perhaps one of my neighbors was having something delivered. I hoped so. If someone were moving out, I would have to wait longer to sneak past unnoticed. I couldn't risk being seen by anyone who knew me—or even someone who didn't. I looked like a walking skeleton. I would not go unnoticed.

The tree directly across from my apartment was sturdy, its trunk thicker than my body. I leaned against it, letting it support me. I just needed a minute. Hopefully, by the time whoever was there cleared out, I would have recovered enough to continue. Curiously, I noticed that I was breathing hard, as if the rising and falling of my chest could help me, as if it was a matter of catching my breath or oxygenating my blood. I held my breath and listened.

Nothing, still nothing.

There was no rapid beating of my heart, just stillness. Breathing, it turned out, was a habit, and I sank back into the rhythm gratefully. It was comforting and familiar, like the building across the street.

At first, I didn't see anyone moving around. The fronts of the downstairs units had small windows that opened into tiny kitchens. The ones upstairs were larger and allowed the light from the main rooms of the studio apartments to shine through. Lights were on in three of the four units, including mine. I couldn't recall if I'd left the lights on when James and I were here two nights ago. It felt like years had gone by since that night.

I waited, feeling the rough tree bark against my cheek and under my fingertips. My skin felt thin, stretched, and sensitive. The sensations were distracting, and I almost missed it as someone stepped out of the building toward the truck carrying a large box.

When I recognized the figure, I forgot my body and

parted my lips to call out, but caught myself at the last moment. The sound died in my throat, and my legs gave out. I slumped to the ground. My knees crashed against thick roots, and my shoulder caught painfully against the tree trunk. It was the only thing that kept me from face-planting into the gutter. I reached out and clutched the trunk as my mother disappeared behind the back of the open truck.

If I'd had enough strength left, I would have gone to her. I wouldn't have been able to stop myself. I realized it was a blessing that I was so far gone. This was what I needed.

I watched as she reappeared from behind the truck, arms empty, shoulders slumped, her back to me. The truck should have been a giveaway. I should have realized that it was my apartment being packed up.

I was the one moving out.

A minute later, as I sat frozen and unable to decide what to do next, my mother reappeared. She carried one end of my futon frame while walking backward. When the other end came into view, the breath left my lungs, and tears over-flowed, slipping down my face. Sara, her curls piled on top of her head and muscles straining, helped my mom with her burden. Of course she would, I thought.

I was far enough away that I couldn't sense their emotions. My strange ability was useless at this distance, and I was glad for it. I had no idea what they were feeling, but I could imagine. All I wanted at that moment were my own emotions. The misery and hopelessness I'd felt since waking were drowned out by love and gratitude. I was happy that this would be the last thing I saw and felt.

I sat back on my heels, allowing my bones to bear the weight of my body as I watched my best friend and my mother. I didn't need to go inside. This was enough. I'd decided before falling asleep the night before that I wouldn't drink. I would not trade my life for one devoid of the people I loved. I wouldn't go through with it. My time had been up when I was hit by that car. It was taking my mind a bit longer to accept that fact. However, my body was well on its way. I would not turn into a monster. And I would not spend an eternity beholden to James.

It was a relief when I woke up and realized I wouldn't have to endure another day.

My plans didn't extend much beyond coming here. I thought about wandering off and finding a quiet place to lie down and wait for the sunrise. That idea appealed to me. I would go somewhere no one would discover me. I hoped I would pass before dawn. I wasn't entirely sure I wanted to face the pain of burning to ash. But James assured me it would be complete. He told me vampires turned to ash when exposed to daylight. I was relying on him to be right.

I sat for a few more minutes, watching my mom and Sara work.

It was time.

My legs felt stiff as I pulled myself up to stand. I took a deep breath, ready to push on, but halted suddenly as frustration and anger washed over me. These weren't my feelings, I thought, just a split second before an arm gripped my shoulders and jerked me roughly around.

"What the fuck are you thinking?" James hissed, then gasped as he saw my face. The emotions radiating from him were drained away, replaced with shock and disgust. "Oh God, Kate. What have you done?"

His grip on my shoulders relaxed, and his mouth dropped open as he looked me up and down.

"Hi, James," I said calmly as he stared. "I haven't done anything." I offered him a small smile. "How did you find me?"

His face went cold as he regained his composure. "I followed the stench of famine and hunger. It wasn't hard."

I nodded and looked back at my mother as she carried another box to the rental truck.

James followed my gaze. "Your mom?" he guessed. I smiled in response.

The wind blew toward us, tugging at my coat and ruffling James's hair. He lifted his chin and sniffed the air. "She smells a bit like you," he said wistfully, though his brows furrowed. Just then, Sara stepped onto the porch, intercepting my mom as she headed back inside. The two stood there talking too softly for me to hear. James stiffened.

"Who's the witch?" he asked, his voice tinged with something dark...almost accusatory.

"What?" I asked, confused by his question and startled by his tone. "What are you talking about?"

"The witch. Speaking to your mother," he growled.

"Sara?" I asked. "That's my best friend, Sara. Why would you call her that?"

James turned to face me. "Because that's what she is," he said, looking at me with exasperation. "For God's sake, wipe your face. You look ghoulish."

I'd completely forgotten my tears. Scrubbing my face with my sleeve, I was pretty sure I was only making a bigger mess. "What do you mean she is a witch?" I said, as I attempted to clean myself up.

His eyes darted back to my apartment. Sara and my mom had gone inside. "I don't know what's so hard to understand. Didn't you know? I can still smell her from here," he said, wrinkling his nose.

I took a deep breath but didn't detect anything other than the earthy scent of the living and decaying things around us. It smelled like life.

My mind struggled to catch up with the revelation. A witch? Sara was different, as was her family. She was private and, like me, had secrets. Taking a moment to consider it, the idea made a lot of sense. I couldn't deny the possibility that witches existed. I stood there with a vampire, not to mention my special ability and everything I'd been through over the past few days. This opened up new possibilities.

"Do witches know about vampires?" I asked.

"Yeah, of course," he said.

"Well, do you all spend time together?" I asked, my tone a bit short. His mounting agitation seeped into me, and I craved answers. "Are there any witch members in your House? Do you have friends who are witches?"

The disgust on his face was answer enough. "No, we don't spend time together. We keep to ourselves, and so do they," he said, gripping my elbow. "Now come on. We need to get you back home and fed. Quickly," he added.

I pulled back from James, trying to think. This wasn't the plan, but I glanced at my apartment.

Sara was a witch.

Maybe I didn't have to lose everything after all. Perhaps there was a way to build a life I could be happy with.

At that moment, Sara walked out of my front door and headed toward the truck with a lamp cradled in the crook of one arm. Partway there, she froze. Slowly, she lifted her head, turning her face in our direction, and stared directly at me.

James turned to leave, letting his hand slide down my arm to grasp my hand. I allowed myself to be pulled along, but I kept my eyes on Sara until she was completely out of sight.

12

SARA

We had been at it for over two hours. The job turned out to be bigger than either of us expected. It was just one room, I thought, how much stuff could Kate have packed into it? A lot, as it turned out—a whole lot.

I agreed to meet Kate's mother after work. Melanie had been packing for at least an hour by the time I arrived, but she'd hardly made any progress. She attempted to organize as she went, but it felt like a lost cause, forcing me to question why it was necessary. No one would likely want the mostly used-up art supplies or well-worn clothing. Even a charity shop would probably reject most of what we were carefully packing away. Nonetheless, I understood the sentimental reasons behind it.

It seemed Kate's mom needed to be there just as much as I did. It felt comforting to handle Kate's belongings, saying goodbye as the objects called up memories I would hold onto no matter where the things ended up. Melanie asked if there was anything I wanted for myself. It was a good question. I liked the idea of keeping something of Kate's—something to carry into whatever life had in store for me, something tangible to bring home.

My eyes swept over the piles of Kate's belongings. It was an easy choice. I picked a small painting that Kate created during our senior year of high school. She loved it enough to display it in her Senior Show, and I loved it too. It depicted us sitting side by side, our heads leaning against each other. We were both smiling and relaxed. She painted it from a photo taken at a party we attended earlier that year. It was a beautiful memory and was exactly how I wanted to remember my best friend—an image of her that I'd been trying to recall over the past few days.

I placed it carefully aside and continued to work. Soon, the room was mostly cardboard, and Melanie and I began moving the boxes to the rental truck she parked out front. I was hot from working and left my coat inside as we went back and forth, first with the boxes and then with the larger pieces of furniture. The more we worked, the better I felt. With each trip to the truck, I felt a stronger sense of resolution and finality. I supposed that was what closure felt like. I was glad I'd come.

Next were the larger items that Melanie wanted wrapped in moving blankets. Picking up a lamp, I went back outside. As soon as I stepped out, I stopped in my tracks. My feelings of acceptance vanished. Like a physical thing, I felt energy flow from across the street. There was something there, something both familiar and dangerous. I turned my head and saw her.

I knew it was Kate the moment our eyes locked. She wore a dark coat with the hood up, and I couldn't see her face clearly, but I knew it was her.

And it wasn't.

Oh, Gods, what was I looking at? And she wasn't alone.

A man stood beside her, exuding a dark energy. It was the dangerous energy that had drawn my attention. It crawled and prickled, burrowing beneath my skin and making me shiver. I clutched the lamp tightly to my chest as I felt a surge course through my body, momentarily causing the bulb to flare to life. Had I not held it so tightly, I would have dropped it for sure. Seeing my dead best friend was startling enough, but it was also the first time my gift manifested outside my hands. I started to shake as I watched Kate being led away by the other figure.

At that moment, the door behind me opened, and Melanie stepped onto the porch with more items for the truck. I wasn't sure what I'd seen, but I knew I should keep it to myself. Whatever it was, it wasn't something Kate's mother needed to know. Even if the creature across the street was her daughter, Melanie was human, and I knew better than to open my mouth around humans.

I made my body move, stepping forward toward the back of the truck. I picked up a blanket from the small pile and wrapped it neatly around the body of the lamp I carried. I didn't look up when Melanie joined me, swaddled Kate's field easel, and tucked it between two boxes.

"Hey, are you okay?" Melanie asked.

I blinked at her. Fresh concern was etched on her kind face, layered over the grief that had lingered for days. I nodded and attempted a smile. "Yeah, I'm fine. It's just a lot," I said. It truly was a lot. I still couldn't feel my hands, and my body vibrated with unspent electricity. I struggled to control my breathing and forced myself to step back so Melanie wouldn't be tempted to come in for a hug. I didn't understand what was happening to me at that moment, and I didn't want to hurt her.

Melanie smiled at me. "Thank you for coming, Sara."

She ran her fingers through her gray-blonde hair. "I don't know how I would have gotten through this without you," she said. "It *is* a lot, and I appreciate it."

I hugged my arms around myself and returned her smile. "I don't mind. It was good to be here, to help. I'm glad you called me." As we talked, I couldn't help but glance over my shoulder at where Kate had stood just moments ago. Had I really seen what I thought I had? I shook my head, refocusing as I realized Melanie still spoke to me.

She tilted her head, eyeing me critically. "I think we're about done if you want to go home. I can manage the rest by myself." She looked so tired, both physically and emotionally, but the overwhelming energy I felt from her was strength.

Tears welled in my eyes, and I turned before she could see, quickly dashing them away. "Yeah, I think I will. I'll just grab my things," I said.

"Sure, I'll lock up the truck and be there in a minute," she replied.

I nearly raced to the building. Before I grasped the door handle, I slapped my hand against the metal trim and released the electricity from my palm. A massive surge left my hand, and I gasped. The lights in the apartment brightened, and I heard a bulb pop from somewhere within, then everything dimmed. I glanced back, but Melanie still faced the truck. She hadn't noticed it.

Before she finished, I had my belongings in my arms and was back outside. We said goodnight, and I promised to call her soon, then headed straight for my car. Guilt churned in my stomach as I fled, but I had to get out of there. I needed to think.

Unlocking my car, I sat in the driver's seat for some time before turning the key in the ignition and pulling away. As I headed back north, I tried to decide what, if anything, I should do. What could I do? I decided I couldn't talk to my mom or aunt about my suspicions. I already knew what they would say. I knew what my entire community would say.

How could this even be possible? I didn't want that glimpse in the dark to be the last time I saw my best friend. If what I thought was true, she was still here, if not alive. I toyed with the idea that maybe I was wrong. I'd never seen one or felt one before. I could be mistaken. But deep down, I knew I wasn't. Tears streamed down my face as I pulled onto the highway—tears for myself, but also for my friend.

When I got home, I had a hint of an idea. My mother was setting the table for dinner when I walked in. I said a quick hello and took the stairs to my room. Dumping my stuff on the bed, I pulled my phone out of my jeans pocket.

Nervous laughter bubbled up in my throat, but a quiet sob escaped instead as I considered what I was doing. I'd always thought about how great it would be to talk to my best friend about things like this. Okay, not exactly like this, but about the witchy problems in my life. While driving home, I thought, *maybe I could talk to Kate.* They'd never found her phone. She could still have it. If she were... around, I could learn exactly what had happened from her. I knew I was grasping at straws, but didn't know what else to do.

I wiped my fresh tears away and gazed at the blank screen. Of course, it hadn't survived my little electrical storm. I sighed and chucked it in the trash. Pulling out a drawer from my desk, I took a small white box from the stack, opened the new phone, and plugged it in. My text would have to wait.

I checked my face in the mirror. I didn't want the looks

of concern and pity I knew I'd get if I looked a mess. Satisfied, I went down to dinner.

I did my best to maintain a level mood and calm thoughts. Despite my efforts, the revelations of the past several hours clung to me, disrupting my energy like an approaching storm. I shifted in my chair, trying to get comfortable, when all I wanted to do was scream.

My mother passed me a dish of green beans, a pleasant smile on her lips. I knew that look in her eye, however. She was concerned.

My mother, Sybil Heartwood, wore linen and was wrapped in her customary apron, the large front pocket concealing all sorts of useful items and, more often than not, something green and growing. Her talent lay with all things plants; she took her green thumb to a whole different level and could practically conjure life from anything. But that wasn't her only skill.

When it came to her only child, she was incredibly perceptive. I focused on my plate, hoping she would let it go.

My mother dipped her head to catch my eye. "So, how was it?" she asked.

I glanced up. My mother and aunt were staring at me from the other side of the worn kitchen table.

"Oh, it was fine," I said, picking up my mug.

"Was Kate there?" my mother asked.

I took a big gulp of hot tea and almost spat the burning liquid back out. I cleared my throat and coughed.

"What?"

"In her apartment, surrounded by her belongings, did you feel her presence? Were you able to say goodbye?" my mother asked, tilting her head, her expression unreadable.

"Are you okay?" my aunt asked. "You look a bit strange."

"I'm fine. Really," I said. "And yes, it was good to go...say goodbye." I blew across the top of my steaming mug, trying to recover.

I considered confiding in them about what I had seen, but I was afraid. I loved my family and trusted them. Yet, they were traditional. They couldn't even handle my crush on Silas. They suspected I liked him, of course, but disapproved. Not because he wasn't great—he was. And not because they didn't like him—they did. But Silas wasn't from a witch family. Worse, he was a shifter. They might have gotten used to a human, as it had happened before. And while shifters and witches got along fine, they didn't date. Ever. Telling them I suspected my best friend was one of the undead was more than I thought they could handle.

Before thinking about what I was saying, I asked, "Have either of you ever known a vampire?"

My mother and aunt weren't twins, but when I looked up, I saw two identical shocked expressions.

"Oh, Gods, no. Why would you ask such a thing?" my aunt replied, her disgust replacing shock. My mother kept spearing beans with her fork but glanced up at me with a worried look from beneath her dark lashes.

I cringed. "No real reason. I think I saw one the other night while I was in the city," I added, trying to act like it was no big deal.

"That's why you should stay up north," my aunt said. "I've told you before that the city isn't a good place to be so late at night." She shook her head.

"Why do we have relationships with shifters but not with vampires? It seems we all have things in common," I said. While it was widely known that vampires existed, they were rarely a topic of conversation, and I'd never learned much about them.

"We have nothing in common with bloodsuckers," Aunt

Lucia said, nearly spitting. "They're killers. We work in harmony with life. If anything, they're our complete opposite."

My aunt was never warm and fuzzy, but I was shocked by the venom in her voice. It reeked of the prejudice I'd come to expect from my elders, and it irritated me. "But have you ever met one? I mean, these days, they follow different rules, right? They can't all be killers," I said.

My mother set down her fork and spoke. Her tone was calm, more measured than her sister's. "Every one of them surrendered their human life to survive off the lives of others. They are Other, but they're not like us. We were born to be what we are. They are a perversion of life itself," she said.

"Their Council may claim they've changed their ways. They might pretend to be tame, but deep down, they're all monsters. Never forget that," Lucia added.

I let the subject drop, and we fell into silence. It was no more than I expected from them. I was frustrated that they couldn't be more open-minded. It was no surprise that the Others couldn't coexist as long as attitudes like theirs continued. It wasn't the Dark Ages anymore; whether or not my elders agreed, things had changed. At least, I hoped they had. If there were ever to be any hope for a better way of life for people like Silas and me, and now possibly Kate…

As I considered it, my resolve grew stronger. I wanted my community to be more modern, but that was beyond my control. I could only make choices for myself. If Kate were out there, I wouldn't turn my back on her, regardless of what my mother or aunt thought. But I wouldn't tell them about her either.

I excused myself from the table and cleared my place, washing my dishes and placing them on the rack to dry.

After saying good night, I returned to my room and closed the door.

My new phone sat on my bedside table, beckoning me. I felt different as I picked it up and turned it on. It felt like I'd chosen to do what I believed was right for the first time, and I rushed through the setup, eager to get on with it. I knew there would be no turning back. I was committed to following through if I made contact. I typed my message, but my thumb hovered over the send button. I wasn't sure which I feared more: that Kate was out there somewhere, changed and different, or that I imagined it all, and she was truly gone. Taking a deep breath, I pressed send and waited.

13

KATE

James yanked me forward toward his apartment. I fought to keep my balance as we quickened our pace. I was dizzy and weak, and the speed wasn't helping.

"James," I rasped, trying to get his attention. I needed to slow down. I used his momentum to move forward, leaning my weight onto our clasped hands. But I couldn't keep it up for long.

He ignored me and pulled harder.

I cried out as my shoe struck a raised lip of pavement, and I went down.

My hand was ripped from James's grasp, and I barely managed to catch myself before my face slammed into the wet sidewalk. James cursed from somewhere above me, but I didn't have the strength to look up. I lay my cheek against the damp leaves. So cool and soothing. Closing my eyes, I inhaled the chilly air. The scent of leaves, dirt, and blood—probably mine—filled my nose.

I still mulled over the various scents in my mind when I felt strong arms under me, turning and lifting me. The scents shifted from an earthy, natural scent to expensive cologne and new leather.

James.

If I hadn't recognized his scent, I would've known him by his emotions: frustration, impatience, and concern—his own unique bouquet. I sighed and let myself be carried along. There was no choice at that point; I was too far gone to do anything else.

The next time I opened my eyes, we were in a familiar elevator. James still held me in his arms, my head resting against his chest. My limbs felt heavy, and my headache returned with a vengeance. I kept my eyes closed until we were in the darkened interior of the apartment.

James gently set me down on the sofa before heading to the kitchen. By the time he returned, I'd managed to push myself up and slip the heavy coat from my shoulders. He carried a wine glass filled with steaming red liquid. Even in my sorry state, my body reacted. My nostrils flared, eager to capture more of the scent wafting toward me, and my canine teeth throbbed.

"Are you done fighting this?" James asked, looming over me, glass in hand.

That was a good question. Was I finished fighting? I hadn't planned to return here. I hadn't intended to drink. But learning about Sara and realizing there was so much I didn't understand about this world changed my perspective. Maybe there was a way forward for me. One I could accept. Yes, I was done fighting, at least this particular battle. I'd made my choice.

Extending my hand, James placed the wine glass into my bony fingers. I cupped both hands around the bowl of the glass. The liquid felt hot, almost uncomfortably so. However, its aroma was heavenly. I hadn't felt hunger since waking, but now it crashed over me with a force that bent me in half. I arched around the glass as the spasm rocked my body. I opened my mouth to pant through the pain, inhaling more of the delicious scent into my lungs, causing my body to tremble with anticipation. Had I not already decided to drink, I'm not sure I could've stopped myself at that point.

After the worst of the spasms passed, I lifted the rim of the glass to my lips. My hands still shook so badly I was sure I would spill half of it down my front, but I couldn't bring myself to care. The only important thing at that moment was getting the blood to my mouth.

When I thought about this moment over the past few days, I expected to have to force myself to drink. I thought it would be hard, that I would have to choke down the blood while my mind and body revolted against it.

I was so wrong.

I didn't just drink; I poured the hot liquid down my throat. It tasted like rare steak and ambrosia, and I couldn't get enough of it. My mind had no room for struggle or second thoughts—there was no hesitation in my body, only greedy acceptance.

Breathing heavily, I pressed myself back into the sofa cushions as warmth spread throughout my body. My headache diminished, and the ache in my belly and joints loosened. My skin prickled all over. I could feel my clothing against my skin, and the individual hairs on my body rising and falling. My mind was clear, and my vision noticeably sharpened. The numbers and letters on the clock across the room were easy to read. Glancing toward the window, I could practically count the individual leaves on the tree a block away. I inhaled the leather scent of the nearby chair and the fabric softeners and detergents from my clothing. And blood.

I looked down at the glass I still held. It was empty, and I felt a pang of disappointment and loss. Noticing my hands, I observed the scratches on my palms from the fall fading, and my skin took on a pinker hue. I was still skeletal, but I felt much better, stronger.

"You're gonna need a lot more, I think," James said.

I jumped at the sound of his voice. I'd been so distracted by the new sensations that I forgot he was even there. As I focused on him, the force of his emotions smacked into me: satisfaction, curiosity, impatience, and relief. I rocked backward. It wasn't what he felt that was so surprising; it was the intensity of the emotions. For as long as I could remember, I sensed the feelings of people around me, but this was on another level. He screamed his feelings at me, and it echoed in my head as if he were shouting in a silent room.

He left the living room again, presumably to get me more blood. I looked away from his retreating figure, like it would help muffle his emotions. I searched within myself for my feelings, the emotions that belonged solely to me. It was an exercise I'd practiced when I was younger and overwhelmed by the flood of others' feelings. It took longer than it should have, but the farther away James moved, the easier it became. I clung to my emotions and pushed back against the rest. I struggled with the space between them and managed to create a greater distance, a sort of internal barrier.

"Hey, are you okay?"

I snapped my head up. James was back, holding another glass of blood, with several bags stuffed under one arm. I nodded, staring at the glass. I momentarily forgot my internal struggle and refocused on the sustenance my body craved. A part of my mind observed the scene, marveling at the overwhelming amount of information I grappled with and the unexpected reactions from both my mind and body.

This time, as I took the glass he held out, a sharp pain shot through my mouth. While lifting the glass to my lips, I probed with my tongue and discovered that my canine teeth had lengthened. Normally, this would warrant significant contemplation, but I didn't have time to panic or marvel at the revelation. I was still starving, and my body was focused on getting what I needed to survive.

I quickly downed the second glass and stared at the bag James held out.

He tilted his head and examined me. "Better, but not quite enough." He paused, glancing at the bag in his hands. "On second thought, maybe we should do this in the kitchen. I don't want you to spill on my rug," he said.

Before I considered moving, I found myself standing in front of him. One moment, I'd been on the sofa, and the next, I stood chest-to-chest with him, my lips drawn back from my teeth. *What the hell is happening?* I wondered.

James raised his eyebrows in surprise. "Alright, no problem. I suppose I can always get it cleaned," he said, handing over the bag.

I stepped back with my prize, shocked by my reaction yet still so hungry. I swallowed hard and breathed deeply, convinced I could smell the blood through the plastic. I lifted the bag to my open mouth.

"Whoa, hold on there. Don't bite it," James said, irritated. Stepping closer, he reached for the bag.

A growl rose from deep within my throat. The sound startled me, but I held tightly to the bag.

"There's an easier and less messy way," he said. Watching my face intently, he placed his hands on the back of mine, rotating them and turning the end of the bag toward the ceiling. Slowly, he reached up and grasped one of the tubes protruding from the bag, pinching the end clean off with his nails. He somehow knew not to try to take it from me.

As he withdrew his hands, I relaxed and looked down at what I held. Yeah, that made more sense. I repositioned my grip, being careful not to squeeze the bag, and brought the tube to my mouth. It was difficult to close my lips around the small tube with my teeth as long as they were. I was properly motivated, however, and it was only a moment before I got the hang of it.

The blood was cold, but I didn't care. I finished every last drop from the bag I could without tearing it open and licking the inside, which I seriously considered. Before I could start ripping, James passed me another bag, open and ready. I drank that one down and two more after.

I felt pleasantly full, almost tipsy, as I handed James the last of the empty plastic bags.

"Feeling better?" he asked. I could hear the smirk in his tone.

"Yeah," I admitted. "I do." I licked my lips, tasting a lingering metallic flavor. "Is that it? Is it over?" I asked. I wasn't sure what I expected, but overall, it was easier than I imagined.

"Yeah. The hardest part was done by the time you woke up in the hospital," he said, walking to the kitchen and tossing the empty, blood-stained bags into a covered trash can. "Fortunately, you were pretty out of it." He ran his hand through his wavy, dark hair. "I remember everything about my transition, and let me tell you, that part was no picnic."

"How long ago was that? Who changed you?" I asked. I hadn't thought to ask until just then.

James straightened up and tugged at the hem of his shirt, smoothing out the wrinkles. His face shifted from whatever he'd recalled to an unreadable, blank expression. "It's not considered polite to ask a vampire that, but you are new, so I'll give you a pass. It was in the eighties, the nineteen-eighties. And it's not important who turned me," he said. It was clear from his tone and the feelings of dread radiating off him that the subject was closed. "Why don't you go get cleaned up, and I'll tidy up in here?"

I looked down at myself. My shoes were dirty, and my leggings were torn at the knees. I couldn't see the rest, but I was probably a mess from head to toe.

"Yeah, sure," I said and turned away. I kicked my shoes off near the front door and disappeared into the bedroom, closing and locking the door behind me.

I tossed my clothes into the corner of the bedroom and went straight to the shower, avoiding all reflective surfaces along the way. The last time I looked in the mirror had been traumatic, and I wasn't sure if I was ready to assess the new changes.

It took a while to adjust the temperature to something I could tolerate, and once I was under the water, I winced at the sharp sting of the spray against my skin. Everything felt more intense. The changes and sensitivities I noticed after waking up in the morgue had intensified a hundredfold. I gritted my teeth, soaped up and rinsed my body as quickly as possible, shutting off the water with a sigh.

Grabbing a fluffy white towel from a hook next to the shower, I wrapped it carefully around my body before stepping out. The large mirror above the sink was fogged with steam. Before I could chicken out, I wiped away the mist, revealing my reflection staring back at me. And I looked... normal. Or normal-ish.

The deep hollows and dark circles were gone. My face was a bit leaner than usual, but not drastically so. My skin and lips were paler, but my eyes were the same brown color. I turned my head from side to side, and everything seemed to be in its proper place.

I unwrapped the towel and looked down. My body was a bit thinner, but not the skeleton it was when I first awoke. The torn skin on my knees was now smooth, with no sign of damage. I placed my hand on my chest. Frowning, I waited. It took almost ten full seconds, but then I felt it—a single thump. I waited another fifteen seconds, and another thump pushed back against my palm. Okay, that was my new normal, I guessed.

I flexed my toes, feeling the springy mat beneath my feet. Nothing hurt, nothing ached. I reached up, stretching my arms overhead. All I felt was the strength of my muscles and a growing urgency to move, to use those muscles.

Before I could think, I sprinted out of the bathroom and into the bedroom. Like in the living room with James, I moved almost faster than I could process. I felt a grin tugging at my mouth and remembered my teeth. I ran, just as quickly, back to the mirror. Sure enough, there they were. Fangs.

I pulled my lips back and poked at one. It was sharp. Blood welled from the tip of my finger, and I stared down at it. My stomach growled, and I felt movement behind my lips. Looking back into the mirror, I opened my mouth and watched as my fangs slid from my gums, lengthening. I shook my head and licked the blood off my finger. Food. Hunger twisted through me again. How much would I need to drink to feel full, I wondered. And what would I be willing to do to stay fed? Could I go out? Could I be around people?

First things first.

Returning to the bedroom, I dressed in my jeans and a T-shirt. Everything felt too tight, too scratchy, too restrictive. Properly dressed, I was about to head back to the kitchen to search for more food when I spotted my phone. It was still plugged in next to the bed where I left it. I hadn't planned on returning, on seeing it again. But that had changed. Everything had changed. And there it was.

No sooner had I decided to retrieve it than I found it in my hand. Flicking it open with my thumb, I saw I had a message. It was from Sara. Relief washed over me. I remembered two nights before when I leaned on Sara to get through an art opening. How would I get through all this without my best friend? I wouldn't.

The hunger in my stomach was replaced by excitement and anxiety. I glanced toward the bedroom door, hearing muffled footsteps and a soft rustling of fabric as James moved about the apartment. He wasn't near the door.

As I tapped on the notification to read Sara's message, I felt like a naughty kid hiding from a parent. I knew James wouldn't approve of my contact with Sara, but that wouldn't stop what I intended to do.

Kate?

I feel a bit crazy for sending this, but I'm pretty sure I saw you outside your apartment tonight.

I wanted you to know that it doesn't matter what's happened. And it doesn't matter what you are. (If you're reading this, you'll understand.)

I love you, and I'm here for you.

My eyes welled up, and my vision turned pink as I read her message for the second time. Blinking away the tears, I considered what I wanted to say. There was so much. I wanted to tell her that I was sorry. Sorry, I let her think I was dead. Sorry, she had to deal with the fallout of my "death." Sorry, I hadn't reached out to her earlier. Sorry, I wasn't a better friend.

In the end, I typed back;

I love you, too.

And hit send.

14

———

JAMES

I decided she'd been in there long enough, and I grew impatient. I approached the bedroom door and knocked softly, not wanting to startle her. A fledgling vampire could cause a lot of damage before they learned to control their newfound strength.

I was about to knock again when the door swung open before my knuckles touched the wood.

Kate stood in the doorway. She wore fresh clothes, and her face was blessedly clean of blood and dirt. Even with her wet hair, she looked fairly presentable.

"Hey. Everything alright?" I asked.

"Yeah," she said, smiling. "But the clothes are driving me crazy. How do you stand it?" She pulled her T-shirt seam away from her shoulder, which undoubtedly rubbed.

I chuckled. I'd forgotten how annoying that was at first. "You get used to it," I said, stepping back to let her into the living room. "It feels awful, but it's not actually hurting you. You're just extra sensitive right now. Your brain will filter it all out eventually."

As Kate passed by, her scent lingered in her wake. The

smell of starvation I'd followed to her apartment was gone. She smelled only of warm rain and honeysuckle, along with something else. Something I couldn't name but found incredibly intoxicating. Kate glided toward the kitchen, and I followed, unable to resist. She was truly beautiful, yet still too pale, even for a vampire.

"You look better," I said from behind her, my voice huskier than intended.

She laughed. "Don't flatter me. I saw myself before. I couldn't do much worse," she said. She paused, looking uncertain. "Do you mind if I have a little more?" she asked. She ran her tongue over her descended canines, and I swallowed hard.

"No, of course. Help yourself," I said, pointing to the fridge. Given my reaction to her, it was probably best if I didn't get too close. This, I reminded myself, was why I knew I did the right thing. I was protecting her and keeping her safe from Alexander's cruelty and his volatile nature.

"Ah, okay," she said and went to the fridge.

She hesitated again, pausing briefly, her face blank as if she were listening to something only she could hear. I listened as well, but didn't hear anything unusual. It made sense that she would feel hesitant, but she needed to be comfortable preparing her food. And I was no one's maid.

There was plenty to choose from, and she reached toward a stack of B-negative.

"No. Not that one," I said. "Take from the next shelf. The O-neg."

She looked over her shoulder, a curious expression on her face.

"Your blood type was O-negative," I explained. "You can drink any type, but consuming a compatible one will give you more energy, especially at your age. It may become less important as time passes, and you might develop a prefer-ence as you age. Some vampires do."

She took a bag from the bottom shelf. "Do you want some?" she asked.

I smiled. "No, I...fed yesterday," I said. Pressing my lips together, I tried not to picture the lovely brunette I'd loaded into the back of my car.

"You don't eat every day?"

"No. Not if I've fed well. I can go a couple of days without eating anything but a snack or two. The older you get, the longer you can last between meals." I walked over to a glass cabinet and met her on the other side of the kitchen island. I slid a wine glass across the marble toward her. "In case you want to be a bit more civilized."

She smiled and took the glass, filled it, and tossed the empty bag. I pointed her toward the microwave.

"Twenty seconds should take the chill off. Heating it in the bag is easier," I said, winking at her.

Considering how hard she had fought the past several days, she was taking this well, which pleased me. It was time for her to get on board.

"I just drank six of these," she said, lifting her glass. "And I'm still starving. I'm glad to hear it won't always be like this." She tucked her long, dark hair behind one ear and sipped the red liquid from her glass. She took small, delicate mouthfuls, but I could see how she gripped the glass and the tightness in her jaw. She was holding back, trying to be polite.

I remembered what it was like at first—never feeling truly satisfied, always hungry, distracted by the blood flowing through the veins of the humans around me. Of course, I still craved it; it was just easier now, less of a fixation.

I glanced down, running a finger along the edge of the countertop. I didn't want to stare, especially while she drank. I needed to maintain control. Besides, it seemed rude to watch her trying so hard to hold it together, and she'd already proved to be territorial when it came to blood. That wasn't unusual or considered rude. In fact, I found it quite attractive.

I couldn't help picturing what it would be like to take her out to the clubs and places I liked to go at night, to have her on my arm, enjoying all the delights she didn't know existed. The thought thrilled me, and I felt my fangs elongate.

"James?"

I looked up as she said my name to find her staring at me. I shook myself out of my fantasizing. This was not helpful. I needed to focus.

Kate finished drinking and set the glass aside. Her eyes were narrowed, and I grew self-conscious that she could read what I'd been thinking on my face.

"Yes," I said, pushing away the images of us drinking, dancing, and moving together.

She cleared her throat. "Nothing, I just wanted to thank you for your help tonight. I don't think I would have been able to make it back here on my own," she said.

It was difficult to envision her as she was before. Now, she was the epitome of health, with a glow in her cheeks and a spark back in her beautiful eyes.

"It's no problem. I'm glad it's over and you're feeling better." Remembering that I'd come with a purpose, not just to watch her, I said, "I came tonight not only to check on you but also because I have some things for you." I went to my bag, which was propped against the wall, and fished out a large envelope.

"Here you are," I said, holding it out.

She took the envelope and opened it, peering inside. "What's this?" she asked.

"It's your ID and a few other documents you'll need. The ID shows your House affiliation and allows you to access credit lines at most vampire businesses. I'll get you a regular credit card for use at human establishments."

"Vampire businesses?" She shook her head. "I have a lot to learn."

Holding up her ID, she examined it. Her face took on an expression that gave me pause. Speculation? Excitement? Suddenly, I regretted giving it to her. After finding her missing earlier, the thought of her being out on her own made my chest tighten. I definitely didn't want her wandering around without me, getting into trouble, or falling into someone else's hands.

"I think it's best if we go out together, at least at first," I said. "There's a lot for you to learn, and I don't want you to get into a situation that could be dangerous for you...or others," I added.

It was the right thing to say. She whipped her head up, her eyes wide. "Am I a danger? I mean, could I hurt someone without meaning to?" she asked.

I masked my face with grave concern. "Yes, you could be," I said. "But don't worry; I'll be with you and help you get through your first few outings."

She nodded and glanced back at the ID, a slight frown on her face. My chest relaxed a little. I hoped it would be enough to keep her in the apartment while I handled things, doing what I needed to satisfy Alexander. Alexander. He would expect things from me soon. I needed to hurry this up. I needed to follow through on my promise to deliver candidates.

"I should probably go," I said. And it was true. I needed to get out of the apartment and clear my head. If I stayed any longer, I would find an excuse to spend the entire night, and I wasn't sure I could hold it together for that long. Kate was irresistible, and I was certain she would be a willing companion as soon as she found her footing in our world, but I didn't want to rush things with her. She felt too important.

"I have business in the city tonight," I told her. "I'll stay there overday."

"Okay," she said, nodding slowly. "When will I see you again?" She gazed at me with her deep brown eyes, cocking her head. She looked like a bird of prey, watching and waiting to strike. So lovely. She was the perfect vampire. And she was all mine. I shivered at the thought but remembered she waited for an answer.

"Tomorrow night, I'll clear my schedule for the evening and take you out with me," I said. I hadn't meant to suggest it, but it felt right as the words escaped my lips. Offering her a chance to go out soon seemed like a good idea, and I was sure I'd be on my best behavior in public.

"Out?" she said. "Where are we going?"

"I want to show you where I spend most of my time. I want you to see how other vampires live. I think you'll enjoy it," I said. I'd always wanted more time to enjoy my social life, after all, and I was excited to share my world with her.

Her posture shifted, and the raptor vanished, replaced by a wide-eyed, frightened creature. "Don't worry. It'll be fun. I promise." I smiled at her, trying to be reassuring.

"Other vampires?" she asked.

"Sure. I'll take you to the area of the city where we usually hang out."

"What about the other vampires from your House?" Kate asked.

Her question caught me off guard. I wasn't worried we would run into Alexander—he rarely left the manor and wouldn't be caught dead in a bar downtown. And, my only other housemate in the city, Josephine, never left her room. We were safe from discovery as long as Kate didn't get too chatty with anyone. I straightened up and grabbed my jacket.

"No," I said. I considered my response before I added, "There is only you."

She seemed to relax at this. And it made me consider her point of view.

If I learned I was the only fledgling of a young vampire, I would have felt disappointed, but she seemed relieved. Then again, she wasn't like me. She wasn't like any vampire I'd ever met. And I realized I liked her more than any other vampire I'd known, even in our short time together. The reason I liked her was also the same thing that annoyed me the most about her. She hadn't chosen this life. She didn't seek to be an immortal killer. She was normal. She liked her old life and had been living it, not running away from everything she knew, like most of our kind had. Like I had.

She seemed happy to be my only companion, even if it was a lie. Perhaps she was possessive of more than just blood. The idea brought me more pleasure than I expected. I'd never experienced that—someone who valued me for who I was, not for the work I did for them or the convenience of my presence, but for my true self.

The lies I told her should have bothered me, but they didn't. The only regret I had was that I hadn't turned her myself. I would have liked the lies to be true. I'd never considered that things would turn out the way they did. But it didn't matter. She was mine, and I would be hers.

I looked back at Kate. She waited expectantly. I really couldn't stay. Before I could change my mind, I reached for the door. "You should find everything you need here, but if you think of anything, just text me," I said. I didn't plan on returning, but I felt a concern I hadn't expected. I needed to make sure she would be alright. "And don't answer the door for anyone. I don't usually entertain here, and the house-keeper isn't due in tomorrow, so no one should bother you, but just in case."

She nodded.

I felt a growl rise in my throat at the thought of someone coming to the apartment while I was away. As soon as I realized what I was doing, I swallowed it down and coughed, attempting to disguise the sound. I needed to leave.

In the hall, with the door closed between us, I felt calmer. I took a deep breath, inhaling nothing but the stale air of the apartment corridor. I sighed. There was a lot to do before tomorrow night. I would finish my chores for Alexander and then make sure that tomorrow evening would be perfect. It had to be. Kate needed to understand how wonderful her new life was. She would see how much fun she could have. She would realize how perfect it would be to spend forever together.

15
___

KATE

The apartment went quiet as the elevator closed in the hall. James had vanished again. It had become a habit, but I didn't mind. He'd started to creep me out. The thought made me feel a bit guilty. I owed him a lot—my life. Yet, I appreciated the space.

I would learn whatever I could from him and then figure out how to make the separation more permanent. I needed to understand what this Council would demand of me and how closely it would connect me to James. There had to be a way for me to live this new life on my terms.

Thinking about my new life, I took my phone out of my back pocket and hurried back into the bedroom, locking the door behind me. It was excessive, but I felt the need to create as much distance as possible between James and me for what I would do next.

I settled onto the bed, leaning back against the head-board and pulling my legs up. Finally, I glanced down at my phone.

My face split into a grin. Sara had texted back.

Kate!!!!

I knew it! I knew you were alive.

I've missed you.

There is so much to say.

Call me!!

I took a shaky breath, joy bubbling up from my middle. It was my first good feeling since waking up in the morgue. God, that seemed like a lifetime ago.

Before I could chicken out, I tapped the camera icon next to Sara's name to initiate a video call. Even though I'd done this hundreds of times before, it felt different. As the phone began to ring, my joy morphed into a frantic sort of anxiety. How would I explain everything that happened?

"Kate!" Sara's voice came through the phone in a loud whisper, clearly trying not to be overheard by anyone in the house. Yet, as her smiling face filled the screen, the happiness radiating from that one word was a relief. She was my best friend. A witch, maybe, but still my best friend.

I smiled back, and her eyes widened in response.

"Uh, yeah," I said, bringing my hand up to my mouth and my exposed fangs. "We have some catching up to do."

Sara nodded, her expression softening. "We do," she said seriously. "Where are you?"

"Oh. I'm in an apartment close to my old place."

I gave her the name of the building, and she nodded once more. "I'm on my way. I'll be outside the front door in thirty minutes," she said.

"But, Sara—" I began, only for her to hang up in the middle of my sentence.

I scowled at the phone in my hand and redialed Sara's number. It was a bad idea for her to come for so many reasons. It rang once, and then the call was rejected. I cursed. She wouldn't let me talk her out of it.

My anxiety intensified as I surveyed the bedroom—James's bedroom, his apartment. I remembered how he tracked me by scent to my place and how he could smell Sara from across the street. There was no way he wouldn't know she'd been in the apartment.

I sighed and pushed myself off the bed. I was certain that if I didn't meet her downstairs, she would call every apartment in the building until she found me. The thought made me smile again. I wanted to see her. I wanted to talk with her and not be alone anymore. But I didn't want to put her or anyone else in danger.

I paced back and forth, shaking my hands, trying to decide whether I felt particularly homicidal or if I could pull it together to see Sara. I just didn't know. But I couldn't stay locked behind a door forever, cut off from all human contact. Could I? No. I'd decided to go along with becoming a vampire because I believed there was a chance for a life with those I loved. I would not live in fear, even of myself.

I went back to the kitchen and yanked open the fridge door. There was still plenty of blood left. My stomach rumbled again when I saw the bags neatly stacked on the clear plastic shelves. I placed a hand on my belly. How could I still be hungry? I took two more bags off the bottom shelf and closed the stainless steel door.

I didn't bother with a glass; I just ripped off the end of the first bag, like I'd seen James do. It didn't taste as good cold, but my body didn't seem to mind. After I finished both bags and cleaned up the mess, I went to the bathroom mirror to check my reflection. The last thing I needed was to show up downstairs with blood smeared on my face.

I glanced into the mirror and contemplated what I saw. I looked like myself, more or less. My skin appeared smoother, and my hair seemed shinier, or maybe that was just the lighting. My face had filled back out, and my body looked the same as before. I leaned in closer to examine my eyes. They were different. I studied the brown irises and felt a thrill of fear run up my spine. It was like gazing into the stare of a wild animal. I shivered and stepped back from the mirror.

I wondered what Sara would see. Would she be afraid of me? She knew I'd changed, and her texts made it clear that she had some idea of what happened. Neither of us was what the other thought. Would I look at her differently now?

Glancing at my phone, I noticed it was nearly 2 a.m. Sara would be here any minute. I slipped on my shoes and gazed at the back of the front door. Peering through the small peephole, I saw no one in the corridor. I listened but couldn't hear the elevator. Cautiously, I opened the door and stepped out.

The air in the hall felt different and smelled different. I could barely keep track of all the scents that registered: carpet cleaner, damp dog hair, cooking oil, and the smell of people. I could smell three distinct types of perfume and cologne, along with body wash, hair spray, and blood. I swallowed. It wasn't like the smell from the bags in the fridge; it was something warmer, deeper, and yet faint.

My canine teeth tingled, but I didn't feel out of control or especially hungry. I shook my head and exhaled through my nose, clearing the scents from my nostrils and mind. I held my breath as I stepped onto the elevator and pressed the button for the first floor. I focused on relaxing my body before taking another breath. I waited for the urge to build, for my lungs to tighten and cry out for air, but the feeling never came. *Do I not need to breathe?*

I didn't have time to marvel at my discovery before the doors opened, revealing a blessedly empty lobby. I drew in a relieved breath and was nearly knocked off my feet by the new scents that assaulted me. I quickly stopped breathing once more and glanced around. The lobby wasn't as empty as I thought. There was someone on duty behind the front desk in the corner. I didn't notice him at first; his head was down like he was reading something or, more likely, looking at his phone. Now that I was aware of his presence, I realized I could hear his heart beating.

I pictured the muscle in his chest. Thump, thump, thump. Pumping blood through his veins, warm beneath his skin. My teeth elongated, my muscles tensed, and my vision sharpened. *Whoa.* I needed to stop this train. This was heading nowhere good, and quickly. I turned away from the desk, breaking off the vision I'd conjured in my mind. He was a person. Not a meal, I reminded myself. Instead, I focused on how the man felt.

Throughout my life, my ability to read people's emotions had been both a blessing and a curse. However, I had never appreciated it more than I did at that moment. As soon as I focused on the man's feelings, everything changed. The complexity of his emotional landscape completely over-shadowed my vampire senses' more basic observations—and it was beautiful.

Never before had a person's emotions registered with such precision. Even in his boredom, sadness, and loneliness, he was rendered in such lovely detail. Although I'd never met this man before, I felt like I knew him, and I wanted to ease his sadness. I couldn't help myself; I turned back and stepped toward him. He glanced up at my approach. His bland expression was replaced with a mask of professional greeting.

"Good evening," he said as I neared. "Can I help you with anything?"

What was I doing?

"Umm, No. I'm just waiting for someone," I said.

He nodded pleasantly, waiting for more.

I used up all the air in my lungs and realized I would have to take another breath to continue talking. But as I looked at him, with no oxygen moving into my body, it wasn't my lungs that ached, but my heart. The urge to ease this man's pain overwhelmed me.

I took a deep breath, and while his scent was drawn into me, triggering all my vampire instincts, none was so powerful as to overwhelm me. I would have felt relief had I not been struggling with the man's sadness.

"Are you okay?" I asked, pushing right up to the desk. I was close enough that I could've reached out to touch him if I wanted.

He blinked at me in confusion, and then his smile slipped. "Uh. Yeah. I'm okay. It's just..." He took a shuddering breath. "My dog recently died." He offered a tight smile. "I'm just missing him, I guess."

When he smiled, I caught a flicker of the love he felt at the memory of his pet. I nodded. I'd lost pets before, and I recognized his emotions as the ones I'd felt at the time—the ones that still sprang up occasionally.

He squirmed a bit in his seat, and his emotions shifted to embarrassment. I realized I stared at him and was the cause of this shift.

"I'm sorry," I said. "I know what that feels like." I smiled and turned away, wanting to give him some privacy. I reached again for that internal space I'd created between James's feelings and mine. It was still there, and I used it again. I placed myself safely back on my side, not cut off from the man's emotions but separate from them. As I moved farther across the lobby, his feelings faded until they were just a gentle nudge against my own.

Walking toward the front doors, I felt euphoric, as if I had passed a big test. Filtering out other people's feelings would be a considerable challenge, but it would be well worth it if it kept my vampire nature in check.

When I stepped in front of the glass and saw Sara on the other side of the double doors, I reminded myself to move slowly. I was nearly bouncing with excitement. I pressed the button to open the inner doors, and she came rushing in. Before I could even greet her, her arms were around me.

I hugged her back. I wrapped my arms around her, tilting my head, and my face ended up buried in the crook of her neck, close to her shoulder. I flinched when I realized how near I was to her vein, but then I noticed her scent. She didn't smell like anything I would want to eat. She had an herbal, spicy scent that burned my nose. The thought shocked me so much that I pushed her back and looked into her face.

"You don't smell human," I blurted.

Sara's eyes opened wide, and she shot a glance at the front desk and the man sitting behind it. He paid no attention and was too far away for his human ears to pick up on what I'd said.

Sara smirked at me. "Nope. And you don't feel human, sweetie," she said in a soft voice, motioning up and down with one hand. "The energy coming off of you is way powerful."

"Energy," I said, confused.

She grinned. "We have a lot to talk about." She looked around expectantly. I realized she waited for me to lead her up to the apartment where I was staying.

"We can't go upstairs," I said.

"Is he here?" she asked in a flat tone.

Her question took me by surprise. "You know him?"

She shook her head. "No. I saw you with a man outside your apartment earlier, remember? I assume he's the one who got you into all this?" she asked.

I stopped to think. Of course, she'd seen James with me earlier. Was that just this evening? It felt like a lot more time had passed.

I surveyed the lobby. The desk was positioned to one side, while an open seating area was located on the opposite side of the front entrance. As I looked over the seating options, I noticed two chairs tucked away in a corner, nestled between the wall and a large plant. It seemed like a perfect spot for a meeting, reading a book, or catching up with your best friend to share the story of how you became a vampire. I took Sara's hand and led her to the chairs, out of direct view of the grieving receptionist.

"No. He's not here," I said as we settled into the cafe-style chairs' soft upholstery. "But I can't take you into the apartment. He would know you'd been there."

She studied my face as I spoke. Her initial joy disappeared. I opened up to her, trying to gauge her emotions, and it took my breath away. My first reaction was to put the wall back up and shut down the onslaught of feelings rolling off her, but I didn't. I needed to know what was going on with her. It seemed important not only to hear what she had to say but also to understand her emotions. I couldn't speak, however, so I waited, hoping she would fill the silence while I wrestled with the conflicting feelings of my best friend.

Finally, she spoke. "I thought you were dead," she said. "You let me think you were dead."

I just shook my head, not yet able to respond.

"I saw your body. I took your mother to see your body, Kate," she said, her voice cracking. "Why couldn't you tell me? Why did I have to go through that? Do you know how many people are hurting because of this?"

I didn't know what to say. Did she really think I'd done this on purpose? I swallowed the lump in my throat and opened my mouth, but no sound came out. I tried again. "Sara, I can barely dress myself without your opinion. Do you honestly believe I would choose to become a...become a *vampire* without talking to you first?" I tripped on the V word, still not comfortable with the idea, let alone the term.

She blinked at me, her emotions becoming jumbled and confused. "You didn't agree to be turned?"

"No," I blurted. "I was hit by a car. And, I guess I did die. At least I would have. But then James, the guy you saw, changed me at the last minute." Then the full effect of what she said hit me. "Wait, you saw my body? You and my mom?"

She nodded, and there was a shine of tears in her eyes. She sniffed. "Yeah. It was terrible. Your mom needed to identify your body, and I went with her." She sniffed again, and my guilt spiked. I hadn't known.

"Are you sure it was me?"

"It was definitely you." She cocked her head. "I could feel it was you. It freaked me out, actually. I could tell you were still around, your energy, anyway. I thought you just hadn't crossed over yet or whatever. I never expected that you were...undead," she said.

I huffed out a laugh. "Yeah, I was pretty freaked out, too, when I woke up in a morgue drawer." I crossed my legs, trying to appear more comfortable than I felt.

Sara froze, and her mouth hung open. Then, she nodded slowly. "Okay. Yeah, that's fucked up."

"Forgiven?" I asked.

She rolled her eyes, but I felt her hurt ease, and she smiled. "Yeah, I didn't realize. I'm sorry I got mad."

I smiled in response. "So, you've been holding back a few things from me, haven't you? Witch."

She had the good sense to look guilty, but I wasn't angry.

"I wanted to tell you—," she started, but I held up a hand.

"It's okay. I understand. Now, better than ever." I sat forward, resting my elbows on my knees, bringing me closer, and grinned at her, teeth on full display.

She sat back and shook her head, but grinned back. "Okay, you need to stop; that is too freaky."

I leaned back into my chair but couldn't get the smile off my face. "Tell me, though, what is all this 'energy' talk?" I asked. "Is that a witch thing?"

Sara glanced toward the receptionist again, but he was screened from view, and no one else was around. She held up one hand, her familiar wooden ring around one finger, and a spark of blue light ignited on the tip of her index finger. The spark grew into a rivulet of electricity that flowed between her fingers and back again, wrapping around her hand like glittering thread. Then, it vanished.

She smiled at the expression on my face. "I can manipulate electricity, and I can sense energy, including that of living things. Everyone feels a bit different, and trees feel different from people or insects, for example."

"Can your mom and aunt do that, too?" I asked.

She shook her head. "No. We all have our own gifts. I take after my dad. His gift was energy, too," she said, and I felt that familiar melancholy she felt when she mentioned her dad in the past, just more intense.

Everything felt more intense since becoming a vampire. I sighed. It felt like a time for coming clean, revealing secrets.

"Sara, there is more," I said.

"More than you being a vampire and me hiding my species from my best friend for the past twelve years?" she asked. Her tone was light, but I sensed her unease.

"Yeah. I think... I think I might be a witch too," I said.

I watched her face, analyzing her expression. Her emotions were all over the place. She looked back at me blankly before bursting into laughter. "No, sweetheart. Sorry to disappoint you, but you're definitely not a witch," she said. I started to protest, but she interrupted me. "No. I understand what you're trying to say. For a while, my mom and I thought you might be, too. But you're not. If you were a witch, there's no way a vampire would've gotten close enough to bite you, let alone turn you. No. I've known you were different since I met you, but you're not one of us."

I considered Sara's scent, still tickling my nose with its astringent quality. The thought of biting her was repulsive.

"But you don't understand," I insisted. "I can sense people's emotions. I can tell how others around me are feeling. And that was before I became a vampire. What else could that mean?"

"Not only that, but you can push on the emotions of others," she said, smiling at my shocked expression. "Yeah, you think I haven't noticed? I'm your best friend."

"Well, now I feel bad. I should have been more observant and figured out your secret years ago, too." I tried to sound playful, but it didn't come across that way. I sighed, feeling a bit cheated for some reason.

Sara reached out and took my hand. "I'm sorry, Kate. I wish we could have talked about this stuff, but I just couldn't. I've never discussed any of this with anyone outside my community. But please know that I would have if I could."

I understood. Now that I was caught up in this other world, I respected the need to keep quiet.

"But, if I'm not a witch, what am I?"

Sara patted my hand. "Well, we know for sure that you are a vampire. As for what else you might be, we'll have to figure that out."

Sara shifted in her seat, her gaze fixed on me. I could sense her weighing what to say next. Finally, she spoke, "I want you to come home with me. I don't know who this James guy is, but from what little I've heard about vampires, they're not safe to be around. Let me put you up at my place while we figure out what to do."

I blinked back at her. I hadn't expected the offer and was grateful, but it wasn't that simple. "Does your mom host many vampires at the house?" I asked. Sara bit her bottom lip but didn't respond. "I didn't think so. Do you guys have any vampire friends? Neighbors?"

Sara sighed. "No. The two groups don't really have anything to do with each other," she admitted. "But this is different—"

"It's not that easy, Sara. I want to come with you; I truly do. But this is all new to me. I still have a lot to learn about what it means to be a vampire. There are apparently rules and a political structure I know nothing about. Not to mention, I have no idea how to keep myself fed."

Sara wrinkled her nose at that, and I flashed her a toothy

grin. "Yeah, it's not like I can just grab what I need at the local supermarket."

Sara smiled back in understanding, but I could sense her disappointment. "I don't know," she said. "I get what you're saying, but I'm worried about you. You can't trust vampires, Kate."

I nodded. "James is taking me out tomorrow night. I'll call you when we get back and let you know how it went. We'll find a way to make this all work. I'm not cutting you out of my life or choosing him over you. I promise. And he's not so bad. He can be annoying, but he did save my life, after all," I said, reaching out to squeeze Sara's hand.

She shook her head. "I feel like I just got you back. I don't want to leave you here."

"You're not. I just need some time to figure things out. In the meantime, maybe you could ask your mom and aunt and see what they have to say about it. Do they know any independent vampires? How do they get by?"

Sara shifted uncomfortably, and I could sense the apprehension at my mention of her family.

"They don't know about me, do they?" I asked, but I already knew the answer.

Sara shook her head. "No, not yet... It's complicated." I could tell from her response that there was a lot I needed to learn about witches, too.

"Sara, are we ok?" I asked.

"Yeah," she said, and I could tell she meant it. "You're still you, right?"

"Yeah. I'm still me, just with a few changes."

"Then we're great," she replied.

We stood together, and I pulled her into a gentle hug. I was cautious not to squeeze too tightly. I caught the ocean scent of her tears before we pulled apart, and I could see them glistening on her face. One tear rolled down her cheek, and I brushed it away with my thumb.

"Thank you for coming," I said. "Seeing you has been the only good thing that's happened to me in the past three days." Her face crumpled at my words, and she started to cry in earnest. I wrapped my arms around her again and held her as she sobbed.

When she finished, I walked her to the front doors and said goodbye. It was hard to let her go. I wanted so badly to take her up on her offer and go with her. I wanted to be done with the apartment upstairs, and James, and the blood, and everything, but I couldn't. If I were going to survive, if I were going to have any hope of taking care of myself, I had a lot to learn about being a vampire.

16

KATE

The following evening, I stepped out of the bedroom and smoothed my hands over the black fabric of the dress that James brought me. I resented his need to dress me, but my wardrobe was severely limited. I would need to get more clothing soon. A pair of ruined stretch pants, a single pair of jeans, and two tops wouldn't last me very long, and weren't suitable for wherever we were headed.

The outfit I wore wasn't something I would have chosen for myself, but I had to admit it was beautiful, especially when paired with the pointy heels he provided. The gown—because calling it a dress didn't do it justice—was a fitted, floor-length masterpiece. The top featured intricate lace in a delicate pattern reminiscent of Art Deco design. My skin peeked through, and I could barely feel the fabric against my shoulders. The rest of the gown, starting at my bust, was made of the softest material that flowed down my body like water, with a high slit up one thigh allowing for movement. I thought it might actually be silk, though I was fairly certain I'd never worn real silk before.

"Where are you taking me?" I asked, looking up to find

James watching me in a way that made me uncomfortable. I let my senses peek out from behind the wall of space inside me, the distance that separated my feelings from his. Yeah, he had different expectations for the evening than I did. Ugh.

"It's a surprise," he said and rose to retrieve his coat.

"Is it cold out?" I asked. "Do I need my jacket?"

"You don't really *need* a jacket," he said, handing me a new black coat. *Where did he pull that from*, I wondered. "But it's a good idea not to draw attention," he continued.

"What do you mean I don't need a coat?" I asked, watching the smug look on his face as I wrapped myself in the thick wool he'd given me. He clearly delighted in my ignorance.

"I mean, the temperature doesn't affect your body anymore. You feel it, of course, until you acclimate, but the cold won't harm you. It might feel uncomfortable, but you'll get used to it. Wearing a coat won't really keep you warm. You can no longer regulate your body temperature; you're the same temperature as whatever environment you're in."

"You mean that if I take my temperature right now, it would match the room's? Like seventy-two degrees?" I asked.

"Exactly."

I pushed the sleeve of the coat up and rubbed my hand along my arm. "But I don't feel cold," I said.

"Not to you, but humans will be able to tell the difference, and you should be aware of that."

I nodded but wasn't entirely convinced.

James chose a black convertible for the evening, but thankfully kept the top up. The weather was cool and rainy, and I believed James when he said the temperature wouldn't harm me, but I was glad to be protected from the elements.

We made good time despite the traffic and wet pavement. The convertible sure beat the bus for comfort and speed, but I could have done without the glances from James and the waves of satisfied possessiveness coming off of him.

We exited into the heart of the city, where the lights were so much brighter than those on the highway. James pulled into a parking space, and I realized we were only a few blocks from the theater that hosted the art exhibit. It was the same street where I'd gotten off when I missed my bus stop just days earlier. I looked around as we got out, and James locked the car. I had no idea I'd been in an area frequented by vampires.

James offered me his elbow, and I allowed him to escort me half a block, where we paused in front of an old bookshop wedged between a hardware store and a real estate office. The shop had a large window filled with vintage tomes and advertisements. The door was painted green with a brass handle. A sign painted in gold across the window read *Top Shelf Books*. James yanked the door open, and bells chimed overhead.

The bookshop resembled any you might find in a large city. It was a cramped space with narrow passageways through towering shelves filled with both used and new books. The air was saturated with the smell of old paper and ink. I took a deep breath, savoring the familiar scent, but there was something more to it. A mix of overlapping aromas floated through the small space—books, paper, leather, and dust, but also vampires and blood. It made my stomach twist, and my fangs tingle as we walked to the front of the shop to greet the man behind the counter.

"Hello. Good evening, Mr. Whitlock," the shopkeeper said as he reached under the countertop. A buzzing sound filled the air, and we moved past the counter, deeper into the shop, stopping in front of a large wooden shelf. James pushed against the shelf, swinging it to the side and revealing a set of carpeted wooden stairs leading downward. The passage was illuminated by glass globes mounted at intervals that flickered as if lit by gas instead of electricity. From the depth of the passage, I could see that our destination lay deep underground.

James steadied me on the steps, but I didn't truly need his help. Although I'd never felt entirely comfortable in heels, my newfound strength apparently came with superior balance, making walking easy, even in three-inch stilettos. As we descended, I heard the low rumble of voices and soft music playing in the distance.

The stairs led to a spacious two-story restaurant featuring a bar styled with a turn-of-the-century vibe—the 19th century. However, it was more richly appointed than any restaurant or bar I'd ever visited.

There were tables and booths with dark marine-blue velvet upholstery. The fixtures were either gold or brass, and dark wood shelves lined a wall of mirrors stocked with every liquor imaginable. The lighting made the glass on the shelves sparkle, and I noticed an upper level that encircled the space's perimeter with smaller tables and low chairs.

The room was half full of patrons, and to my surprise, I realized I could easily identify the vampires among them. It wasn't that they looked so different from the humans; it was more of an impression I got. The way they moved, the way they smelled, even from a distance. Then I listened with all my senses, and the differences between them clarified even further. The emotions of the vampires were completely different from those of the humans, and I wondered why I hadn't noticed it sooner. They operated on an entirely different frequency than the people in the room.

Focusing on so many people and vampires at once threatened to overwhelm me, so I tightened my grip on the barrier in my mind, leaving my other senses bare. Blood. Without the distraction of swirling emotions, my vampire senses sharpened, and the scent of fresh blood crashed into me.

I looked around a second time and saw what I'd missed at first. Some of the vampires I'd identified had their heads bent over the outstretched arm of a human sitting next to them. The sight kindled something within me that remained mostly dormant until then. My teeth punched painfully into my mouth, and I parted my jaw to make room.

"What is this place?" I asked, the words escaping in a hiss because of my elongated canines.

"You might call it a speakeasy, I suppose," James said. "This is the Tap House. It's a safe place for us to get together and...dine."

I didn't respond to that. I should have been horrified, but I wasn't. I was intrigued, more than intrigued, and I reminded myself that I was there to learn, not to indulge my baser vampire instincts.

At that moment, a woman stepped forward. She took our coats and offered to guide us to our seats. James took my arm, and we followed her to a table along one side of the room. When my hand made contact with James's arm, I was bombarded by his emotions. Contact seemed to make it impossible to shut him out completely, even with my guard up. He was excited and anticipating what would happen here. That knowledge made me nervous, and I gratefully dropped my hand as soon as we reached our table. Once we were seated in the plush booth, a waitress greeted James by name and handed us both menus.

I was grateful for the distraction and glanced down at

the words printed on the folded brown paper in my hands. It was a typical menu. The artistic style was minimalist but leaned more toward hipster than practical. It listed what appeared to be dishes or even full meals. There were names written beside each listing. Where one might expect to see a symbol for food allergens, there was a letter followed by a plus or minus sign. There were no prices.

"What is this?" I asked.

"The menu," James said, affecting a bored tone. "It lists the human's most recent meal and blood type. You can order by the glass or straight from the tap, so to speak."

I looked over the offerings with a new eye. "You're kidding? I don't..." I didn't know how to finish the thought. This was not something I'd come prepared for.

James smiled at me knowingly. "Don't worry. I'll order for you."

I shook my head. "No. I'll just take something in a glass."

"Oh no, you won't. You need to feed properly. I'm getting you something warm and fresh." He waved the waitress over and pointed to the menu. She nodded politely and disappeared before I could object.

I opened my mouth to speak, to call her back and refuse, but I couldn't. I closed my mouth as best I could and swallowed hard. Blowing out a breath, I looked around again. "All those liquor bottles," I said, trying to distract myself from what was about to happen. "Do people here drink?"

"They aren't for the diners; they are for the meals. You can order a beverage or a dish for the human to consume before you drink. It's not your typical establishment," he said. "It's a bit more upscale, but I thought for your first time it would be nice."

I licked my dry lips, revealing my fangs. The evidence of

my desire to feed should have embarrassed me, but I was too nervous to care. I glanced around at the other tables. Some vampires held glasses of ruby liquid, drinking and chatting like patrons at any bar. A few others were feeding from the wrists of humans. I was surprised they weren't drinking from their necks, as I'd imagined, and I asked James about it.

He laughed softly. "No," he explained. "This isn't that sort of place." He narrowed his eyes as he spoke. I didn't understand what he meant, but I nodded. "There are other places for that kind of thing," he said. "This is a more wholesome establishment."

I didn't have time to consider the difference before our waitress returned, accompanied by a large man. He appeared to be in his early thirties, with short, spiky black hair, a hint of a beard, and tattoos peeking out from the collar of his black button-down shirt.

"This is Bruce," the waitress said, and the man next to her nodded politely. "If you need anything else, just let me know," she added before walking away.

Bruce stood there waiting until James pointed at me. Then Bruce walked to my side of the circular booth and slid in next to me. He was enormous, even more so now that he was seated so close. I tried to create some distance between myself and the hulking man by inching closer to James until my hip pressed against his leg. It was a mistake. James's anticipation only intensified my own, prompting me to move away quickly so that I wasn't in contact with either of them.

I looked up into Bruce's strikingly blue eyes. He smiled encouragingly and began to roll up his sleeve, uncovering a forearm wrapped in tattoos. He turned his wrist over, revealing an uninked patch right above a pulsing blue vein that ran up the inside of his arm. Suddenly, I forgot all about James and everything else around me.

My eyes were locked on that blank patch of skin. I watched the rhythm of his heartbeat within the fragile vessel there, and my mouth began to water. He twisted, reaching across his body, and extended his arm toward me. "Whenever you're ready," he said in a smooth, deep voice. I opened my mouth slightly but didn't move. I flicked my gaze back up to his.

"It's her first time," James said from over my shoulder, his voice startling me.

Bruce's face brightened. "Your first time here?" he asked, but I found I couldn't speak.

"No. Her first time ever," James explained, and I swear I could hear the grin in his voice.

Bruce's features change. His smile vanished, his eyes widened, and the muscles in his jaw flexed. He glanced over my head at James, his expression tense. "You got her?" he asked. The smoothness faded, and his voice sounded tight.

"Yeah, you're good. I've got her," James said.

Bruce nodded and brought his arm closer to me, but I noticed his hesitation this time. I reached out with both hands, placing one under his elbow and the other gently around his wrist. His fear thundered into me. It should have deterred me, made me reconsider what I was about to do, but instead, it only intensified my desire for him. His skin felt warm, and it was surprisingly easy to hold the weight of his massive arm. I had no plan when I bent my head over the outstretched limb, but my body knew exactly what to do.

I struck swiftly, sinking my long fangs into the flesh of his arm. I'd found my mark, the punctures precisely where they needed to be. I pressed my lips against his smooth skin, and my mouth filled with his blood.

This felt completely different from drinking from a cold plastic bag. What touched my tongue and slid down my throat was warm and fragrant. The taste was bold, yet at the same time, delicate flavors were layered beneath. I tried to appreciate the bouquet, but my focus was solely on its warm vitality. I inhaled and exhaled through my nose as I drank swallow after swallow. The warmth of the blood pooling in my belly spread throughout me. It was raw. It was thrilling. It was life. And it was mine.

17

JAMES

I had chosen well. Bruce was a true professional. He didn't even flinch when Kate attacked his arm. Although she would learn the delicacy of the act in time, she was doing well for her first attempt. She was a natural, and it was a thrill to watch her feeding from the man. It made me imagine her at my throat.

As much as I was enjoying myself, the feeding had gone on long enough. I locked eyes with Bruce, and we nodded at each other. It was time. I leaned forward and gently placed my hands on Kate's shoulders. Instinct took over, and she tensed, her body going rigid. She tightened her grip on Bruce's arm and began to growl in warning, her body hunched protectively over her meal. Pain flickered across Bruce's face, but he quickly regained control of his expression and waited patiently. He knew better than to jerk his arm away or struggle. Besides, she had him in a vice grip, and he couldn't escape even if he wanted to. She might be half his size, but she was magnitudes stronger than the large man.

"Kate. Katie, you're hurting him. It's time to let go," I said in an even tone.

Her body suddenly softened, and she paused. I couldn't see her face from where I sat, but I could see Bruce relax as she withdrew her fangs and sat back. Bruce immediately clapped a black cloth over his wounded arm and waited.

"Here. I've got it," I said, bringing a finger to my sharp teeth and making a small cut. Leaning forward past Kate, I offered my bleeding finger to Bruce, who lifted the cloth. I rubbed my finger over the punctures until they sealed and the bleeding stopped.

Kate watched all of this with a look of fascination. She turned her head back and forth between Bruce and me. "Is he going to be okay?" she asked, sounding genuinely concerned.

She focused on Bruce, who pulled down his sleeve. "Are you okay? I'm really sorry about your arm. Did I take too much? I didn't mean to," she stammered.

Bruce rolled his shoulder but shook his head. "No, I'm just fine. You did well."

He looked pale but smiled reassuringly at Kate as he pushed himself to his feet. He stood for a moment to test his balance before wishing us a good evening and walking toward the kitchens. Another employee, on hand in case Bruce needed support, met him halfway. And then it was over.

Kate watched the man leave, her face still etched with concern. She needed to get over that. This was precisely why I had brought her here. This place was safe and discreet. Even if she drained the poor guy, the repercussions would be minimal. Obviously, I would have to compensate the Tap House, and the Council would issue a warning, but it would amount to little more than a slap on the wrist. It was one of the advantages of dining in an establishment with contracted humans: more paperwork, but fewer consequences. Almost no one risked hunting in the wild anymore.

But the thought of consequences made me hesitate. If Kate were to stumble in public, there could be serious repercussions for me. Any report involving me would eventually reach Alexander, and then I'd really be in trouble.

I hoped the young human male I'd left with him last night would distract him. I recalled how Alexander purred and stroked the man's reddish-brown curls. I prayed he would connect with the man and decide to change him. I wanted my search to be over so I could focus on creating a real life and a routine for Kate and me. Maybe if Alexander liked the man enough, he could eventually forget all about me, and I would be free.

I glanced back at Kate, who still seemed lost in thought. "Hey, you okay?" I asked, patting her hand. Her entire body jolted at the contact, and she pulled away.

"Oh. Yeah. That was...really different," she said, but her body revealed more than her words. Her cheeks were flushed, she avoided my gaze, and her heart had just started to settle back to its normal rhythm. She'd enjoyed it—a lot.

I smiled, feeling satisfied. It was good to see her this way, experiencing the pleasure of being a vampire.

Our waitress came back to the table and asked how we were doing.

"Is Tanya still available this evening?" I asked.

"Of course," the waitress said with a smile. "A double of Oban, eighteen year?"

I nodded.

"I'll send her over when she's ready."

I thanked the woman and turned back to Kate. "I hope

you don't mind if I eat too. I wanted to let you go first and offer a hand if you needed it. Plus, I didn't want to tease you with my meal before you had a chance to feed."

She smiled tentatively. "I don't mind. I probably should have watched you first so that I could have done a better job. I'm worried I hurt that poor man."

"Forget about him," I said, annoyed that she was so preoccupied. "You did an amazing job, especially for your first time."

She smiled again, though it resembled more of a grimace.

It took a moment before she spoke. "So, all these humans here—the waitress, the guy in the bookshop, and the...donors—they all know what goes on here, what we are, but they don't say anything?"

"No. They're all very discreet, and they know the consequences of speaking to other humans. It's severe," I said.

"Then why? Why would they work here? Why would they...?" she trailed off.

I tilted my head and watched the tall, beautiful blonde woman heading in our direction. "Because they are all extremely well compensated, and some of them hope to be adopted into one of the Houses, either as employees or transformed into vampires like us."

"Houses? Like your House, you mean?" Kate asked.

"Yes. There are five major Houses and dozens of smaller ones. But enough of that for now," I said as Tanya arrived, tumbler in hand. It was good timing. I stood and kissed the back of her free hand. I'd had her several times before, and we were well acquainted.

Tanya was tall for a woman, nearly six feet. She had an athletic build and wore a uniform of black slacks and a black button-down shirt with her sleeves rolled up to her elbows. I motioned for her to slide into the booth between Kate and me. She took her seat, sipping from the glass of scotch. She'd already finished half of it before arriving at the table, as was customary. The scent of the familiar liquor and the woman made my fangs ache.

Sitting beside her, I took one of Tanya's hands in my own and gently turned her wrist over. "There are ways to make the experience more pleasant for the human," I said, glancing at Kate as I spoke.

I brought Tanya's wrist to my lips and kissed the underside of her arm, licking gently with my tongue, all the while keeping my eyes on Kate.

Kate watched me, her mouth open slightly. "Our saliva numbs the skin. If you wait a minute or two, the human won't feel the sting as intensely," I said. I continued kissing Tanya's arm as she sat working on her drink with detached professionalism.

After a minute or two, I opened my mouth, revealing my elongated canines. I bent back over Tanya's arm and slowly bit down through the skin, puncturing the vein below. The taste of her blood and the scotch was what I'd been craving. Even as I drank, I kept my gaze on Kate. Tanya's blood was wonderful, but not half as good as the expression on Kate's face.

She watched me, her throat moving as she swallowed, her tongue flicking out against her lip while her fangs descended once more. She fed well, and I doubted she was hungry, but she focused on the feeding, intrigued. Perhaps even intrigued by me, and that thought was exhilarating.

The feeding was over sooner than I would have liked. Although my hunger was sated, and I enjoyed the momentary buzz from the alcohol, I was far from satisfied. I bade

Tanya a good evening, and the waitress returned to check on us. I told her we were ready to go and signed our bill.

As we gathered our coats, Kate asked, "Where are we headed now?" Her cheeks were still rosy from feeding, and she had an excited glow about her.

"I thought we would go back to the apartment," I said, raising the corner of my mouth and offering her my arm.

Her expression changed, and she knit her brows together. "I'd hoped to see more. You mentioned vampire-owned shops and businesses. I don't want to go back just yet," she said. "It feels like I've spent weeks shut in that place." She crossed her arms and waited for a reply.

She shifted from foot to foot on her delicate heels. Her long, dark hair and liquid brown eyes were simply lovely. Even with a frown on her face, she was beautiful. The dress I'd chosen was perfect for her, just as I knew it would be. It would be a shame not to show her off some more, I decided.

It wouldn't hurt to take her somewhere else. I wasn't keen on the idea of introducing her around, but it might be fun to take her to a dark, crowded place where we could get to know each other better. We would just be two vampires in a sea of bodies, finding anonymity in the crowd, and there were plenty of clubs nearby. We would avoid my usual haunts to ensure we wouldn't run into anyone I knew well, someone who might ask questions.

"Okay. I'll take you to a place that's a little more lively and a bit less exclusive. It's one of the places vampires go to socialize," I said.

She grinned at me, and I extended my palm toward her. She glanced down at it and hesitated briefly before slipping her hand into mine. We climbed the stairs and exited the bookshop. I led her deeper into the darkened streets, away from where the humans were still eating, drinking, and dancing.

We walked along the mostly empty sidewalk until we reached an alley illuminated only by a naked bulb hanging over a door set halfway down the passage. Approaching the door, I knocked softly on the thick metal and glanced at the security camera overhead. No signs or indicators revealed what was inside. It was one of many places you had to know about to find. No humans entered here uninvited.

The door swung open, and the man on the other side looked us over. He smiled at me as I extended my ID for him to inspect. His eyes widened, and he nodded. "She have ID?" the man asked.

"She does, but she's with me," I said.

The man inclined his head and then stepped aside for us to pass.

We entered a dark hallway illuminated by blue light from above. "He's not human, is he?" Kate asked.

"Nope. He's one of us," I said, pulling her down the hall toward the sound of loud music.

"Was he asking if I was underage?" Kate asked over the growing noise.

"No. He was asking for your new ID. He didn't recognize you and wanted to ensure you were properly registered."

"I thought you said this place was less exclusive."

"It is. But it's a legitimate business and doesn't admit the unaffiliated. They wouldn't want to risk being on the wrong side of the powers that be. The Tap House caters to a wealthier clientele but would also refuse anyone without proper identification, no matter how substantial their line of credit. They just ask fewer questions if you're with a regular like me. They know I wouldn't risk breaking the rules," I said, flashing her a smile. *If only they knew?*

"And that guy back there?" Kate asked. "He didn't seem to recognize you."

"He recognized the name of my House," I said, cutting off any further questions by turning away to guide her toward the crowd.

We entered the main area of the club. I hadn't been there in years, but very little had changed. A dance floor filled the center, with blue lights strobing across the bodies of several dozen dancers crowding the small space. The rest of the room was divided into tiered sections; some held tables and booths, while others featured small seating areas, including sofas, armchairs, and low tables. The place was mostly full, with an even mix of vampires and humans—fortunately, no one I recognized.

Kate hesitated on the edge of the crowd, her expression pained. I tugged on her hand, prompting her to follow me up a short staircase to one of the seating areas. We settled onto a plush, dark-colored sofa, and a human waiter approached to take our drink order. Kate just stared at me. I ordered us both glasses of warm O Negative, and the waiter went off to fetch our drinks.

"Sorry if this is too much," I said over the loud thumping bass.

Kate shook her head and glanced around. It had been so long since any of this was new to me. I'd forgotten how overwhelming it was at first. There was plenty to capture her attention. Groups of vampires drank from glasses, but most fed from wrists or necks. I followed Kate's gaze to a human-vampire couple caught up in the throes of feeding, hands roaming, and bodies moving.

I leaned closer to Kate. "Not wholesome, but a lot of fun," I said into her ear.

She whipped her head in my direction, her eyes wide.

"Don't be embarrassed. They aren't," I said, and reached for her hand again.

She pulled it away. "Do all these humans work here as well?" she asked, avoiding my gaze as well.

I sighed. "Some do, but vampires bring their own humans, too. You know, people from their Houses who aren't vampires—mostly hopefuls. They can feed out here on the floor, but there are private rooms in the back for... other activities."

The waiter returned with our drinks, and I took a sip. I nearly spat it back into the glass. I could taste the preservative in the blood; it had likely been sitting in a fridge for weeks. Now I remembered why I hadn't visited this place in years. Kate either didn't notice or was too polite to mention how terrible the blood tasted. She took small sips and continued to survey the club.

I watched her, marveling at how lucky I was to be sitting there with someone as lovely as Kate. I was sure that every male in the club, along with quite a few females, envied me. However, we would have to find new places to spend our time, places out of the city. I would avoid my usual spots for a while, but there were plenty of clubs to try. We could venture as far as Vancouver in a single evening. I would make new friends—ones who didn't know me before—and I'd introduce us as a couple.

Eventually, when I was free from Alexander's control, we would travel anywhere we wanted. I'd vanish for years, just like Miguel, and Alexander would never find out about Kate. It would be perfect.

At that moment, Kate's attention shifted. She was no longer casually scanning the room; instead, she was focused entirely on something across the dance floor. I glanced over to see what she stared at so intently, and froze. My body turned cold, and my heart picked up speed. This was bad, very bad.

The tall figure in black moved with a powerful stride. His short, dark brown hair caught the light, shining blue in the club's darkness. I recognized him, but he wasn't a friend. Worse, he was an unforeseen complication. It would have been better to try to introduce Kate to a room full of nosy friends than to be caught with her by one of the Council's enforcers. And yet, here one was, heading right for us.

18

KATE

The night had been enlightening so far, but I hadn't learned anything about taking care of myself. I didn't think most vampires went to clubs or upscale bars to feed each night; James's fridge confirmed that. I had no idea how most vampires made their money, either. What other businesses did they own? What kinds of services did they provide besides food service? I still didn't have a clear idea of how the society worked or how it was all laid out.

I looked at the many clubgoers, trying to figure out how to broach the subject with James, when I noticed a dark-haired man heading our way. He was large, at least a head taller than the people around him, with wide shoulders and a muscular build. But he crossed the dancefloor, easily avoiding the flailing arms and legs, moving more gracefully than any of the dancers.

As he drew nearer, I noticed his clothing. He wore a black muscle shirt paired with black cargo pants and boots. He seemed dressed more for a fight than a night out unless this club wasn't his usual scene, and he typically frequented much rougher places than this.

As the man climbed the steps to the area where we sat, James reached over and grabbed my hand. The intensity of his emotions shocked me. He was terrified. Fear and dread flowed into me from the contact of our hands, and I snapped my gaze to his face. James's expression was calm, almost disdainful, but his feelings were anything but. It made me pause and reevaluate the man approaching our table.

"James," the man said in greeting and inclined his head just a fraction.

"Marcus. I'm so pleased to see you," James replied.

Liar, I thought. I couldn't imagine anyone feeling less pleased.

Then the man, Marcus, turned his gaze on me.

His steely gray eyes didn't seem to hold any threat, but the way he moved and stood... He had a military air about him. There was clearly something dangerous about this man. I had my guard up against the rolling emotions of the crowd, but with him so close, I caught a glimpse of him. Just a hint of what he felt, and the impression I got was vampire in nature.

James didn't seem inclined to introduce us, and I wanted to get a feel of him for myself. I wrenched my hand from James's grip and extended it to the man. "I'm Kate," I said as Marcus reached out and shook it politely.

His grip was strong, and his palm felt neither warm nor cool, confirming that he was indeed a vampire. As I held his hand for that brief moment, I felt no malice or anger, only curiosity and confidence. It was a relief after James's swirling alarm.

"It's nice to meet you, Kate," Marcus said in a smooth, low voice that cut through the loud music easily. "May I join the two of you?" he asked, looking toward James.

"Of course," James said, but I couldn't help but notice his rigid posture and the tight set of his jaw. I scooted farther from James, afraid he might reach for me again. I didn't understand what was happening or why James was so upset, but I didn't like the feeling of his emotions, and I wanted a chance to sort things out for myself.

Marcus settled into a chair across the low table that held our drinks.

"I don't see any weapons tonight. Are you on duty, or are you here for pleasure?" James asked.

"I just got off, actually," Marcus said. "It's been a slow night, and I thought I'd stop by on my way home to grab a drink." He smiled at us, and it seemed both genuine and professional.

"Marcus works for the Council," James explained. "He's an enforcer. Something like our version of the police or investigators. It's his job to enforce the Council's laws." He returned Marcus's smile, but it was anything but friendly.

Marcus nodded. "Kate, were you recently turned?" he asked, shifting his gaze to James. "A new House member?" His tone was friendly, yet it felt more like an interview than a conversation between friends.

James froze. He glanced back and forth between me and Marcus before taking a breath and nodding. "Yes. Kate has just joined us. I thought it would be nice to take her out and show her how some of the others spend their evenings. It's tough being young and cooped up all night."

Marcus smiled widely at me, flashing his fangs. "Welcome. It's always nice to see a new face. And it's good to see that Alexander is letting you both out for an evening of fun. I know he can be...demanding on one's time."

Alexander? What was he talking about?

James shifted next to me, drawing my attention. His gaze

flicked to me and then away, but his expression spoke volumes. Before I could talk, however, he answered Marcus.

"No more than usual," he said. "How are you doing, Marcus? The Council keeping you busy as well?"

Marcus heaved out a sigh and leaned back into his chair. "Like you said, no more than usual. Things have been pretty quiet lately. Everyone is behaving themselves, which is just plain boring." He smiled and gave us a wink.

At that moment, a waitress walked by, and Marcus waved her over to order a drink. With Marcus distracted, James leaned toward me and whispered in my ear, "It's time to go. Keep your mouth shut and follow my lead."

I stared at James. I'd clearly missed something. James looked ready to have a panic attack, and there Marcus was, as cool as a cucumber. I didn't see the threat, but I was new to this world, new to the players, and didn't understand the game.

James stood, and I stood with him. "Marcus, I hate to leave you just as you've arrived, but I'm afraid we have to go," James said. "I'm sure you understand."

Marcus widened his eyes and jumped to his feet. "Of course," he replied, shaking James's hand and mine. He didn't seem annoyed or angry; instead, he was filled with curiosity like before. "It was nice to meet you, Kate. I hope to see you again soon. And, James, pass my regards to Alexander if you would?"

"Of course," James replied, putting a hand on my back to usher me along.

As soon as his fingers made contact, his annoyance, anxiety, and alarm surged through my system, making me gasp. Something was wrong. I nodded politely to Marcus in farewell and then hurried ahead of James, back the way we came. Whether it was James's emotional state or my own, I found myself increasingly frightened and seriously confused.

We burst from the metal door back into the crisp night air of the alley where we'd entered. Everything appeared the same; no one was around, but everything felt different. James rushed ahead of me, grabbing my hand and pulling me along.

"James, wait," I panted as he dragged me quickly from the alley and onto the sidewalk toward his car. "What the hell is going on? Why are we running away? What happened?"

"It's not safe. I'll explain in the car," he hissed, pulling me harder.

If I'd been human, I never would have managed to stay on my feet. We moved so quickly, and my shoes were certainly not designed for sprinting. If I weren't so scared, I would have reveled in how effortlessly I could move over the pavement in those beautiful stilettos. I was scared, though, and irritated. I didn't understand why we were forced to flee.

We reached the car, and James practically shoved me in before getting into the driver's side and slamming the door. I winced at the sound. I didn't know him well, but I knew he loved his cars and didn't usually handle them so roughly. Something must be really wrong.

"Now, will you tell me what's going on?" I asked as he peeled out of the parking space and raced down the street.

He kept his eyes on the road, not even glancing my way. "We're in trouble. We have to get out of here," he said. I noticed his hands gripping the steering wheel; they were shaking.

My shoulder slammed into the door as he took a corner at high speed. "I don't think he's following us," I said, glancing back. "Do we have to go so fast?"

He chuffed out an unamused laugh, but he did slow down as we turned the next corner and followed the signs for the highway. "It's not Marcus I'm worried about. It's who Marcus talks to that is the problem," James ground out. "What had I been thinking? This was so stupid. I should have known this was a mistake."

I still didn't understand the problem, and as he spoke, I only had more questions.

"James," I said, drawing his attention. He glanced at me as he took the ramp for I-5. "Who is Alexander? Why did Marcus seem to think I knew him?"

James gazed at the road as he merged into traffic, weaving in and out of lanes, moving ahead of the other cars, and leaving Seattle behind. It took a little while before he answered. "Alexander is my sire," he said.

"Your sire? So, was Marcus asking if I was a new member of your House or Alexander's?"

"It doesn't matter," he hissed. "It's all gone to shit now anyway. As soon as Alexander finds out about you—and he will—I'm fucked, totally fucked." He slammed his hand on the steering wheel in frustration.

"I don't understand any of this. Why would Alexander knowing about me be bad?"

"Because he thinks you belong to him. He doesn't understand. He would never understand." James practically shouted now. "He's a selfish, arrogant, violent bastard. If he gets hold of us, he'll kill me. Maybe both of us. And if he doesn't kill you, he'll make your life a living hell. Trust me. This is what I tried to protect you from. This is why I hid you from him. There is no way I would let you fall into his hands. I won't allow it, Kate."

As James spoke, a feeling of dread came over me. A feeling that was all my own.

He lapsed into silence, but my mind kept spinning. I needed more.

"James, why does Alexander think I belong to him?"

He didn't answer; he just kept driving.

"James, tell me why Alexander would think I belong to him," I repeated, my body growing numb with fear of what he would say.

James's nostrils flared as he breathed heavily. His anger was banked, not burned out.

"James—"

"Because he's your sire," James spat. "He's the one who turned you, not me."

I nodded, thinking back to my hazy memories from that night. "He had a beard and dove-gray eyes," I whispered.

James snapped his head in my direction. "You remember him?"

"Not really," I said. "Just his face." I felt detached. It was all a lie.

"If you remembered him properly, you would understand," he said. "We aren't safe."

I gazed out the window at the dark pine trees whipping by. Now I understood why James was always in a hurry to be somewhere else and why he kept me in the apartment by myself. It all made more sense. He'd been hiding me. But then, why take me out at all? Why risk it if he was worried he would be found out?

I asked him, and he sighed. "I wanted to have you on my arm when I went out. I guess I thought I could have it all. Plus, I wasn't sure you would stay in the apartment if I left you there again. Not after you sneaked out to return to your apartment. And not after I smelled the witch's scent all over the lobby and your clothes from last night."

That got my attention. "You knew?" I asked. "You knew I'd seen Sara?"

He smirked at me. "Well, I wasn't sure until just now, but I had some idea," he said as we exited the highway. "I was mad, but it doesn't matter anymore."

He drove into the parking garage beneath his building and parked. I couldn't believe we were back so soon. Before I could reach the handle, James opened the door for me, and I stepped out. He grabbed my upper arm, and I could feel his fear still, but also his determination and rage.

"What are you going to do?" I asked as he dragged me toward the elevator. I didn't want to return to that apartment with him, but he wasn't giving me a choice. The grip on my arm was like a vice, and he was much stronger than I was.

"What are *we* going to do, you mean," he said as he pushed me onto the elevator. "We're getting out of here. We'll pack and leave first thing tomorrow night. It'll probably take him a few nights to discover you're still alive. I don't think he'll come after us if we get far enough away. He's vicious, but he's also lazy. I can't imagine him going to great lengths to get us back." As he spoke, he appeared more certain, more determined.

He ushered me down the hall and into the apartment, closing and locking it behind us. "This could be good for us," he went on. "Yeah, this is for the best. We'll just leave and start over somewhere new. This could be good."

As he spoke, he paced back and forth, becoming increasingly manic with each pass. Then he stopped and turned to me. What I saw in those green eyes frightened me.

"Kate, can't you see? This is just what we needed. We'll leave, and then we can be free. Just you and me, forever," he said, walking over to me and taking my hand.

His emotions chilled me to the bone. He believed every

word he said and more. As I tried to process what was happening, he brought my hand to his lips. I was too shocked to resist, as he kissed the back of my fingers.

He inhaled deeply as he held my hand to his face. "It's the way you smell," he said, his eyes closed, his voice smooth, almost dreamy. "I knew we were supposed to be together. Something pulled me toward you even then. From the first moment I saw you." He brushed his lips over my fingers and took another breath.

I tried to pull back, but he was too strong. He reached out with his other hand and locked it around my wrist, pulling me closer.

He dipped his head again and bit down on the back of my hand. I struggled wildly, but it was no use. He held me still as he licked the blood off my skin, where it welled from the two punctures he'd made.

Through our contact, I could feel his emotions surge as he licked at my hand, tasting my blood.

"From the first moment I saw you," he breathed softly. "You stepped off that bus and ran across the street right in front of me. I forgot everything else but you."

I froze.

"You were so beautiful, and your scent..." he sighed. "I knew I had to have you. I knew you were destined to be part of my life. I waited so patiently. I followed you, but you were with the witch, and by the time you were free of her, you had already caught another bus. Then I realized you were headed toward where I worked most nights. You got off the bus just blocks from here, and I knew it was meant to be."

He gazed into my eyes, like a lover, rubbing the backs of my knuckles softly with his thumb. "I couldn't let you slip away. I couldn't risk you saying no. It was a risk with the car. I knew you could have been seriously hurt, and I'm sorry. I never intended for you to be injured so badly. But it worked out in the end. Didn't it? The only thing I regret is calling Alexander. We wouldn't be in this mess now if I had never involved him. I just never considered what you would mean to me."

I couldn't believe what he'd said. "Mean to you…," I said, feeling numb. I gently pulled my hand, and he let it go. I took a step back, keeping my eyes on him. The way he looked at me, with such hope and expectation…

"You hit me with that car. On purpose. You did this to me. You… You killed me." I stammered.

"It seemed like the easiest way." His voice cracked with emotion. "I was under a lot of pressure from Alexander to help him build his family. It seemed so perfect. I'm sorry, Kate, but you're missing the point. Can't you see how much better this is? I'm sorry I got you into this mess, but it doesn't matter now. We'll leave here and never come back. We'll be happy, I promise."

I was missing the point? "No," I said. "You are seriously deluded if you think I'm going anywhere with you." I turned toward the door, but then he was there, blocking my way. His expression was no longer hopeful. His face was a stony mask of disapproval and anger.

"You don't have a choice," he bit out. "It's the only way. The only way to be safe from Alexander. You can't leave."

"The hell I can't," I said, trying to push past him. But it was no use. He was bigger and stronger, and it was like trying to push through a mountain.

He locked his arms around my middle, lifting me off the floor, and walked me backward to the bedroom. I kicked my feet against his shins, losing both my shoes in the process, but not causing any real damage. He tossed me onto the bed and stepped back.

"Pack what you need. There's a suitcase in the closet," he growled. "We leave at sunset tomorrow. I'm staying here overday to make sure you behave." He exhaled sharply and tugged his shirt back into place. "It's for your own good, Kate. Please don't make this harder than it needs to be."

With that, he closed the door.

I just stared at the back of the bedroom door in disbelief. I had to get out of here. I had to get away from James. I couldn't stand the thought of being in the apartment with him all day. I couldn't believe he'd done this to me. It was all because of him.

He was my murderer.

I swallowed the tightness in my throat. I had to think. Looking down at the evening gown I still wore, I decided to start there. I changed back into my jeans, sweater, and tennis shoes.

The metal cover was securely shut over the only window in the bedroom. I needed to find the remote. It usually hung on the wall by the door, but it was missing. I realized that my coat, cell phone, and wallet were also on the other side of the door with James.

After an hour of thinking but getting nowhere, I cracked the bedroom door and peered out. James moved from the sofa to the door faster than I could blink.

"I don't think so," he said and pulled the door shut again.

I was trapped. But before panic could fully set in, I felt the pull of sleep. Dawn approached, and no matter how hard I tried, once the sun rose, I couldn't stay awake. I sank to the floor. My last thought before my eyes closed was that at least James would be in the same predicament. He, too, would lose consciousness with the dawn. I was safe from him, at least for now.

19

KATE

B linking once, twice, I was back online. It wasn't so much waking up as it was reanimating, I thought with a shiver. It was not like any sleep I'd ever experienced. My mind resumed right where it left off the night before. I had to find a way out and fast. I couldn't let James get his hands on me again.

Pushing myself up to sitting, I listened. Nothing.

Not waiting, I rose as quietly as I could and cracked the door open again. There was no rush of movement, no deranged, delusional vampire staring back at me this time. I widened the gap and stuck my head out, straining to hear any footfalls. I heard the pipes behind the walls, the neighbors above, the cars outside, the hum of electricity from the appliances, and a soft, rhythmic beat of a very slow heart coming from the direction of the sofa.

Was he still asleep? There was no time to think it over. I seized my chance. Sliding out of the bedroom on tiptoes, I made my way to the front door. I rifled through the pockets of the new black wool coat to retrieve my things and snagged my old coat from the hook. I wouldn't take anything James had given me, besides the ID. My hands shook as I fumbled with the lock. The damn thing let out a horrid "curthunk" as it turned over, and I shot a glance toward the sofa, but there was no movement.

I let out a wobbly breath and slipped out the front door.

Sprinting down the hall, I dashed past the elevator in favor of the emergency stairs. With no one around to witness, I let my legs move as quickly as they could, and they carried me at a blinding speed down three flights of stairs and to the lobby before I could take another breath.

I paused at the bottom of the stairs to collect myself before pushing into the lobby. I glanced up, but there was still no sound or movement from above—nothing to suggest that James was in pursuit.

Pressing the bar on the emergency door, I shoved it forward. But instead of exiting into the lobby, I recoiled quickly, backing again into the stairwell and throwing an arm over my face. The last rays of the setting sun flooded the lobby, and the glimpse of them stung my eyes.

My heart raced, and my breathing was labored, but I realized it was from fear rather than pain. I examined my hands, the only exposed skin I could see, and they looked completely normal. My exposure was brief enough that I remained unharmed. Glancing up again, I listened. If the sun were just setting, James would be waking soon. I didn't have time to wonder why I had awoken early. The only thing that mattered at that moment was getting away before he woke up.

Putting my jacket on and zipping it all the way up, I pulled the hood over my head and tucked my hands into my sleeves to shield my skin as best I could. Bracing myself, I opened the exit door again and squinted into the dim glow. It wasn't terrible, but it wasn't great either. The light was so bright that my eyes watered, and I dabbed at them quickly with my sleeve before any tears could escape. I swallowed hard and stepped into the light. I needed to keep moving, regardless of the pain. As soon as James realized I was gone, I knew he'd be after me.

Aside from my eyes, the fading light was bearable. I walked as quickly as I dared toward the front doors. I drew a few stares but ignored them as I stepped out into the soft evening air. By the time I reached the sidewalk, the sun had sunk well below the horizon, and full night wasn't far off. Turning left, I noticed a bus pulling up to the corner ahead. I hurried toward it and boarded. Pulling out my phone, I tapped to pay the fare. I didn't even know where it was headed; I just knew that going away from here would make it harder for James to track me by scent.

Sinking into one of the seats, I wrapped my arms tightly around my chest. I pressed them firmly against my body, trying to contain the hurt and panic that felt like it was spilling out. I still couldn't believe it was true. How could James have done all that to me and acted like everything was okay? How could he expect me to be fine with everything and want to run away with him? It was ridiculous—a betrayal. Tears pricked at the corners of my eyes. I turned away from the other passengers and dabbed at them again. There would be time to cry later, but this was not the place.

I raised my head and looked out the window. It was time to figure out where I was and where I was headed. I could tell we were moving south towards Seattle from the streets flashing by. The only place I could think of going was Sara's, but I knew there was a more pressing matter than where I would sleep come dawn. There hadn't been time to take what I needed before leaving James's apartment. Fleeing had been the only thing on my mind. But now, as the bus moved closer to the city and its resources, I felt grateful. I needed blood.

When I calmed down enough to take a breath, it carried with it the scent of the people sitting uncomfortably close by. I smelled the blood in their veins, and my mouth began to water, my teeth sliding from my gums. I needed to eat, and soon.

It was completely dark out by the time we reached Seattle. When I got close to my destination, I got off the bus and walked the last few blocks. My steps led me back to the bookshop where James and I were the night before. I waited across the street, watching. I wasn't sure what my plan was. I didn't know if this was the best place to get what I needed, but I didn't have any better ideas. The thought of going down into the luxurious dining room, dressed as I was, and with no clue what to ask for, made me pause.

I was about to turn and head for the second place we'd visited, hoping that the bar might be an easier target, when I saw two figures emerge from a narrow alley between the bookshop and the hardware store. I recognized the larger man by his tattoos and kind face. He walked arm in arm with another man, their heads bent close together, their breath visible in the cold night air. As the wind shifted, I caught the scent of fresh blood. Yes, this was exactly what I needed.

I tried to walk calmly, but no one else was around, and I couldn't let them get away. I skidded to a stop in front of the two men, blocking their path. Bruce wore a cap covering most of his dark hair, but if I hadn't remembered the distinctive tattoos running up his neck or his bright blue eyes, I would have known him by his scent.

His eyes were now wide with fear. But, instead of

running away, he stepped forward, gently pushed the other man behind him, and raised his hands.

"Hi," I said, my voice a little breathless. "Do you remember me? I need…" I paused, looking at him, uncertain how to phrase it properly.

"Hey there," he said, holding my gaze. His voice was soft and steady. "I'm afraid I won't be on the menu for another couple of weeks." He offered me a small smile, but his eyes remained wary.

"Oh, no. I mean, I thought about going in, but…" I glanced away and took a deep breath. "Do you know anywhere else? Somewhere I could get something less fancy? Something to go?"

Bruce visibly relaxed but kept himself between me and the other man. His expression was confused, so I tried again.

"Something that would fit in a take-out bag? This is all a bit new for me," I explained, clasping my hands in front of me. My body felt twitchy, but I didn't want to do anything to worry this man further.

His eyes softened, and his posture relaxed. "Yeah, the Tap House probably wouldn't appreciate me sending a customer elsewhere, but yeah, I do."

My shoulders sagged in relief. "Thank you. I didn't know where else to go."

He continued to study me but nodded. "Do you have a phone?" he asked.

I handed over my cell phone, and he began to enter the address. "It isn't far from here. It's a legit place, registered and all that. It's a tattoo shop that does a separate needle business on the side. I used to sell there sometimes before I got the job here," he explained. "The guy who runs it is one of you. Which is ironic." He quirked his mouth in a smile as he finished and handed me back my phone.

"Why is that ironic?" I asked, confused.

"Um, well, because you all can't get tattoos. Your bodies reject the ink," he said, narrowing his eyes. "You really are young, aren't you?" He studied me intently, and his scrutiny made me uncomfortable.

Before I could turn to leave, he said, "Hey, listen, tell whoever's working there that Bruce sent you. They'll do right by you. Okay?"

I nodded, but my body began to tremble. He was so kind, and walking away from him felt like letting go of a lifeline.

"I didn't choose this," I blurted out.

I wasn't sure what compelled me to say it. I didn't know why I wanted him to know. Was it to make him think I was a good person? To confide in someone about what was done to me? Either way, it opened a door inside, and the tears began to flow. I felt them slip down my cheeks, wet and unwelcome. I reached up with a sleeve and tried to wipe them away.

"Oh, hey there," Bruce said, fishing a black cloth out of his pocket and handing it to me. I wiped my face, and Bruce reached out a hand and patted me on the shoulder.

"Thank you," I said, but my eyes were drawn to his outstretched arm. The sleeve of his coat was pulled up just enough that his wrist was exposed, and even through the ink, I could see his vein pulsing below. Just inches away from my face. I felt through the connection the moment Bruce realized his mistake.

I looked up at him.

He'd gone completely still.

I opened my lips to speak, but my fangs crowded my tongue. The smell of him so close made the hunger in my gut twist painfully. I eased back out of his grasp and slapped a hand over my mouth. And then I turned and ran away as fast as I could into the night.

I quickly found the address Bruce entered into my phone. It was just as he'd described. The tattoo shop had lights on inside, and I saw a man behind the counter to the left of the door. I sighed with relief and pushed it open.

Now that I stood inside, I felt a bit nervous. First, I'd never been in a tattoo parlor before, and the walls lined with pictures of tattoos and artwork were visually over-whelming. Second, I'd never tried to purchase blood before, and I wasn't sure how it worked.

The shop was empty, except for the guy behind the counter and a woman at the back of the store. She straddled a chair, staring at her phone. Next to her was what looked like a black dental chair, surrounded by carts and shelves filled with items I couldn't even begin to name. She didn't even look up as I entered.

I approached the counter with hesitation. "Hi," I said, trying to sound like I belonged there. "Um, Bruce sent me. He said you might have what I need...?"

The guy appeared to be in his late thirties. He was tall and thin, with a bald head that gleamed under the overhead lighting. He had numerous piercings—his ears, lips, nose, and forehead all sported a good amount of metal—but no tattoos that I could see. He smiled at me, and I caught sight of his fangs, confirming what my senses suggested, and that I was indeed in the right place. I relaxed slightly and smiled back, flashing my own sharp teeth.

"I sure do," he said. "You got a cooler?"

I shook my head.

He fished under the counter and pulled out a small soft-sided cooler. "How much do you need, and do you have a type preference?" he asked.

"Um, O negative. If you've got it, and I'm not sure how much. Enough for a week?" I said.

The man looked a bit annoyed. "Hey, I hate to ask, but how old are you, kid?"

"Twenty-six," I answered without thinking.

He sighed. "No, I mean, how long has it been since you were turned? It'll help me do the math," he explained.

"Oh. Yeah. Two days," I said, feeling embarrassed for some reason.

His eyebrows rose so high that some of his piercings clicked together. "I see. You got ID?" he asked.

I reached into my wallet and pulled out the new ID card James gave me. It felt odd between my fingers as I handed it over.

"I do an above-the-board business. I can't sell to someone unregistered," he said as he took the ID. "Oh, Damn. I don't think I've ever sold to someone from your House before. They not feeding you at home? I bet those big Houses keep a well-stocked fridge or whatever," he said.

I shook my head. "Are you going to tell them I was here?" I asked. I didn't know the rules, but I didn't want to leave a trail for James to follow, and I also didn't want to get Bruce into trouble.

The guy narrowed his eyes at me. "No. I assume, since you are here, you've left home. I'm not going to report you. Your ID is in order. But, if someone comes looking, I won't lie either. Not for someone I don't know, even if Bruce did send you." He crossed his arms and studied my face. "That is, if you want to buy. If you walk away now, I can forget I ever saw you. What will it be?"

I licked my lips. "That's fair," I said. "I'll take a week's worth."

He nodded and disappeared through a curtained doorway behind the counter. He came back carrying a slightly larger cooler, filled and zipped shut. Just thinking about what was inside made my stomach rumble. He placed the cooler on the counter and then quoted a price that made me blink up at him in shock.

I gaped at him. "That's more expensive than a month's worth of groceries," I said.

He chuckled. "We're higher up on the food chain, my dear. And that's with the friends-and-family discount courtesy of Bruce." He winked at me. "Do you want me to bill it to your House? I'm sure they're good for it."

"No, I got it," I said, sighing as I handed over my well-worn credit card.

20
___

SARA

Lying on my bed after dinner, I attempted to watch Netflix on my laptop. It was propped on a pillow beside me instead of in my lap. After my little electrical storm at Kate's, I'd been extra cautious with anything electronic. I used the mindlessness of auto-play to distract myself from the fact that I hadn't heard from Kate. She told me she would text me when she got back from her night out with James. It was the next night, and I still hadn't heard from her.

I reminded myself that it didn't necessarily mean anything was wrong. Kate had always been forgetful, and I wasn't sure that becoming a vampire would change that. However, as the night wore on, I began to feel uneasy. Even if she'd fallen asleep soon after getting in last night, she should be awake by now and would have seen my text messages. I'd sent ten.

I was about to check my phone for the hundredth time when I heard it buzz on the bedside table. I snatched it up and looked at the screen.

It was a message from Kate.

U still up?

I glanced at the clock. It was after midnight.

Yeah. Everything okay? How was last night?

I fired back.

I waited for a reply and jumped when my phone rang instead.

"Kate?" I said, bringing the phone to my ear.

"Yeah, it's me," she said.

"You okay? You don't sound right."

"I need help, Sara. I'm sorry. I didn't know where else to go." Her voice was rough with emotion.

"What happened? Where are you?" I jumped off the bed and reached for my bag. If I left now, I figured it would take me at least half an hour or more to get to the apartment where she was staying.

"I'm outside," she said, stopping me in my tracks. "At the end of your driveway."

"I'll be right out," I said and hung up the phone.

As I hurried down the stairs and through the house, I was vaguely aware that my mom and aunt were still in the family room watching TV, but I didn't pause to say hi.

Instead, I flung open the front door, crossed the wooden boards of the porch, and rushed down the steps. Gravel crunched under my shoes as I sprinted down the drive. Just before I reached the end, a dark figure emerged from behind a tree and stepped into the moon's light. It was Kate, and she was alone.

"Kate," I called out as I neared.

"I'm so sorry," she said again.

"What's going on? Are you in trouble? Why didn't you call me sooner?"

She pulled in on herself, her shoulders hunching over. "I guess I was afraid. I was afraid you would tell me not to come, and I don't have anywhere else I can go right now. I…" Kate burst into tears, and I put my arms around her, rubbing her back.

"I told you I would take you home with me. You are always welcome here," I said, hoping it was true.

"But what about your family?" she hiccuped. "I don't want to make things difficult for you."

"Shh, now. Tell me what's happened?"

But before Kate could pull herself together and explain, my aunt called from the porch.

"Hey, just give me one minute, okay?" I said as I let go of Kate. I don't want them coming out here and freaking out. "We can figure this out, I promise." She nodded, covering her face with her hands, and I turned back to the house. My mother joined my aunt on the porch. *Great*, I thought. How was I going to explain this?

I tried to project calm as I walked back to the house, but my legs felt rubbery, and my knees threatened to give out.

"Sara?" my aunt called again. "What's going on? Who's out there with you?"

"It's alright, Auntie," I said as I continued, my long strides quickly covering the distance. If I'd been thinking more clearly, I would have taken smaller steps and given myself more time to come up with the right response. But before I'd decided what to tell the two women, the breaking of a branch sounded behind me, and my aunt and mother stiffened.

"Sara," my mother hissed. "Get up here now. Get into the house."

I'd never heard my mother's voice sound like that before. It was full of warning and fear.

My aunt stepped forward, and suddenly, the porch, steps, and the entire clearing in front of the house were brightly lit by the immense ball of fire cupped in her outstretched palm. The firelight cast harsh shadows on her face and danced in her dark eyes, making her look fierce.

"No!" I yelled, holding both hands out to forestall whatever my aunt planned. "It's Kate," I gasped.

Both women glanced in my direction, faces blank with shock.

"It's Kate," I repeated.

My aunt lowered her arm but didn't extinguish the fire. A giant ball of it rolled and hovered over her palm.

My mom stepped closer, her eyes on me. I wasn't sure if it was hope or fear I saw there. "Kate. Like, Katie, our Katie?"

I nodded as tears spilled down my cheeks. "Yeah. She needs our help, Momma." My voice cracked.

My mother heaved a great sigh, her shoulders sagging, but she nodded. "Okay, Baby."

My aunt glanced between us and huffed her disapproval, but the ball of fire shrank smaller until it was no bigger than a golf ball.

"Kate. It's okay. You can come out," I called to my best friend.

Slowly, Kate made her way up the gravel path, carrying a large square bag. She walked with her head down, eyes focused on the stones beneath her feet. I tried to see her as my family would. She appeared tired and worn down, but her stride was a beat too quick and her movements too fluid. Her once peach skin was now a creamy white, and she had a new edge to her features.

When she reached the steps, she stopped beside me, and I reached over and grabbed her hand. Her icy fingers gave mine a quick squeeze. Kate looked up, and my mother gasped. The sound tore my heart out. It was the eyes that gave Kate away. Her once soft brown irises were now reflective and sharp—the eyes of a predator.

I knew the pain and sorrow my mother felt for Kate.

For what she'd become.

For what was lost.

My mother let out a small sob. "Oh, Katie. What have you done?"

Kate's lip trembled as she looked into my mom's eyes. I felt like we were fifteen all over again. Like we'd gotten caught sneaking out or drinking beer behind the school. The disappointment on my mother's face was evident.

Before I could defend my friend, Kate spoke, "I didn't... It's not my fault." Her voice cracked.

My mother shook her head. "Sweet girl," she said. "Are you in control of yourself? Can you behave?"

Kate swallowed hard and nodded.

"Well, let's go inside out of the cold, and you can explain how on Earth this happened," my mother said with a sigh.

Kate didn't move at first. I glanced over at my aunt. Aunt

Lucia still held a palm full of fire, which, though impressive, was also very intimidating. It was Lucia's behavior, not Kate's, that concerned me most. Lucia shot a look at my mom and then glanced back at Kate. She wasn't pleased but allowed the flames swirling over her hand to go out, plunging the front of the house into the shadows of night.

Still holding Kate's hand, I gently tugged her up the steps. My mom and aunt moved back and let us pass. I led Kate through the entryway, down the hall, and into the kitchen. The kitchen was the right place for our discussion. It was the heart of our home, the nerve center, where all important decisions were made, and where we would listen to what Kate had to say.

We all took seats around the well-worn table. Kate set her bag down and pushed it underneath with the toe of her shoe as if trying to hide it from sight. The two older women looked grim as they regarded Kate, and I couldn't blame them. But this was Kate, someone they considered one of their own. Surely, they could see her for who she was, not as a monster who'd come to invade their place of safety.

Kate took a deep breath and began to tell us everything. I was surprised when she started her story with the art show we attended together, and even more surprised when she recounted how a vampire unknowingly stalked her. I remembered the feeling I'd experienced that night. Knowing that James was there, watching us, sent a thrill of fear down my spine.

My mother and aunt listened, only interrupting occasionally to ask a question. They nodded at times and shook their heads at others. Once she finished, Kate took another deep breath and looked around the table.

"Oh, Kate. I'm so sorry," I said, and reached for her hand again.

"I'm sorry too," my mother said. "That should never have happened. Vampire laws are very specific. Humans are supposed to choose freely. Your transformation was a violation."

I looked at her curiously. *What did she know about vampires?* I wondered.

"She shouldn't have been in that position in the first place," Lucia snapped. "He hit her with the car, for crying out loud!" she huffed and leaned back in her chair, arms crossed.

"Of course," my mother replied. "Their Council should be made aware of both issues." The two women nodded at each other and glanced back at Kate.

"But what would they do about it? James said Alexander is my maker. That gives him authority over me, right? Wouldn't the council just make me turn myself over to him?" Kate said, her voice growing frantic. "I don't know anything about him other than that he was willing to break the Council's rules and that James is afraid of him."

"They could try," Lucia said, looking ferocious again despite the lack of fire. "No one, not even a vampire, could get in here if we didn't want them to."

My mother and I nodded, and the tension in Kate's face eased a bit. "I don't want you all to get into trouble. I don't want to cause problems, especially for people I care about."

"And what about the people we care about?" my mother asked. "You matter to us, Katie. We will protect you. I promise."

A sob escaped Kate's lips at my mother's words. I leaned in and wrapped my arms around her. She hugged me back and held on tight. It felt good to be able to comfort her, to let her know she wasn't alone. We would all get through this together.

After a minute, we pulled apart, and Kate wiped her eyes. I tried not to gawk at the red streaks she cleaned off her face. Glancing at my mom and aunt, I caught their looks of shock as they, too, noticed the bloody tears.

My aunt cleared her throat. "Then it's decided," she said, pointedly ignoring the reminder of what Kate had become. "You'll stay with us until we get this figured out."

"Agreed," my mother said, echoing her sister. "We'll ask our Elders to reach out to their contacts. It may take a few days, and you'll be safe here in the meantime."

Contacts? I shook my head. I would ask her more later; Kate was my priority for now.

"Thank you," Kate said, sniffing. "I don't know what I would do without you guys."

"I assume that bag you brought has something for you to eat?" Lucia asked boldly.

Kate nodded. "I can't go long without eating. I think I have enough for several days at least."

"Good. Do us a favor and stay well-fed," Lucia said. "Not that we couldn't stop you, but no one here wants to be bitten."

Kate balked a bit but smiled at the stern warning. "Don't worry. None of you smells like food," she said.

"Well, we don't want you eating the mailman either," she sniffed.

Kate smiled and nodded reassuringly. "Promise."

Ok, this had gotten too weird. "Kate, I'll set up a space for you downstairs," I said before Aunt Lucia could say more. "I'm afraid we don't have a proper bedroom down there, but there is a finished sewing space my gran used. There are no windows, and I can set up a cot."

"Thank you," Kate said. "I don't need much. Anything really will do."

I glanced back at the two women still seated at the scuffed wooden table, their heads leaning together, speaking softly. They appeared much as they had the day before, but I viewed them differently now. I was proud of them and how they were handling all of this. They possessed so much more power and strength than I'd ever given them credit for—a power and strength that had nothing to do with their abilities as witches. I blinked back my gratitude and led Kate downstairs.

After getting Kate settled in the small basement room, I found my mom and aunt in the living room. It was well past two in the morning, and the women looked tired but clearly wanted to talk to me before going to bed. I entered the room and sat on the floor facing them, wrapping my arms around my knees.

"So, this is what all those questions were about?" my mother asked.

I nodded. "Yeah. It's been a lot. I wanted to tell you earlier, but..."

"We didn't make it easy for you, did we?" my mother said.

"No. Not really. I should have just come out and told you, but I was nervous. I didn't want you to think less of Kate or me," I admitted.

"How much of that story had you already heard?" my aunt asked.

"Only some," I said with a shrug. "The stuff about James was a surprise. We can't let him get her. Him or Alexander. Who knows what would happen to her if they did? We might never see her again."

"That won't happen," Lucia said. "Your mother and I will see our Elders tomorrow morning and insist they reach out to the Vampire Council. If anyone has authority over those two, it would be them. And I don't think the Council will be pleased with what they've been up to, especially now that witches have gotten involved. But either way, we aren't giving her over to them."

"You know," I said. "If you two had shared a bit more information with me from the start, we could have reached this point sooner. Why didn't I know our Elders were in contact with the vampires?"

The two sisters exchanged glances, and my mom let out a sigh. "You're right. We should have been more open. It's difficult not to want to shield someone you love from all the dangers out there, though."

"Keeping things from me isn't protecting me," I said. "I'm an adult, and I'm in the world. The danger will find me, or it won't, but keeping me in the dark isn't the solution."

Both women had the decency to look ashamed, but neither said a word.

We were quiet for a time, and then my mom asked, "Is Kate still...different?"

"Yeah," I said, nodding. "She's still got her gift, wherever it came from."

"She definitely isn't a witch," my aunt said.

"I think we knew that," I replied.

"Well, all we know for certain is that she is a vampire," my aunt responded. "A vampire in need of our help. Although I never would have thought to hear myself say those words. Strange times," she trailed off, staring at her hands.

"It's late," I said, getting to my feet and wishing them a good night. "I'll see you both in the morning."

As I went to my room, I considered our conversation. I wanted to believe it would all work out with the Council, but I didn't know the first thing about them, or how they enforced their rules. I only hoped we wouldn't be put in the position of defending Kate or our home from a group of angry vampires.

21

JAMES

Opening my eyes, I stared at the shutters over the window across from the sofa where I'd slept. My ears told me Kate wasn't awake yet, which was to be expected. She was only days old; it would be years before she'd wake right as the sun set. I stretched, inhaling deeply, and froze.

Kate's scent was stronger than the previous night, and I could smell the damp air drifting in from the hallway. Launching off the couch, I turned to see the front door ajar and the bedroom door wide open. I knew, before I glanced inside, that Kate was gone.

I studied the scene. There were no signs of a break-in; nothing was out of place except that Kate was gone and the apartment was wide open. This left me with only one conclusion: somehow, Kate had woken up early and run off. As unlikely as that seemed, it was the only thing that made sense.

Grateful I'd slept in my clothes, I sprinted out the front door and followed Kate's scent down the stairwell and through the lobby. She could only be moments ahead of me,

I thought. The sun just set, for fuck's sake. Given that there was no charred body in the lobby, I headed out onto the sidewalk.

Once outside, tracking her became harder, though not impossible. I paused briefly and inhaled deeply, seeking her scent—that lovely, intoxicating fragrance that was Kate. As I searched the night air for even a trace of her, memories of the night before flooded in: holding her hand, pressing her skin to my lips, and then biting down. I breathed in again, recalling the taste of her blood on my tongue. My body shivered at the memory, but then I caught it. My head whipped around as I moved as quickly as I dared down the street, but her scent faded to nothing at the end of the block near the bus stop.

Fuck!

There was no way to track her now. I was truly fucked, we both were. By now, Marcus could have told dozens of people about Kate and would surely have mentioned it to someone from the Council. And if he'd tried to look her up, he would have discovered that there were no official records of her anywhere, and Alexander would've been notified.

No. I needed to halt the downward spiral of thoughts. Things moved slowly in the vampire world. It could take several nights before Alexander found out what I'd done. It would be okay. I just needed to get Kate back, and we would leave just as I'd planned. There was still time. I would explain everything to Kate again. This was all just a misunderstanding.

I returned to my apartment, replaying the fight with Kate from the night before. What had I been thinking? I should've just denied it. Why did I admit to her what I'd done? It was her fault anyway. She didn't understand vampires or our world. How could she know that for any vampire, hitting a human with a car was nothing? Humans were food—disposable. True, the new laws meant that vampires had to be discreet, and the preferred method of feeding was from live, willing hosts. But one human death or maiming would hardly turn heads. No, the real crime I would pay for was having Alexander turn her without prior consent—that and hiding her from Alexander and the Council.

I should've realized she'd be upset about the car situation. And she was right; I'd done it intentionally. I'd seen her as soon as she'd gotten off the bus that night. She'd been in a hurry and run right past me, smelling so wonderful I almost chased her down in full view of the humans walking by.

I couldn't help myself. I followed her. From a distance, I watched as she met the witch and entered the old theater. I walked inside, through the crowd, while they admired the art and chatted with the beautiful redhead. Afterward, I trailed her back outside and watched her board another bus headed uptown. I would've approached her immediately if she hadn't been with the witch. I would've tried to talk to her in the theater; she would have left with me one way or another. Instead, I went to get my car.

Back behind the wheel of my Portofino, my mind was clear. Why would I limit myself to this creature for only one night when I could have her forever? I could speed through this "searching for candidates" business Alexander kept harping about, and have someone to share the burden of caring for the family. Someone lower in the pecking order, and someone I found captivating. At that moment, I hadn't considered the greater implications of bringing someone so irresistible into the House. All I knew was I wanted her and couldn't let her slip away.

As I drove on, I'd grown increasingly frantic. How would I approach her? How would I convince her to believe me, to trust me? I followed her north, and when she got off the bus, we were just blocks from the hospital where I worked. At that moment, I realized it was meant to be. And a thought struck me: *what if she were in an accident and brought to my hospital?*

What if I saved her?

The rest was fairly straightforward. I was worried she might've remembered the car or me behind the wheel, but she didn't. And then, I'd put it out of my mind, for the most part.

She'd come around. She had to come back eventually. Where else would she go? She couldn't go back to her old apartment, and everyone else she knew thought she was dead. She was still mad from the argument, but would return by the time the sun was down. I just had to wait for her. I only hoped there was time.

When I got back to my apartment, I pulled out my phone. There was a new message waiting, and hope flared in my chest. Maybe it was Kate. Perhaps she realized her mistake. But no, it was from Alexander. My hands shook slightly as I opened the message and read it.

This one is acceptable.

He's not as good as the girl, but he will do.

I will change him this evening.

Make the appropriate arrangements and
have the documents drawn up by midnight.

Relief washed over me. It wasn't about Kate. It meant I had to return to the manor, but it would also buy me even more time. *Okay, I could work with this*, I thought. It would be all right. And this would give Alexander the diversion I'd hoped for. I remembered the first weeks after he turned me, how he doted on me, spent all his time with me, and showed me off to his friends. Back when I'd craved his attention. Before he became a burden, yes, this was good.

Pulling up to the manor, I parked in my usual spot. I tried to act as if nothing was wrong. Alexander would know something was off if I deviated from my normal behavior. I just had to do what he asked of me, and then I could escape. I knew if I failed to answer his summons, he would become suspicious, and I'd be caught before I could get Kate back and slip away.

So, I masked my face in my usual subservience and did everything that was expected of me.

As it turned out, that wasn't much. Just as I'd hoped, Alexander was infatuated with his new toy, and there was little for me to do other than shuffle paperwork and make appointments for the two of them at Alexander's favorite tailor and jeweler. I didn't even see the new guy, whom I'd chosen myself, but whatever.

I checked my phone over and over—still nothing from Kate. I sent more than a dozen messages, and not a single reply. Apologies, even though the fight wasn't my fault. Warnings about the danger if she didn't return. Reassurances that she'd be safe with me, that I was the only one who could protect her from Alexander. I even promised to buy her anything she wanted, just to wipe away whatever debt she still thought I owed. And still—silence.

By 3 a.m., Alexander finished with me, and I was free to go. I walked down the front steps of the manor expecting to feel something as I left for the last time, but I didn't. I was done with this place. A new, better life waited for me with Kate, and I was excited to start living it.

By 4 a.m., I started to panic. It was getting late, and Kate still wasn't back. I continued to text and even tried calling, but the messages and calls stopped going through. Perhaps this would take more than one evening to fix? Why did she have to make things so hard?

I had no idea how long it would take for word to get to Alexander about Kate, but I knew it would happen eventually. I had hoped that Kate and I could be away the next evening, if not sooner, but that became less and less likely as time passed.

Just before dawn, I climbed into bed feeling miserable. The sheets still carried her scent, which didn't help. I lay there, wondering how everything changed so quickly. A week ago, I'd been bored and frustrated, longing for more time to myself, for more excitement. Then I met Kate. And suddenly, I was ready to change my whole life to be with her, but I was also struggling for my very survival.

The only thing I knew for certain was that there was no going back to how things were before. I decided I would act within the next twenty-four hours. I would find Kate, and we would leave; there was no alternative. I just hoped she found somewhere safe to bed down for the day.

22

KATE

The next evening, I opened the door at the top of the basement steps and emerged into the hall separating the kitchen from the front of Heartwood's old farmhouse. I was anxious. It was too early for news from the Council, but my nervous system didn't seem to care.

My stomach twisted at the thought of what they might decide about me. I had no idea what kind of power the Council held over my fate. I lacked any understanding of the pressure they could place on the leaders of Sara's community. If the community agreed to give me to the Council, what could the Hearwoods do about it? And what would the women in this house face if they chose to go against their Elders?

I blew out a breath, trying to steady myself, and turned toward the voices coming from the kitchen.

Sara, Sybil—Sara's mom—and Lucia were gathered around the kitchen table again. They were in the middle of dinner. It made me feel like an intruder, stepping into a ritual I was no longer part of.

"I'm sorry," I said. "I didn't mean to interrupt."

"Don't be silly," Sybil said. "Please sit." She motioned to the empty chair I'd occupied the night before.

I swallowed. The food didn't smell appetizing, but I was hungry. I glanced at the refrigerator in the corner, where I'd wedged the entire cooler onto the bottom shelf. Somehow, bringing my meal to the table didn't seem appropriate. I sat down and put my dinner—or breakfast—off until later.

"We went over and talked to a few of the Elders like we'd planned," Sybil said, setting her spoon down beside a bowl of what smelled like chicken soup of some kind. "A message has been sent roughly outlining the manner of your... change and the dilemma now faced. They expect to get a reply sometime tonight and promised to call and let me know what they said. Now we wait," she finished.

I shifted in my seat. "Okay. But, does the Council know where I am?" I asked.

Lucia nodded. "Yes. We wanted them to know."

Sybil shot her sister a look. "It was a matter of some discussion with the Elders, but we felt it was important to let them know you are under our protection," she explained. Her mouth was pressed into a thin line, and I understood how hard that discussion was.

"Are you sure you want me to wait here, though?" I asked. "I don't know how the Council will react. I don't know much about vampires, actually." It was an embarrassing admission, given the fact that I was a vampire, but it was the truth.

Sara smiled warmly. "It's okay. We want you here. We understand the risks." She looked to her mom and aunt for confirmation, and they nodded in agreement but didn't return her smile.

The trio continued their meal, and the table fell silent except for the sounds of spoons scraping against bowls. I glanced up at the fridge again and swallowed hard. I didn't want to be rude, but my hunger was becoming uncomfortable, nearly painful.

"Oh dear, do you need to eat?" Sybil asked, sounding motherly and concerned.

"Uh...yeah. I do. Could you please excuse me?" I asked, the embarrassment nearly overpowering my hunger.

"We told you we want you to stay well-fed," Lucia said, her tone straightforward. "Do what you have to." She continued to focus on her bowl of soup, completely ignoring me. Somehow, her bluntness made me feel better. After all, it was a necessity, not a moral choice I'd made.

I got up, took the cooler from the fridge, and quietly returned downstairs to feed privately. No matter how open-minded these women were, I doubted they wanted to see me eat, especially during their dinner.

It didn't take me long, but I lingered downstairs until I heard the dishes being cleared and footsteps fading into other parts of the house. I came back up and returned the cooler. The kitchen was quiet and empty.

I was washing my hands at the sink when I heard a noise behind me.

"Hi, Sara," I said before turning around.

Sara stood in the kitchen doorway, watching me. "I can't sneak up on you anymore, huh?"

"Nope. Humans are noisy."

Sara chuckled. "Not human, remember? But I understand what you mean. Witches can be noisy, too. It's weird to hear you talk about humans like you're no longer one. I know you're not, but it still feels strange," she said with a shrug. She wore a small smile, but I could feel the sadness beneath it.

"Don't worry," I said. "I'm okay. I mean, I'm going to be

okay. At least, I think so." I swallowed hard but then brought my head up sharply. "Someone's here," I said.

"At the door?" Sara asked.

"No, turning up the drive."

Sara's eyes widened, and she bolted from the room, calling out to the others. Her mom and aunt met us at the front door.

Lucia peeked outside and opened the door, leading the four of us onto the porch. She positioned herself in front but didn't summon the ball of fire from the night before. But she must have come to the same conclusion I had; an attack likely wouldn't come in the form of a solitary figure driving a silver Honda. At least, I didn't think it would.

The car pulled up to the mouth of the driveway, the engine cut off, and the headlights went dark. The person got out and stood without approaching, giving us time to get a good look at him.

"I know him," I whispered, which was silly, considering the vampire across the clearing could hear me either way. "His name is Marcus. He works for the Council."

Marcus stood in the moonlight, arms relaxed at his sides, hands empty. He wore the same clothes from the night we met, but this time, he had on a black leather jacket. I wondered if it concealed the weapons James mentioned at the club and if he'd come to use them on me.

"Do you trust him?" Lucia asked over her shoulder, not taking her eyes off Marcus as he stood, unmoving.

"I don't know him that well. We only met once," I admitted. "But James was afraid of him."

"What does he feel like, Kate?" Sara asked from beside me.

"What?" I asked, momentarily confused. I looked at Sara, and she motioned toward Marcus with a nod of her head. "Oh, yeah. Of course," I said, embarrassed I hadn't thought of it sooner. I glanced at Marcus. He was a good way away, but I opened my senses to give it a try.

As soon as I did, a flood of information came at me. The emotions of the three women on the porch threatened to overwhelm me; they were so strong. My ability, or whatever it was, was definitely growing. I stepped away from the group and tried to shut out their alarm, concern, worry, and determination. I focused on the man beside the car. Instead of a wall of distance I tried to keep between me and those around me, I tried to create a sort of tunnel—a way to focus and let in what Marcus felt while ignoring the others.

It took me a moment, but as soon as I could visualize what I wanted, it snapped into place, and all I felt was him. I took a calming breath. His emotions were tranquil and steady. He wasn't alarmed, angry, or ready for a fight. He was concerned, but it felt more like empathy than fear or worry. He still radiated confidence as he had in the club, but it didn't feel like a threat.

"I think we're okay," I said. "I think he's just come to talk." At least, I hoped so.

"Well, let's see what he has to say," Sybil said.

As soon as she spoke, Marcus began to move toward the porch. He paused after only a few steps, turning his head and sniffing the air, then continued his approach, but his brows were drawn together, and his eyes kept darting left and right, scanning the area. He sensed a threat. I could feel it, and it made me bristle with anxiety. I hoped it wasn't us he'd reacted to. I didn't want this to turn into a fight.

"That's far enough," Lucia said when Marcus was still several yards from the bottom of the steps.

"You aren't going to invite me in?" Marcus asked, smiling

up at them, his canine teeth glinting in the moon's silvery light.

"No," Lucia replied.

"Kate," Marcus said, nodding in my direction. "Nice to see you again."

I nodded back but didn't respond.

"The Council sent you?" Sybil asked, her tone expectant.

"I volunteered," Marcus said. "But yes, I come on their behalf. And, not too soon, it seems. Kate, you are the only vampire in residence, I presume?"

"Of course she is," Lucia snapped.

"Well, someone else was here a moment ago. You need to be on your guard."

I started, whipping my head from side to side, but saw no movement other than the swaying of the trees. And I couldn't be sure, but I didn't feel anything either.

"We are more than capable of keeping Kate safe," Lucia said, raising a hand, as a warm glow appeared in her palm, but no fire burned there yet. "From you or anyone else."

Marcus raised his hands. "Just the messenger."

"Say what you came to say," Lucia said, not lowering her hand.

"The Council has received your message and will convene to discuss what actions, if any, to take concerning James and Alexander's violation of council law. In the meantime, Kate may stay at the Council House if she prefers not to live with her sire, Alexander. For now," he finished.

"She's not going anywhere," Sybil said, interrupting her sister, who was about to make her own protest.

Marcus nodded. "Alternatively," he said, raising a hand. "She may remain here if you agree to regular check-ins with a Council representative until the matter is resolved."

I glanced at the three women beside me. They all focused on Marcus, but Lucia's eyes scanned the clearing, alert for any additional trouble, her palm still raised. I hoped whoever was out there had already left. I had a hunch about who might have come looking, and I wanted to avoid a confrontation here at the Heartwood home. I considered going with Marcus. It would keep my friends safer, but I was terrified to put myself at the mercy of a powerful group of unknown vampires. My interactions with vampires so far were limited, and I didn't trust them.

"I'd prefer to say here," I said.

"I thought you might say that," Marcus said, turning and walking back to his car. He opened the trunk and pulled out a large styrofoam box. He brought it back to where he'd stood to address us and set it on the ground. Looking at me, his expression softened. "This is to keep you out of trouble. Consider it a gift. And, stay in the house. I don't know what James was thinking, doing what he did, but I don't trust him to act rationally."

"I will," I assured him.

"Good. I'll see you tomorrow," Marcus said.

"Tomorrow?" I asked.

"Yes, I'll be here each night to check on you and ensure you have what you need. The Council's purpose, after all, is to ensure the safety and anonymity of our kind. We can't allow a fledgling vampire to run around loose and starving in the human world—or the witch world, for that matter," he said. "The clean-up would be a disaster." He shot me a half smile to let me know he was joking, but I didn't find it particularly amusing. This whole situation was a disaster, and I just wanted to be left alone. But then I glanced down at the styrofoam box and sighed. Life was no longer that simple.

"You may return to the property, but you will not be permitted inside the house," Lucia said.

"Understood. Good evening, ladies," Marcus said and returned to his car, leaving the box in the clearing and backing down the drive the way he'd come.

I stood with the three witches and watched him leave. Lucia continued to scan the trees. When I could no longer see the car, I descended the steps to retrieve the box.

"Be careful, Dear," Sybil said. "It could be something dangerous."

I sniffed as I got closer. "No. I think it's just...food," I said, and brought the package back to the house.

Lucia finally dropped her hand to her side and turned away. I followed the trio inside, sticking close to Sara.

"So, is there any truth to the myth that vampires must be invited inside?" I asked Sara in a low whisper as we walked to the kitchen together.

Sara giggled. "No. But the house is well-warded. You wouldn't have been able to get in the first time if I hadn't been holding your hand. Now you can come and go as you like," she said and gave me a wink.

"But I've been here before," I protested.

"Not in your current state," she said. "Besides, we reward the house every year or so, and it's been a while."

I discreetly stowed my new provisions and joined the Heartwoods in the living room. "I'm not sure if that went well or not," I said, taking a seat on an ottoman near Sara.

"Well, I think if they were bent on your destruction, it would have gone differently," Lucia said from her spot on the sofa.

I blinked at her and reached out to see if she was joking. She wasn't. "You really think they would do that?" I asked.

"They might have done it just to resolve the matter, but

now it's more public," Sybil said. "Coming here was a smart move. With others involved, they will likely act with more restraint. However, I imagine Alexander will be in more trouble than he would have been otherwise."

I gulped. I wondered what would happen to James, but then I remembered that I didn't care. He was the one who created this mess in the first place. It was his choices and his delusions that everyone suffered from now. He'd tried to reach me the night before. I read the first few of his texts, but couldn't read any more. I'd finally blocked him.

"That being said, you should stay in the house like the vampire suggested," Lucia said. "If that is someone from Alexander's House lurking about, and if they could get you to your maker, I'm not sure the Council would intervene. They may punish Alexander, but they may not do anything to help you," she warned.

"His name is Marcus," I reminded her.

Lucia just sniffed.

"Thank you all again. For what you're doing for me. For letting me stay here. I know you don't like having...one of us in the house."

"Nonsense," Sybil said. "It's true; we don't generally hold high opinions of vampires, but you're our Katie. Nothing will change that." She offered me a reassuring smile, and I smiled back.

Sybil flinched slightly, and I remembered to pull my upper lip down over my exposed canine teeth. Sybil had a big heart, but she'd likely been raised her whole life to dislike vampires. I couldn't blame her. I wasn't sure I had a high opinion of vampires myself.

23

JAMES

When the sun set the next evening, I barely paused to get dressed and grab a meal before heading out the front door. I'd woken up in the same state of misery I'd fallen asleep in. I knew Kate wasn't coming back, and I would have to find her myself. The first thing I'd do was track down the witch who visited Kate. It was the only place I could think she might go for shelter. And while witches and vampires typically didn't interact, I thought this particular witch might be willing to make an exception for Kate. They were friends, after all.

I walked past my damaged convertible in the parking garage under its cover, hardly able to glance at it, and chose another to take me north toward the valley I knew held the largest communities of witches in the state. At least four small towns were spread along the highway that wound through the mountains. That was where I would begin.

Finding the first of the towns was easy. Locating an individual witch was much harder. I knew no more than her first name, but it didn't matter. There was no way any of the residents would let me close enough to ask about her, let alone tell me where she lived. I'd have to rely on my nose and hope to locate Kate.

I parked off the main road and went on foot. It was a risk to prowl around a community of witches, but I had to take the chance. I'd run out of time.

After quickly scouting the first town, I came up empty and moved on to the next. I was halfway around the community when I picked up Kate's scent. My heart beat faster, and I pushed myself harder.

I paused at a large tree at the end of a gravel driveway that led to a three-story house tucked back into the trees. She was here, I was certain. Her scent lingered on the tree beside me and still hung in the air. I would recognize it anywhere.

I crept closer, determined to get her away from the witches inside. They were undoubtedly poisoning her against me and all other vampires. I could smell at least four distinct individuals, including Kate. While I stood pondering my next move, I heard a car approaching. The sounds from the tires and the engine indicated it was slowing down. I backed off the driveway and hid among the trees.

A few seconds later, the car turned up the drive and rolled past where I crouched. I could see the person behind the wheel in the moonlight. I instantly recognized the driver's short, dark military haircut and square jawline. It was Marcus. *Fucking fantastic.* The only reason he'd be here was that the Council sent him. Which meant they knew what I'd done. Which meant that Alexander would have been notified as well.

As the realization hit me, my phone vibrated in my pocket. I pulled it out and looked at the screen. It was Alexander, of course.

I cursed and sped away from the house before Marcus could get out of his car. I wanted to be out of earshot before I answered the phone. I briefly thought about rejecting the call. I even considered throwing it into the forest and continuing to run until I was hundreds of miles away. I didn't, though.

Kate was beyond my reach, and I realized I didn't want to go alone. I didn't want to sacrifice everything I'd worked for, everything I deserved. I had one more option to try to salvage the situation and, in doing so, hopefully save myself. So, in the end, I did what was expected of me. I pressed the button and held the phone to my ear.

"Hello," I said.

"You will come home now," Alexander said, his voice deep, commanding, and offering no other option but to do as he said.

I hung my head, "Of course," I replied. "I'm on my way, Sire."

When I returned to the manor, Alexander waited in the foyer with his new protégé beside him. Seeing them there together chilled my already cool blood. The message was clear: I was replaceable. What I'd once counted as an advantage could now prove to be my undoing. The young vampire smiled smugly at me from his elevated position, new fangs on full display.

Alexander, on the other hand, was not smiling. To say that he was upset would be a gross understatement. The way his eyes bore into me made it clear that if I didn't talk quickly, I would end up being the lesson for this new vampire. It would be me scattered all over the marble floor, my blood coating the walls.

So I talked. I fell to my knees, and I pleaded my case. I sobbed, I begged, and I bargained.

When I'd exhausted my excuses and promises, I fell silent.

Alexander paused just long enough to hear my words, but as my voice faded, he stepped forward. Not in a rush. There was no blur of movement, no flex of his incredible speed. He didn't need to move quickly. He knew I wasn't going anywhere. I'd submitted to him and his will, and I would accept whatever punishment he doled out.

He extended a hand to me, and I took it. I placed my palm in his, fully aware that this was neither a kindness nor a gesture of forgiveness. His deadly calm was precisely that.

Then he struck.

I blinked only once, and we were up against the nearest wall. He had me pinned in an embrace from which I knew I had no chance of escaping. His eyes met mine for one terrifying moment before he lunged and tore deeply into my throat. In some ways, the physical attack was preferable to his icy gaze.

I wasn't shocked by the pain, and I didn't struggle. I was angry but only with myself in that moment. It seemed to go on forever as he tore my flesh, and my blood poured down my chest, and dripped from my hands, held loose at my sides.

I had miscalculated. I weighed Alexander's desire to recover Kate against his rage at being deceived. I believed my assistance in her recovery would be enough to stay his murderous impulses.

I was wrong.

He pulled back, locking me with his gaze once more, his

face covered in gore and smeared with my blood. I thought that was it. He would finish me. But instead, he let me drop to the ground.

Then he raged and snarled for over an hour and hope crept in.

I spent most of that time kneeling on the tile, my blood pooling around my knees, praying to a god I didn't believe in that Alexander wouldn't destroy me on the spot. That I would survive this and have a chance to make things right. That there was still a place for me. That I wouldn't lose everything.

After a while, the heat in Alexander's voice faded, but his words still echoed in my ears, and his teeth marks still marred my throat. "If you expect me to let you live, you have to do what I say. Be effective. Be brutal if necessary," were the last words he whispered in my ear before he and his companion left me there on the floor.

Only then did I allow my body to relax. Bracing myself up with my arms, I felt the blood drip from my chin into the ever-widening pool. There was only one way out of this, one way back into Alexander's good graces. I had to get Kate away from the witches and smooth things over with the Council.

Not only did Alexander feel betrayed by my actions, but he was embarrassed and shamed in front of his peers because the Council had discovered what I'd done. He was not going to let this go. My only hope was to get Kate to him before the Council ruled so that he could deal with her on his own. This was a private family affair, after all.

Fortunately for me, the Council deliberated slowly on even the simplest decisions, and with the witches' involvement, this was anything but simple. If I could get Kate home before the Council decided what to do about the forgeries and the unorthodox transformation, we might be able to avoid serious repercussions. I realized this meant Kate would either have to agree to drop the matter, or our sire would take care of her himself.

I shuddered.

The longer I was away from her and the pull of her blood, the clearer I thought. I still cared about her, but she'd made her choice by going to the witches. There was little I could do about it now.

I'd made my choice, too.

I'm not sure how long I stayed in that position—on the floor, contemplating my next moves. It could have been minutes or hours.

The sound of nails clicking on marble finally made me lift my head. Alexander's dogs, who'd stayed away during the storm, had come to see what they could scavenge from the wreckage. I wasn't in the mood. I refused to be their prey. I bared my fangs and attempted to growl low in my throat, but no sound came out.

I lifted my hand to my neck and found it ravaged and gaping. The discovery shocked and enraged me. My rage gave me strength, and I pressed a hand against my ruined throat as I pushed myself to my feet before the two hounds could come any closer. I stood as tall as I could and glared at the animals creeping near.

I would not run away.

Whether it was the look in my eyes or the fact that I'd never stood up to them before, it was enough. They backed down, and I walked, as calmly as I could, up the main stair-case. I could still hear the sound of them lapping my blood from the marble as I shut the door to my bedroom.

24

SARA

Several nights passed with no further word from the Council. Marcus came to check on Kate each evening, but apart from that, everything was quiet. Kate seemed a bit withdrawn, and I could tell she was doing her best to pretend everything was normal, that she was normal. I understood where she was coming from. My aunt, in particular, could be a bit prickly regarding Kate's...differences. But I didn't understand why it all had to be so difficult. She was part of the family and had been for years. Was she different? —Yes. But we all changed over time. We didn't all become undead blood-drinkers, but they would get used to her. I was sure of it.

While Kate slept the days away in the basement of our family home, I kept myself busy in the outside world. I spent most of my time at the shop with my aunt, but I also had a special project I'd been working on for a while. Now that Kate was here, it brought a new urgency to my plans and added new meaning.

I shared some details with my mother and Aunt Lucia,

and while I had their blessing, I could sense they weren't exactly enthusiastic about my plans. I was an eternal optimist, though, and I refused to entertain anything but a positive outcome. Knowing we would all get through this together, I wanted to ensure we were well prepared.

Despite my growing to-do list, I made sure I was home by sunset each day. I wanted to be there when Kate woke up, and my aunt insisted we were all back within the warded walls of the house by nightfall. I thought it was overkill. Lucia acted as if there was to be a vampire invasion at any moment. We hadn't seen any other vampires besides Marcus so far, and he seemed nice enough, but I complied nonetheless.

When Kate was awake, in the evenings before I slept, the two of us talked. When Kate's mind drifted to dark places and worry overcame her ability to focus on the here and now, I distracted her with stories about my day, the shop, and Silas. All about Silas.

On Kate's third night with us, I gave her some art supplies. She accepted them gratefully, though with a sad smile. We both knew that her beloved supplies were packed up and headed to a charity shop or possibly the dump. It almost made me regret buying them for her, but later that evening, I found her working on a drawing at the kitchen table, and I knew I'd made the right choice. The look of peaceful concentration on her face was healing for us both.

Kate offered to pay me back for the supplies, and when I refused, she decided to compensate me with art. I was thrilled with the idea, and she began crafting images for us to use on some of our products and in advertising. And they were stunning.

Over the next few nights, Kate was completely absorbed

in the project. I don't know how much time she dedicated to it, but there was always a fresh stack of art waiting for me on the kitchen table when I came downstairs for breakfast.

Sometimes, I would make a specific request, like a label for a particular herb or tonic; most of the time, though, I was greeted with beautiful illustrations of the tools and plants we kept around the house. The colors were soft and earthy, and the designs ranged from simple and instructional, like something you would find in an old botanical journal, to wonderfully intricate, resembling the illumination of an ancient manuscript. They were perfect for what I needed.

We both sat at the kitchen table on Kate's fourth night; she drew while I sipped tea from my favorite green mug. "I wish I could take you to the shop," I said. "I've been working on repackaging most of our inventory featuring your new art. I'll bring some samples home tomorrow so you can see."

Kate smiled but didn't look up from the drawing she was working on. "I want to meet Silas," she said. "I know he doesn't come around here, and I'm not sure how he would feel about meeting me, but I've heard so much about him I'm dying to meet him for myself. Especially now that I know he isn't human, either. It makes him so much more mysterious." She grinned at me, and it was so nice to see her looking relaxed and happy.

"He's not that mysterious," I said, wrapping my hands around the warm ceramic of my mug. It was cold in the old house this time of year, and the heat felt good soaking into my chilled fingers. "I want you to meet him too. I think you guys would like each other. He's been helping me a lot lately. Remember how I told you I'd been working on expanding the business?" I asked.

Kate nodded and looked up from her sketchbook.

"Well, he's been a big part of that. With the construction, I mean."

"And what do your mom and aunt have to say about that?" she asked.

I winced. "That's more difficult," I admitted. "They like him alright, for a shifter, but they don't approve of us spending so much time together."

"You still haven't told them how you feel?" she asked, raising her eyebrows in disbelief.

"No. I haven't even told him," I said, feeling my cheeks heat up. I wasn't sure what I loved more: the way the new property was coming together or the excuse to see Silas so often. "It's been great spending so much time with him, though. I really like him, Kate. And maybe things will change with my family. You're here now. Nothing is impossible. Right?"

"They tolerate me, but..."

"Yeah, I know what you mean," I said. "*Tolerate*" was a good descriptor of the way my mom and aunt were handling Kate's *condition*. While frustrating, I found it humorous how hard the two tried to ignore the fact that Kate was a vampire. They went out of their way to ignore the blood in the fridge, how Kate snuck downstairs to eat, and other reminders that she wasn't the same girl they remembered from years before. Their powers of denial were impressive. But I was grateful they welcomed her in, no matter what mental gymnastics they performed to accomplish it.

"You know it's not about you, though? They love you, Kate."

"I know," she said and bent her head back over her work, her fingers moving impossibly fast as she inked tiny leaves onto the page in front of her. "But I know I can't stay here forever."

I didn't reply. I knew Kate was right. I loved having her in our family home, but this wasn't a permanent solution. That reminded me I needed to talk to Marcus the next time he came. Privately.

25

KATE

In the week following my escape from James, Marcus came by every evening as promised. On his fourth visit, he delivered a letter from the Council notifying me that Alexander requested a delay in their decision about my independence or lack thereof. Marcus wasn't certain when the matter would be resolved.

I was somewhat surprised to discover that Alexander was, in fact, a member of the Council, as he held the position of head of one of the major—meaning old—Houses, and it was his privilege to request the delay. Despite being a member, Alexander hadn't attended a meeting in over fifteen years. I was unsure what that indicated about my chances of receiving a favorable decision. For now, I was to remain where I was. I just hoped I wouldn't outstay my welcome in the Heartwood home.

Marcus was told to continue his regular check-ins. He still wasn't allowed in the house, but was now permitted to sit on the porch. The witches relaxed somewhat concerning his presence, but I saw Lucia peeking out of the windows from time to time during Marcus's visits.

I started to look forward to our discussions each evening. I learned a great deal about the Council, the Houses, and vampires. Marcus was open and willing to share much more than James had. He was shocked to discover that he was only the second vampire I'd ever met. The more we talked, the more I realized how much I didn't know about the world I now inhabited—and how much I didn't know about myself.

"So, I know I can't go out in daylight. And, I can't eat human food or drink anything except...you know," I said one night as we were having one of our chats.

"Yes. And you are going to need to be less squeamish about what you are and what it takes to keep yourself alive. You can't even say the word without choking on it," Marcus said, his tone teasing. "Blood. You drink blood, human blood. From the vein, if you like," he finished softly.

I glanced at the last insulated box he brought with him and pressed my lips together.

"Yes. Well, I'm on house arrest, remember? And I'm not feeding like that in front of the Heartwoods or even in their home," I said.

Marcus nodded, conceding the point. He furrowed his brows. "Have you ever fed from the vein? You weren't out in the world for very long."

I swallowed hard, thinking about my one night out. It was the only time I'd used my fangs for their intended purpose. My teeth throbbed at the thought. I recalled the powerful feeling of gripping the man's arm and sinking my teeth into his warm skin. A shiver ran through me at the memory.

Marcus chuckled under his breath, drawing my attention back to him. "That answers my question," he said.

I felt annoyed that I let so much show on my face, so I

shifted the conversation. "Back to my question," I continued. "I know I'm faster and stronger. My senses are enhanced, and I heal quickly. But is there anything else I need to know?"

Marcus blew out a breath. "Well, a lot. You won't always be so hungry. As you get older, you will require less blood. You'll wake up earlier as well. The very ancient can remain awake after the sun has risen and will awaken before it sets again," he said.

I didn't tell him that I'd already woken up early. I didn't want him to know I was different for some reason. I spent my whole human life hiding my differences from others, and now that I was a vampire, I didn't see any reason to stop.

"Your body will remain as it is now, unchanged," he went on. "You can cut your hair, but it will quickly grow back and never be longer than it is now."

"I heard we can't get tattoos," I said.

"Our bodies have a sort of memory for our physical state. It rejects the ink, heals our wounds, and prevents damage from heat or cold. But not fire. Stay away from fire," he warned.

"Got it. No fire."

"You can't catch any sort of disease or sickness. You won't die of cancer or a heart attack or stroke."

"Hmm, I was never one to get sick before, but that is good to hear." I paused before asking my next question. "What about magic? Special abilities?"

Marcus laughed. "You've been around witches too long. Nope, besides our physical enhancements and our blood's healing properties, we have no special abilities. No magic. No flying. No turning into a swarm of bats." He smirked at me, and I rolled my eyes.

"Okay. So, no sunlight. No fire..." I continued.

"And don't lose your head. Literally or figuratively," Marcus said. "Some vampires are killed, torn apart by others, or sometimes by humans. But many, a great majority, die of loneliness or boredom. They stop eating or lie down somewhere the sun can reach them." He took a deep breath and stared out into the dark woods. "You have to find what you're living for—what keeps you going—and hold on to that."

"What about you?" I asked quietly. "What keeps you going?"

Marcus glanced back at me and smiled, but it didn't quite reach his eyes. "Me? Protecting our kind from what would happen if humans found out about us," he said, and I could tell there was more to that story, but I didn't press. "That and the next adventure, I guess," he added with a shrug.

"What I really want is to get out from underneath all of this. I want my life back. I want to make my own decisions about where I live and what I do." I sighed. "I want to live long enough to have adventures," I mumbled.

"I get that, I really do," he said, placing his hand over mine. "And, don't worry about the Council. I don't think they're inclined to take any action against you. This is all for your protection, you know? You did nothing wrong here. Sure, they would have preferred you didn't run to the nearest witch with your problems, but they aren't upset with you."

"But what if they decide I have to go live with Alexander?" I asked. "I've never even met him."

Marcus considered. "I'm not sure what they will decide on that front," he admitted. "But I wouldn't give up hope just yet. I don't live with my sire or any sire for that matter," he said.

"So you don't have a House?" I asked, intrigued.

"No. I work for the Council, and I'm under their direct jurisdiction. It's one of the few exceptions."

"What happened to your sire? The House you were made into?" I asked.

"Nothing happened to him. My sire is still alive. He lives in the east, and I decided to move out west. He allowed me to leave," he explained.

"So, Alexander could just let me go?"

Marcus grimaced. "He could. But from what I know of him, which is not a lot, he probably won't do that. And, even if he does, you will still need to either find another House willing to take you, or do as I have done and work for the local governing body."

"I still can't believe that vampires have a government and laws," I said.

"Believe it," Marcus said. "It has become increasingly necessary as technology has made it more dangerous for our kind. We must follow the rules to remain safe and unde-tected. The last thing we need is to *go viral* because someone got sloppy or turned someone unwilling and have them live-stream their grievances. It all must be handled with care, but that doesn't mean that we adhere to human laws. You should remember that," he warned. "Vampire law is abso-lute and often brutal. The Council doesn't care about things like hitting a human with a car. It's not their concern." He paused, considering. "You should know that James got in trouble for forging your documents, not killing you."

I couldn't believe what I was hearing. They really didn't care that he stalked me, killed me? All they were concerned about was the paperwork? "You've got to be kidding."

"Nope. Humans are food and sometimes a workforce, but we don't concern ourselves with their general welfare.

He could run over a hundred humans as long as he didn't get caught," Marcus said without apology.

We were both quiet for some time, and then I took a breath and asked, "Is James still alive?"

"As far as I know," Marcus said, looking down at the scuffed boards beneath his feet. "I think Alexander would have let the Council know if he killed him, or if James had run off, if only to help settle the matter."

I nodded.

Marcus looked up and met my eyes. "You know. The first night we met at the club, I thought the two of you were together. I thought that was how you came to be a vampire, came to be with him," he said. It was a statement, but there was a question in his tone.

"No. He wanted there to be something, but it was never like that for me. My...instincts told me I couldn't fully trust him. But I really did think at the time that he'd saved me. It never crossed my mind that he was the one who put me in that position in the first place. I just thought he was a creep."

"What do your instincts tell you about me?" Marcus asked.

I considered him then. Opening myself, I could sense everything he felt. He was exactly as he appeared. He was compassionate, genuinely interested in what I had to say, and generally happy. It was refreshing. Sara was the only other person I knew who was as straightforward in their communication. There was no hidden motive that I could detect, which made me trust him even more than I already did.

I realized he stared at me, waiting for my answer. I shook my head. "You're not a creep," I said, smiling at him. He smiled back, and I felt a warmth radiating from him that made me drop my gaze and restore the wall of space between us. It wasn't necessary for me to feel everything he felt; the man deserved some privacy.

I learned early on that it was best not to know how everyone who looked at me felt. It made things awkward, and in some cases, it provoked reactions I would have preferred to hold back. But now, I didn't have to try at all to sense emotion. I felt it all so strongly. The challenge would be to keep my guard up and maintain a distance between my feelings and the feelings of those around me.

Marcus cleared his throat. "Well, I should leave you alone. I'm sure you have things to do," he said, getting to his feet. "Until tomorrow."

I waved goodbye and watched him walk down the steps toward his car. Marcus had started to convince me that not all vampires were terrible.

"Hey, Marcus," I called after him.

He turned, eyebrows raised.

"Thank you. For...everything," I said rather lamely.

"Don't mention it. For what it's worth, you're handling all this remarkably well. I'm rooting for you," he said and flashed me another smile before getting into his car and driving away.

26

JAMES

It took me over a week to recover from Alexander's lesson. I looked into the ornate mirror hanging over the sink in my bathroom at the manor. I'd not been allowed to return to any of my other apartments since I came back. I examined the jagged scar on my throat. It was still visible, and the skin was tender, but it had closed nicely and was well on its way to being fully healed. In a month, there would be no trace of it at all.

I cleared my throat, and a ripping, tearing sound escaped. I hadn't been able to speak for the first few days, but speech was slowly returning as well. I'd had few opportunities to engage in conversation over the last several days, for which I was grateful, and I tried to stay silent around Alexander in particular. When I had to talk with him, he seemed much too pleased with the evidence of the damage he'd inflicted. His obvious delight made me uncomfortable.

Surprisingly, however, Alexander mostly left me alone. I didn't know whether he was giving me the time I needed to heal or if he was preoccupied with his new companion. Frankly, I didn't care. But I knew that Alexander wouldn't forget what happened, and that my reprieve was temporary. Now that I felt better, it was time to return to work. It was time to fulfill Alexander's demands and resolve all this once and for all.

The first thing I did, once I was strong enough, was send a message to the Council requesting more time. Naturally, I made it seem as though it came from Alexander. Since my sire often left his communications for me to manage, it was easy. Their reply was yes, of course, anything to delay the unpleasantness and give Alexander more time to clean up his own mess so they wouldn't have to.

Reaching out to Kate was the next step. I attempted to message her again, but my messages continued to be blocked. I knew she was still at the Heartwood home. The Council's communications informed Alexander—and therefore me—of her location and that she was being regularly monitored. I considered returning to the witches' house to try to lure Kate out, but ultimately dismissed the idea. I needed to get her away from there, away from the protection of the witches and whatever magic they possessed. If I couldn't convince her to come willingly, I planned to use force. There would be no returning empty-handed this time. I was sure I wouldn't survive another reprimand from Alexander. No, I would reach out to the Council again and let them know about "Alexander's" desire to contact Kate directly. If I was correct, and they preferred Alexander handle this, they might be inclined to deliver a message on his behalf. Now, I just had to decide what that message would be.

27

KATE

Time passed slowly. It had been over a week since I'd first come to stay with the Heartwoods, but it felt like a month. I lay on my narrow cot in the basement sewing room. I didn't mind sleeping there, but I felt unsettled. I was grateful they'd accepted me into their home, and while I felt secure and loved by those around me, it wasn't my home. When I'd first arrived, I was solely focused on survival, but now I needed to start making a plan for what would come next, assuming the Council didn't demand I submit to Alexander.

I thought over what I learned from Marcus. Perhaps there was a place for me in the service of the Council. I wasn't sure what I could do for them. I didn't have a law enforcement background. The idea of me fighting was laughable. I wasn't particularly skilled in any way besides art, and I somehow doubted the Council needed a resident artist.

When I finally climbed the stairs to the first floor, Sara waited at the kitchen table for me, a wide grin on her face. Her expression instantly brightened my mood.

"What's up?" I asked, joining her at the table.

"I have a surprise," Sara said, her hands resting on top of one another on the tabletop, concealing something underneath. Even with my guard up, I could feel the excitement radiating off of her.

"Oh yeah? Is it a new life?" I asked sarcastically, anticipating some new artist's delight, like a kneaded eraser or a fantastic new pigment. What I saw instead, when Sara lifted her hands, was a simple, silver key resting on the scarred wood.

"Actually, yeah," Sara said, raising her eyebrows but not losing the grin.

I leaned forward and picked up the key, turning it over. It was unmarked, and I had no idea what it went to.

"What is this?" I asked.

"It would be easier to show you," Sara said. "Wanna go for a ride?"

"Umm, I'd really like to. But I could get into a lot of trouble if I'm not here when Marcus arrives. You know, house arrest and all that?"

"I already spoke with your parole officer. He'll be here in twenty minutes. He's coming too." Sara's eyes sparkled the way they did when she was genuinely happy, and it warmed my heart to see it.

"Okay. Do I get to ask questions?"

Sara considered for a moment. "Nope. Go eat, and I'll meet you on the porch."

Thirty minutes later, I found myself in the back of Marcus's silver Honda, Sara riding shotgun and pointing out directions as we went. It took less than ten minutes to reach our destination. It was in the same river valley, farther out of town, but not far off the main highway. We pulled up a short driveway that led to a large two-story log home.

The house featured a circular gravel driveway and a parking space in front of what looked like a commercial addition. Marcus parked the car near the house, and all three of us got out.

My eyes were drawn to the main building. It was beautiful. Constructed of sturdy, light-colored logs, with a red shingled roof and a large front porch, it looked right at home among the cozy pines. The home appeared to be relatively new, though there were signs of neglect. The brush was overgrown, and moss covered most of the roof and a significant portion of the steps leading up to the porch and front door. The walkway and driveway were blanketed in fallen leaves, but there was a stack of freshly cut timber to one side and a work truck parked nearby.

"What is this place?" I asked.

Sara's grin grew wider—if that was possible. I couldn't help but return the smile as I waited for an explanation. From Marcus's expression, I knew he was in on the surprise.

"I bought a house. Well, not just a house," Sara explained. "You know how I've been saving, planning to expand the business?"

I nodded, waiting for her to go on.

"The current shop has become too small, and we've been looking to sell and buy a bigger place. Somewhere with more storage, since most of our business is online these days. Well, I found this place a while back. It was built as a B&B, with guest rooms in the main building and on this side," she said, pointing to the addition. "Was the dining room and gift shop. The people who built it were humans, though, and the locals didn't like having them around. I'm afraid it's been empty for a while."

She licked her lips, her smile slipping a bit. "So, about a month ago, I bought it. And since you came to stay with us, I started thinking that maybe this property could solve a few of our problems."

"You own this?" I asked in wonder, looking back up at the structure. It was impressive, larger than the Heartwood family home, and imposing with all the massive timber.

"Yeah, well, the family business owns it, but it's also a place to stay. I thought, if you want, we could live here together," she said, looking at me. Her smile was gone now, and her eyes held an equal measure of worry and hope.

"You want me to live here with you?" I asked. I couldn't believe what I'd heard. It seemed too good to be true.

"Yes. I do. You would have to put up with store inventory all over the place, and the occasional customers over in the shop. There is a lot of work to do, but I think we could make it nice."

As she spoke, I could imagine it. A place for the two of us. A place I could live in, not just stay.

A home.

A moment passed. Sara stared back at me blankly, and I realized I hadn't given her an answer. "Yes. Oh God, yes. I would love to live here with you," I said, glancing back at the house in wonder. "But, Sara, I don't know what is going to happen with the Council or Alexander. And I can't afford to pay rent. At least, not yet. But I'll work that out. I promise."

Sara lunged forward and pulled me into a tight hug. "I'm so glad. We'll figure out the rest later. Oh, and my mom and aunt brought someone by earlier, and we warded the entire building except for the shop. Marcus checked with his bosses, and they said they didn't care where you stayed as long as he checked on you, so... It's all set," she said. "Oh, and I almost forgot the best part." She grabbed my hand and pulled me up the steps, Marcus following behind, smiling as he watched the two of us.

As I crossed the threshold, I felt my skin prickle, and a feeling like a small jolt of electricity shot through my body. I jerked slightly, and Sara looked back at me. "That's the fresh warding you're feeling. You should be good now."

I stopped and looked around. I was in a massive entryway, open to the wooden rafters two stories overhead, where a large circular wrought-iron light fixture hung from the ceiling. To the left, there was a large open space. Although there was no furniture, I suspected this once served as a sitting and living room. A river-rock fireplace dominated the far wall, framed by large windows that opened onto the dark forest outside.

"Excuse me?" Marcus said from behind us. I turned back toward the open front door. Marcus stood just outside on the porch, an eyebrow raised and arms crossed over his chest. "Will I be allowed in this one?" he asked.

I looked at Sara, who nodded back at me. I went to the front door and extended a hand. Marcus placed his palm in mine and took a step. Once fully inside, he shook slightly, like shaking off a chill. "That was unpleasant," he said. "It won't be like that each time I come over, will it?"

"No," Sara said. "You're good now." She gave Marcus a reassuring smile.

I turned to Sara. "So, what's the best part?" I asked.

"Oh, yeah," Sara said brightly. "Follow me." She headed off in the direction of the central staircase. It was one of the most beautiful staircases I'd ever seen, featuring twisted wooden railings crafted from natural branches. I ran my hands along the wood as I followed Sara down the steps, Marcus trailing behind us.

At the bottom of the stairs, Sara paused and opened what looked like a newly installed door. I went to follow her inside, but as soon as the door swung open, I stopped in my tracks.

Every hair on my body bristled, my lips pulled back from my teeth, and my canines elongated. I don't know what I was more afraid of: the danger I sensed or that my body reacted automatically to whatever was in the room ahead.

Just then, I heard a low growl, and Sara's head whipped in my direction as I felt Marcus lock his arms around my middle from behind. *Couldn't they hear that?* I thought.

"No!" Sara screamed, throwing her hands up in front of me.

With a shock, I realized that the growling came from my own throat.

"Whoa there," Marcus said from over my shoulder, not loosening his grip. "Sara told you about Silas, yes? What you smell is him. Everything is okay."

That thought sank in, and I relaxed a little. As I did, Marcus cautiously withdrew his arm, and I felt him stepping back. Once I felt back in control, I glanced at Sara and nodded. I knew, in theory, that Silas was a shifter, but I'd never encountered one—at least not since becoming a vampire. I breathed in, sampling the scent once more. It was prickly, filled with warning, and ripe with potential violence.

"You okay?" Sara asked. She looked both worried and frightened.

Guilt clogged my throat.

The last thing I wanted was to scare my best friend. I swallowed and nodded again. "I'm sorry, Sara. I didn't expect..."

Sara reached out and squeezed my hand. I saw her eyes dart over my shoulder toward Marcus. Whatever she saw there satisfied her, and she turned and walked through the doorway. I followed cautiously. I knew I was being silly, but my new instincts told me to proceed carefully.

We walked into a construction zone. Sheets of drywall were stacked beside the door, a workbench sat in one corner surrounded by sawdust and bits of wood, and a plastic sheet hung from the ceiling along one side, keeping the dust from an adjoining space. And right in the center of it all stood Sara, alongside a huge, broad-shouldered man with wavy brown hair and piercing yellow eyes, the eyes of a wolf.

As I stared at Silas, he shifted his muscular frame so that he stood slightly in front of Sara. I stiffened again but then saw him put out his arm and gently push Sara behind him.

"Kate," Marcus breathed into my ear. "You're making him nervous."

I blinked and shook myself, trying to dispel the tension in my body. I took another breath and slowly opened myself to understand what Silas felt, hoping it might help calm me down. I nearly stumbled back from the force of his emotions. He was dangerous, but his overwhelming emotion was one of protectiveness for Sara. He wasn't scared of me, but he did see me as a threat. I hastily shut down the connection.

"Silas. Please forgive me," I said. "I've been so excited to meet you. I really have." My voice came out a little shaky. "I'm afraid I'm screwing up and not making a very good first impression."

Silas cleared his throat and dropped his shoulders. He managed a small but genuine smile. "It's ok. Sara explained that this is still new for you," he said. "I'm glad to meet you. Sara talks about you a lot." His voice was deep, soothing, and calm, like the flow of a gentle river, and I relaxed a bit more.

Sara stepped up beside Silas, touching him briefly on

the arm. "Kate, Silas has been working the last few days to get this level ready in case you said yes." She beamed up at him and then glanced back at me. "Can we show you?" she asked.

"Of course," I replied, feeling even guiltier for my reaction.

Silas moved, keeping his eye on me as he urged Sara to go first, positioning himself between her and the vampires behind him. His protectiveness of my friend made me smile to myself, and I knew that Sara's feelings for the shifter were mutual.

Sara pushed the plastic curtain aside and flipped a switch, illuminating a short hallway lined with several doors. She led us to the newest-looking one and opened it, stepping aside to let me move forward and look in.

What I saw was a modern bedroom complete with furniture. I stepped in and glanced around. There was a queen-sized bed with a fluffy green duvet, side tables, a dresser, a plush rug over the honey-colored wooden floor, and a door leading to an attached bathroom. I walked over to the one window. The view was of the property's backyard.

"It's a walk-out basement," Sara said from the doorway. "But Silas installed covers that you can pull down over the windows. They're similar to what you described about the apartment you stayed in. He also added shutters over the large windows and the sliding glass door in the main room down here. I think it used to be a game room. And you noticed the new door at the bottom of the stairs. We wanted to make sure no daylight reaches your bedroom back here for when you wake up early," she said.

I glanced at the doorway, but only Sara and Silas were in view. I wondered what Marcus would think of her comment.

I still hadn't mentioned to him that I'd been waking up earlier and earlier each day.

Then I noticed the painting hanging just inside the room, beside the door where Sara stood watching me. It was one of mine. A painting I'd done of the two of us in high school. It was one of my favorites.

"You kept it," I murmured, gazing at the small canvas, a piece of our history.

"Of course," Sara said, a sad smile on her face. "It's us."

I felt tears welling in my eyes and turned away from the couple standing in the doorway, wiping my face with my sleeve. "I just...don't know what to say. I can't believe you did all this for me."

"I want this to be your home," Sara said. "I want you to feel comfortable here."

I couldn't believe they had gone to so much trouble, not knowing if I would say yes. I collected myself and turned back around. "Silas, thank you. It's perfect."

Silas reached up, placed his hand on Sara's shoulder, and smiled. I knew he hadn't done all this work just for me, but I was grateful nonetheless.

"If you need anything else or something needs changing, let me know," Silas said. "I'm happy to help."

"You can sleep here right away if you like," Sara said. "I spent today moving some of my things over to one of the rooms upstairs. There isn't much furniture in the rest of the house, but I figured we could do it up the way we want. Do you like it?"

"I love it," I said. "It's more than I could've imagined." I wanted to go to my friend and put my arms around her, but I didn't want to get too close to Silas. We were both much calmer now, and I didn't want to spook him.

Plus, he still made me nervous.

Sara must have guessed what I was feeling because she walked into the room and wrapped me in a hug. "Thank you," I whispered into her curls. Sara squeezed me hard and then let go, stepping back.

After exploring my room for several minutes, Sara led us back down the hall, where Marcus waited at the bottom of the stairs. She and Silas gave us a tour of the rest of the house, pointing out all the work they'd already begun and the projects that still needed to be done. I grew more and more excited as the tour continued. I could envision myself living there, a life with Sara, a life I hoped to have the chance to experience.

My stomach tightened when I remembered that all of this could be taken away in an instant. As much as I wanted this, wanted to fight for it, I knew I wouldn't put Sara or anyone else in danger to keep it. If the Council decided I had to move in with Alexander or into the Council House, I would. It would kill me—might actually kill me—but I would do it.

I hadn't realized I felt that way until that moment. Seeing Sara with Silas and how they looked at each other, I caught a glimpse of the future they could have together. I knew that was more important than the life Sara offered me, and I wouldn't be the one to take that chance away from my friend. That was what I would fight for. Keeping my family safe. That's what would keep me going.

28

SARA

I surveyed the kitchen while preparing dinner and cringed. For all my efforts, it was far from what I'd pictured. It was Kate's first night waking up in our new home, and I wanted it to be perfect, but I'd have to settle for just okay.

I'd spent most of the day moving in some temporary, mismatched furniture and setting up enough items in the kitchen to ensure the first floor would at least be functional. I expected Kate to be up in just a few minutes, and I was excited to show her the changes.

I set two places at the wobbly kitchen table and walked over to the fridge. A new start needed a gesture. Kate deserved to feel like this was her place, too. I gulped and reached for the cooler Marcus brought the day before.

With everything set, I felt strangely nervous as I heard the basement door open and Kate's footsteps on the stairs. A moment later, Kate walked into the kitchen with her nose in the air, sniffing, and a crease between her brows.

"Sara. What's going on?" she asked from the doorway.

Clearing my throat, I pointed to the chair across from

me. "Would you like to have dinner with me?" I asked, hoping I hadn't overstepped or done something inappropriate. There hadn't been time to ask Marcus if this was okay. I'd just run with the idea.

"Dinner? Is that what I smell?" Kate asked, a smile tugging at the corners of her mouth.

"I thought we could eat together. I want this to be your house as much as mine, and I don't like the idea of you having to sneak off to a dark room to feed yourself," I said. "It's not right."

Kate smiled widely then, showing her fangs, which were much longer than usual. "You sure?" she asked as she came over to the table and took a seat.

"I fixed it for you, didn't I?"

"That you did," Kate said, picking up the insulated travel mug that I'd arranged for her.

I hadn't been able to bring myself to pour blood into a clear glass. Maybe I would get there someday, but this seemed like a good first step for a mortal witch.

"Cheers," Kate said, bringing the mug up to her mouth. Her fangs banged against the black plastic top, her lips not close enough to drink.

I cringed. "Oh, maybe a straw?" I suggested.

Kate nodded. "Yeah, if we have one. I could take the top off, but..."

I jumped up and got the reusable metal straw I'd tucked into a drawer earlier that day. It was not the use I envisioned for the thing, but it would do the job. Kate took it, fitted it into the lid, and sipped.

"I promise to do the washing up. Since you cooked," Kate said and winked.

Honestly, that was a relief. Pouring the stuff into a cup and tossing the bag in the trash was one thing; washing the blood out of that cup was not something I looked forward to.

"Thanks," I said and dug into my meal of pasta bolognese.

This felt good. This was how I'd imagined it—maybe not with the second-hand furniture and the piles of construction tools lying around, but it was close. On one hand, I already missed living with my mom and aunt, but I savored this bit of independence too. I'd never lived alone or with a roommate. Right after high school, my mom and I moved into the family home with Aunt Lucia. I'd been happy there for the past several years, but I needed to start building my own life. I would still see the two women every day, probably. They would both still be working at the family business, which was now located in the attached shop, but now I had the space I'd been craving and the privacy I needed.

The idea of privacy immediately brought to mind thoughts of Silas and all the time we'd been spending together. I still hadn't spoken to him directly about my feelings, but I could sense something between us. It was in the way he briefly touched me when we talked and the way he looked at me when he thought I wasn't watching.

I was surprised when he tried to shield me from Kate and Marcus the previous evening. At first, I could sense the tension between them. The air practically sizzled with the energy exchanged between the shifter and the vampires. I'd had a moment of real worry, but it turned out okay. I was confident they would grow comfortable with each other, just as I had.

"Someone's coming," Kate said, interrupting my thoughts, and hooking a finger in the direction of the front door. A knock sounded a heartbeat later.

Kate and I exchanged looks. Neither of us was expecting anyone. Marcus didn't usually arrive until around midnight. "I can get it," Kate said, starting to rise.

"No. You stay put. I'll get it," I said, and went to answer. If it were Silas, it might be better for me to be the one to open the door.

But it wasn't Silas; it was Marcus. He stood under the porch light, his expression serious, unlike his usual relaxed and friendly demeanor.

"Hi, you're here early," I said, holding the door wide for him to come in. "Is everything okay? You look troubled."

"Yeah, it's more business than pleasure today," Marcus said as he entered.

"I thought you lived in Seattle. How did you get here so fast?" Kate asked when we walked into the kitchen together.

"I haven't been staying that far away," he said. "I've been sleeping at a friend's place to cut down on my nightly commute. Tonight, when I woke, I found a letter waiting to be delivered to you. It's from Alexander, relayed through the Council office in Seattle." He dug inside his black leather jacket and came out with a slightly crumpled envelope, handing it to Kate.

Kate flipped the envelope over and read the script on its front. She tore it open and pulled out a single sheet of thick paper. I couldn't see what it said from where I stood, but the expression on Kate's face darkened the longer she read. Finally, she looked up, brows drawn together, and handed the letter to Marcus. I read it over his shoulder.

The letter requested a meeting to discuss the dispute over Kate's living arrangements and work out any outstanding differences. As I reached the end, I saw that James had signed it as an agent of Alexander, not Alexander himself. I wasn't sure what that meant. The language of the letter was very formal. It sounded nothing like someone communicating with someone they knew personally.

Marcus nodded as he read. "I think you are going to have to go," he said.

Both Kate and I looked sharply in his direction.

"What do you mean?" Kate asked, a note of panic in her voice. "I don't want to go anywhere near him or ever see him again. And what's all this crap about my living arrangements? Where is the part about how they killed and illegally turned me?"

"I understand, and I get it, I do. But this is an official request, and he has undoubtedly sent a copy to the Council. The friend I've been staying with is a lawyer. I've been consulting with him about your situation. If you want to keep the upper hand here, you need to appear to be the reasonable party," he said, placing the letter on the table between them. "If you refuse, the Council will be more likely to view Alexander as the one who'd tried to handle this responsibility." He raised his hands as Kate began to argue. "I understand. It's not fair or right. But you should still meet with him."

"You were the one who told me you didn't trust him," Kate said. "How can I trust that he's not going to do something stupid, like hit me with another car?"

"Because I will be with you the whole time. We will agree to meet him somewhere public, and you will listen to what he has to say, and then we will leave together."

Kate let out an explosive sigh. "I don't like it," she said, shaking her head.

"I know you don't, but this is how we get this resolved the fastest. Once you've met and have proven that you are unable to work it out between yourselves, then Alexander will have no grounds on which to continue to delay the Council's decision," Marcus said.

Kate sat back down at the table and stared at the letter. She looked miserable. "I guess you have a point. I do want this over," she said. "I'm tired of living in limbo. I want a life here. I want to start living it."

Marcus nodded again. "Text James. Set it up."

I edged closer. "I'm coming too," I said.

Kate snapped her head in my direction. "No. It's best if you stay here, behind the wards. I don't trust James, and I don't want you anywhere near him," she said.

"I'm not without defenses," I reminded Kate, holding up a hand covered in arcing blue light.

"Okay, that is impressive," Marcus said, his eyes wide. "But Kate is right. We don't want to complicate this any more than necessary. I'll be plenty of protection for her. We just need to make an appearance and then get out of there. It'll be pretty straightforward."

"I can stay back, but I would feel better if there were more witnesses," I said.

"There will be plenty. We won't give him a chance to get his hands on her. Don't worry," Marcus said, giving me a tight smile.

I didn't like it. It made more sense to take as much backup as possible.

Kate's hands shook as she took out her phone and retrieved James's number. She started a new message and then held it up for us to see.

Tomorrow night.

Beth's Diner off HW 9.

8 pm

Marcus nodded approval. Kate took a deep breath and then hit send.

"I still can't believe we're doing this. I hoped this could be resolved without ever having to see him or Alexander. This whole thing is making me feel sick." She pushed her chair back and bent her head down toward her knees, placing her hands on her thighs. "I feel like I'm gonna be sick. Can vampires throw up from nerves?" she asked from behind a curtain of dark hair.

Marcus chuckled. "I don't think so. It's going to be okay," he said. "I'm going to head out, but I'll be back early again tomorrow night. I want us to get there well before James, which shouldn't be hard, given that the location is closer to us. I want us seated in the diner when he shows up. And we won't get up until he has cleared the area. Sound good?"

Kate sat up and nodded. "I guess so," she said, still looking a bit green.

"That's the spirit," Marcus said and flashed her a fangy grin. "See you tomorrow." He turned on his heel and left.

Kate got to her feet, and the two of us stood in the kitchen looking at our ruined supper, the offending letter lying between our place settings.

"This was not what I envisioned for our first meal together in our new home," I said.

"I'm sorry," Kate said. "I feel like I'm constantly screwing things up. For you especially."

I glanced up at Kate. "What? You didn't do this, any of this," I said and sighed. "It will all work out. I'm sure it will."

I took my plate to the sink and scraped it into the garbage disposal. I'd lost my appetite.

"Just leave it there," Kate said. "I'm doing dishes, remember?"

I set the plate next to the sink and gave her a half-smile over my shoulder. "Thanks. I've got some work to do. I'm going to go next door to the shop for an hour or so. You can join me later if you get bored," I said.

"Sara," Kate said, getting my attention before I could leave the room. "Thank you for trying. For making me feel wanted."

I gave her a real smile then. "You're welcome. Let's try again in a couple of nights. Okay?"

"Sounds good," she said.

I walked through the passage that led from the house to the extension that would be our new shop. It was in as much disrepair as the rest of the property, but I had big plans. I sat down at my makeshift desk and turned on my computer. I stared at the screen but couldn't bring myself to focus.

I understood where Kate and Marcus were coming from, but I didn't agree. This put Kate in real danger. I was less worried about Marcus. He worked for the Council after all —it was his job—and he seemed capable of handling himself. I liked Marcus, but I wasn't sure I fully trusted him. I wouldn't let them go on their own. No matter what they thought, I would find a way to be there in case Kate needed me. Hopefully, Marcus was right, and this would all be over in a few nights. We just needed to get Kate through one more night.

29

KATE

The muscles in my arms and legs twitched. By the time Marcus arrived the following night, I positively vibrated with nervous energy. I felt an intense urge to run, to escape the dread and fear bubbling up inside me. I wanted this to be over, but the only way was to get through it. There was no escaping or going around.

Marcus arrived in the silver sedan, and I waved goodbye to Sara as I climbed in. She was still upset about being left behind, and I felt a bit guilty. I knew she wanted to help, and I hated that she was upset, but it was for the best. I had no idea what to expect, and I couldn't stand it if something happened to her.

When she'd come in from the shop the night before, I'd gone so far as to ask her not to tell her mom and aunt. I was worried about what they would do. I couldn't risk that they, too, would want to come along. I wasn't sure how much experience the witches had with vampires—I didn't think it was a lot. I didn't have much either, but I knew what James was capable of, and I didn't want them anywhere around him.

We headed toward the highway, and neither Marcus nor I spoke as we drove the winding road out of the valley. The turns made my stomach flutter, and I clenched my jaw tightly, fighting the nausea churning within me. *Just a few more hours*, I told myself. I just needed to hold it together a little bit longer.

The diner sat directly off the road. I could see the cheerful interior from the parking lot through the large windows. Half the booths were empty, but there would still be plenty of witnesses to stop James from doing anything too dramatic—hopefully. There was some time before James was supposed to arrive, which made me feel a little better. I needed that time to gather myself.

Marcus parked, and we went inside. It felt strange to be back among humans again. The aroma of cooking food helped mask the scent of the people chatting merrily, completely unaware that two predators had entered the small restaurant. Had I ever been in their position? How many times had I gone about my life while in the presence of deadly creatures?

The hostess seated us in a booth against the front windows, with a clear view of the highway and the main parking lot. I arranged the paper menu and roll of silverware in front of me, then rearranged them. I looked up, and Marcus watched me, smiling kindly. Placing my hands in my lap, I took a deep breath.

When the waitress arrived, we both ordered coffee that we wouldn't drink and settled in to wait.

I grew more and more anxious as the minutes passed. James was fifteen minutes late.

"Do you think he decided not to come?" I asked Marcus. He, too, began to look worried.

"I'm not sure," he said. "Why don't you try texting?"

I didn't want to text him again, but sitting there waiting became unbearable. I pulled out my phone and sent a quick text.

Are you still coming?

I waited, but didn't get a response. I let out a breath. "Nothing."

"Hmm," Marcus said, uncrossing his arms and shifting in his seat. "Let's go. I don't feel good about waiting around any longer."

"What if he's waiting outside?" I asked, my stomach knotting at the idea of an ambush and a physical altercation.

"It's a possibility," he admitted. "We'll go cautiously. I'll lead. We go directly to the car. Understand?"

I nodded and slowly got to my feet, my legs feeling a bit wobbly.

Marcus took out some cash and left it on the table next to our full cups. I followed him to the front door and waited while he peeked out to look around. He paused, sniffed the air, then cursed softly under his breath and pushed the door all the way open, stepping outside. I was right behind him.

"What?" I asked, but then I smelled it. Sara. Sara was here.

We followed her scent to the corner of the building, where it grew thickest. Marcus scanned the area, alert for danger. As we stepped around the corner, Sara's scent became so strong I could taste it on my tongue. She'd been here and not long ago.

Panic rose in my throat, and I spotted Sara's purse lying

on the sidewalk. I looked closer and saw dark spots on the tan cement. It was blood, but not human. It had a spicy, astringent smell I'd come to associate with witches—Sara's blood.

Marcus circled the area quickly, leaving me staring down at the drops on the ground.

"He was here," Marcus said.

I raised my head, feeling numbness slowly replacing the panic. "Who?" I asked, my thoughts frozen.

"James," Marcus said. "Can't you smell him?"

I blinked and looked down at my hands. I held Sara's purse. I didn't remember picking it up. *James?* I thought. But then I sniffed the air around me and knew it was true. I had been so overwhelmed with the scent of Sara's spilled blood that I'd missed it. James's scent floated alongside Sara's—not as strong, but there. The smell of him stabbed into me. Once I'd found it familiar. Now the scent made me want to vomit.

Marcus disappeared across the parking lot, through a stand of trees. A moment later, he rushed back to my side. "His scent leads to a side road where there are fresh tire marks. There was more of Sara's blood on the road."

"He took her," I said, my voice hollow in my ears.

Marcus nodded, looking down at me. I think he spoke, but I couldn't focus.

I grabbed Marcus's jacket. "What if she's dead? What if he killed her?" My mind came back online, and my thoughts raced with all the horrible possibilities.

Marcus placed his hands on my shoulders. "Listen to me. She's not dead. If she were, he would have left her here. No. He'll keep her alive. The only reason he would have taken her is to trade." He took a deep breath. "You have to let me handle this. Take Sara's car," he said, guiding me over to where it was parked next to a large truck. "Go back to the house."

I shook my head violently and started to protest, but Marcus squeezed my shoulders hard. "No. Go home. Get behind the wards and let me handle this my way. I can't protect you and do what I need to do. It will make this twice as hard if you come along and risk putting yourself right into their hands. Do you understand?"

I just stared back at Marcus. His short hair was caught in the wind, and pieces fluttered back and forth; his steel grey eyes were intense but sure. I knew he would do his best to get Sara back. I knew, too, that Marcus wouldn't let me go with him, and that he wouldn't leave until I agreed.

I nodded and tried to still my features. "Okay," I said. "I understand."

"Keys?" Marcus asked.

I dug into Sara's purse, pulled out a set of car keys, and held them up.

"Go straight home. I'll text you as soon as I have news. And keep trying to reach James. Let me know if you hear anything."

"I will," I mumbled, turning and unlocking the driver's door.

I climbed into Sara's car and choked back a sob as the familiar smell of the interior hit my nose. As I started the engine and backed out of the parking space, my vision clouded with red tears, and I wiped them away. Marcus watched me, making sure I did as I was told. I pulled into the main lot and turned right onto the highway, heading toward home.

30

JAMES

Glancing at my watch, I decided it was time to get ready. It was not the reunion I once hoped for, but it would be sweet nonetheless.

As I dressed to meet her, I examined my feelings for Kate. How had I let it all get so complicated? I'd been drawn to her from the beginning—yes, but she started as an easy target. She was supposed to be an evening's entertainment. And then someone to offload my responsibilities onto. When had I grown to care for her, to need to be with her, to want her for myself? She'd entranced me. That's what had happened.

It was my mistake. It should have been obvious that she was completely unsuited to being a vampire and should never have been turned. I understood that now. She didn't appreciate this life, what had been given to her, or what I'd been willing to risk for her sake. She didn't understand what it took to survive. She was naive, and she'd betrayed me by going to the witches. If she'd just come back, let me explain, this could have worked out so differently. I touched the raised scar on my neck. But it was too late for that. I made mistakes, but I would fix them.

Putting on my coat, I headed for the door. I knew Kate would get to the meeting point before I did. I also understood that she might not be alone.

My excellent timing had me arrive just before 8 pm, but I didn't slow down or turn into the parking lot. I drove past, taking note of the situation. The diner was brightly lit from within, and I caught sight of Kate sitting near the window. She'd brought Marcus with her.

A growl escaped my lips. It would have been easier if she'd brought the witch, as I thought she would. No matter, I would separate them somehow; I had to. I found a spot to turn around and drove back toward the restaurant, turning off just before the parking lot onto a side road.

Hidden by the trees, I parked and approached the building on foot. It was essential to take the time to think, observe, and formulate the most effective way to accomplish my task. I crossed through a stand of pines separating the access road and the side parking for the diner, but then stopped. There was a familiar scent on the cold breeze. As I scanned the parking lot again, my eyes caught movement at the corner of the building. It was as I suspected. She'd brought the witch after all and left her alone outside.

The small, dark-haired witch stood in the cold, stomping her feet as if trying to warm up. She kept glancing at the main lot over the top of the cell phone held out in front of her, presumably watching for me. I froze as her gaze passed over my position among the trees. Her eyes swept over where I stood before checking the lot behind her. There was no one else around. She tucked her phone into a pocket and brought her hands together, rubbing them for warmth. I leaned forward, able to see perfectly in the dim light, but struggling to understand what I was witnessing. Her phone remained tucked away, yet a glowing blue light emanated from her hands, dancing and rippling across her skin like... *electricity*, I thought. That was her power. It appeared to be confined to her hands, but it was hard to be certain.

Given the witchy complication, I started to lose confidence that I could get Kate out of there without alarming the humans or getting myself injured. Marcus was both older and larger than I. Making him more than capable of stopping me if he chose to, and I had no intention of ending up in a pair of UV restraints. I might be able to reason with him; he was, after all, an employee of the Council, but a witch wielding electricity? She might be more challenging. The two of them together...

I grew more and more frustrated. Why did this have to be so difficult? Why had Kate driven us to this? If I could just get her alone, even for a moment, I could overpower her and whisk her away. It would be so simple. Then a thought struck me. It could be that easy.

My attention returned to the witch. She was completely focused on the highway and the parking lot ahead of her. Additionally, she was hidden from sight, standing in a patch of darkness behind the corner of the building. I smiled to myself and rushed forward faster than she could turn around.

31

SARA

When you open your eyes, and the world looks the same as when they're closed, you question whether you're actually awake. The pain was a tip-off, however. My dreams rarely came with pain. I tried to reach up to my face to find out what was wrong with my eyes and discovered that my hands were bound in front of me. Panic flooded my bloodstream, and I struggled wildly for one unproductive moment before regaining my senses and lying still. I needed to figure out where I was and what was happening to me. Inhaling slowly, I took stock.

My head behind my eyes throbbed, and the back of my skull pulsed with a dull ache. I heard the muffled sounds of traffic and felt the car rocking beneath me. I lay on my side in a cramped space, fairly certain I was in the trunk of a car. Reflexively, I reached for my magic to illuminate the confines of the trunk, hoping to find something to help me. As electricity spread over my hands, I yelped in pain. Metal. Someone had wrapped something metal around my wrists. I felt a searing burn across the back of both hands where the metal touched my skin, and I whimpered.

I bit my lip, and my eyes flooded with tears. My wrists hurt, I was trapped, and I was cut off from the one power I possessed. Real fear started to trickle in, and I jerked again like an animal trying to free itself. Thrashing against my bonds had no effect but to exhaust me. My limbs felt heavy, and my head swam from the pain where I'd been struck.

Breathing helped, and I tried to focus on steady inhalations and exhalations. I needed to calm down and think. This had to be James. I hadn't seen him, but I couldn't imagine anyone else who would do this. Taking another breath, I wrinkled my nose at the harsh chemical smell of the trunk. What would a vampire like James regularly keep in his trunk that would need such thorough cleaning, I wondered. The thought made me shiver. Witches didn't make a satisfying meal for a vampire, but James was perfectly capable of killing me and disposing of my body. I hoped to the Gods that he had a reason to keep me alive, and that was why I wasn't dead already.

Having thought that far, I decided it was time to act. Scooting back as far as I could, I brought my knees to my chest. I reached down toward the bindings around my ankles. My wrists screamed out in pain as the metal around them bit into raw, burned flesh. Gritting my teeth, I continued picking at the knots in the rope. As long as I was alive, there was a chance to get out of this.

Lack of circulation made my fingers numb and slowed me down, but I kept working steadily. However, I could barely feel the knots under my fingertips. Finally, the first knot came loose, and I felt a thrill of hope.

The car slowed, throwing me to one side as it took a sharp turn. My head bumped against the side of the trunk, sending waves of nausea and dizziness through me. I gulped in the stale, chemical-laden air, trying to clear my head. It didn't help. Pushing myself back into position, I continued working at the ropes around my ankles. I figured we'd left the highway, which could mean we were getting close to our destination. My heart rate picked up. There might not be much time.

The last knot came free as the car's engine cut off. Elation, fear, excitement—my emotions swirled in a great tempest. I knew I'd probably only get one shot at this. I pushed the rope behind me with my feet and tried to position my legs so that my unbound ankles wouldn't be visible when he opened the trunk. It was difficult to move quietly; I knew his hearing was far better than mine. The car door opened and closed, and I heard footsteps on the pavement. I stilled my breathing and closed my eyes.

The trunk popped open, and the cold night air flooded the tight space. A cool wave of relief washed over my heated skin and lifted the oppressive feel of my confines. I fought the urge to take a deep breath of the fresh oxygen. But along with that sense of relief came a thrill of fear now that I was exposed to my captor.

"I know you're awake," James said. "I can hear your heart beating fast, and the smell of burned skin. I see you discovered the wire I used to tie your hands." He sucked a breath in through his teeth. "Oh, man, I bet that hurts. It looks nasty."

My heart sank, and I opened my eyes, blinking up at a vampire I could only assume was James. His face was harsh, and his green eyes were icy as he looked me over.

"Have you learned your lesson then?" he asked, smirking. "I'm going to pull you out of there, and I don't want any trouble. If you're good, I won't have to hurt you any more than necessary."

I clenched my jaw but remained silent as he reached in

and grasped my upper arms, hoisting me from the trunk with a swift, effortless motion. I managed to get my feet under me before he released my weight, and my boots planted firmly on the paved driveway. Before he could drop his hands, I took a deep breath, filling my hands with as much energy as I dared, and placed them on his chest.

A scream of agony tore from my throat as the raw wounds on my wrists were seared once again. This time, I could smell the burning flesh. James jerked away, but not before getting a serious jolt of electricity. His eyes rolled back, and his body crumpled to the ground in a heap. My breathing was ragged from pain, but I didn't pause to catch my breath. I turned away from the massive grey stone building looming in front of me and shot for the end of the driveway. It led away from the house and to what I hoped was the street beyond.

My boots pounded against the pavement until I was caught short by a wrought iron gate spanning the opening to the street, blocking my escape. I looked from side to side, searching for a button or release, but couldn't find anything that might help. I cast my gaze wider, spotted another opening in the hedge-covered fencing, and sprinted toward the small pedestrian gate. It took a moment to find the tiny silver release button, and I raised my bound hands to trigger the gate, but as my fingers made contact, I was pulled off my feet from behind. I landed hard on the ground, my teeth clicking together. Another wave of pain shot through my head, and everything went black again.

32

KATE

As I drove Sara's car around the first bend in the road, I spotted a place to pull over and shot James another text, demanding to know where Sara was. I waited, gripping the phone so tightly that I heard the case crack. I relaxed my hand but held my breath, staring at the screen. Yet again, I received no reply. I let out a curse as tears flowed freely down my cheeks. There was nothing to be gained by sitting around and waiting for news. If Marcus was right and a trade was what James wanted, I would give it to him. The last thing I wanted was to submit to him and Alexander, but Sara's safety was the most important thing. I would do whatever it took to get her free.

Turning the car around, I headed back toward my old neighborhood. I had the address of Alexander's manor, but I would check James's apartment first. Finding them as quickly as possible was the goal. A shiver rippled through my body as I thought about the blood I found on the pavement outside the diner, and then a heat began building in my cold chest. The steering wheel let out a crack of protest as I gripped it too tightly. I would happily trade myself for

Sara, but I would find a way to make James pay for what he'd done—all of it.

The truth was, I was also angry with myself. The only reason Sara found herself in this situation was because of me. Sara had been in that parking lot for my sake, to make sure I was okay, and James had taken advantage of that.

Another thought twisted my stomach. Others would want to know what happened to Sara. I knew I should call Sara's mom and Lucia; they were her family and deserved to know that Sara was in danger. They would be furious if I left them in the dark. Silas would also want to know that Sara was missing. He cared for her in ways that he and Sara hadn't addressed yet, but he deserved to know.

I almost reached for my phone, but couldn't bring myself to do it. I didn't dare, no matter how mad they got. It was best if I went alone. James and Alexander wanted me. They wanted me to submit, and Sara was their pressure point. Alerting Sara's family would just put the rest of them in danger. And what could they do that Marcus and I couldn't?

I assumed Marcus would go to his boss to report what happened. I knew how slowly they moved, though, and I couldn't sit and wait another week for them to make a decision. The only thing I knew about the Council was that it was made up of other vampires, including Alexander. However, Marcus assured me that even if Alexander bothered to show up, he'd been removed from decisions regarding his own House. Each of the five major Houses had a representative— if they chose to send one—and there were elected representatives from the other, smaller Houses. But when you lived for centuries, a few weeks or months delay didn't bother you. Sara couldn't wait that long, and neither could I.

I reached the familiar apartment building and circled twice, looking for anything that might indicate whether James was there. From the street, I could see the windows of his apartment, and they were all dark. Either he wasn't home, or the shutters were down. I parked beside the building and looked around. His car wouldn't be on the street, even if he weren't bringing in a wounded hostage. He'd park in the garage, and I didn't have access.

Weariness washed over me, and I sighed, resting my head on the steering wheel. How had I thought this would work? I was running out of ideas, and every minute I delayed was another minute Sara was at the mercy of James. I prayed he wouldn't hurt her, but then I thought of the blood again.

He already had.

I knew I had to move, to make a decision. Glancing over at the entrance to the building, I knew there was one way for sure to see if he was there. My hand was on the door handle when my cell phone buzzed. I jumped and scrambled to grab it from the passenger seat, where it lay. I flipped it over. There was a message from James.

> I have something you want. Meet me at the Manor. Come alone
>
> It's time to come home

I let out a soft moan. I already knew he had her, but reading the words was like being hit in the chest. My fingers shook as I entered my response.

Is she okay?

I waited as he typed out his reply. My anxiety built with each blink of the dots on the screen.

She is alive. For now

Get here soon

I tapped out,

I'm on my way

I waited a beat longer. That was all. He wasn't typing.

Marcus had given me the address of the manor earlier, and I pulled it up. I wasn't familiar with the neighborhood on the far side of the city, but the street where it was located had very few houses. It wouldn't take me long to find. I tossed the phone onto the seat beside me. The trip to the apartment had been a complete waste of time, and James was well ahead of me at this point.

As I started the car and pulled back into traffic, passing

one car after another, I tried to remember not to press the gas too hard. I didn't want to be pulled over for speeding, but I knew I needed to hurry. I had no illusions about what James was capable of, not anymore. I shuddered and took the ramp onto the highway.

Red taillights stretched out in front of me as far as I could see. Traffic moved, but not fast enough. I screamed in frustration, slamming my hands down on the wheel, nearly knocking the thing right off the steering column.

This was taking too long.

33

JAMES

Bending down, I picked up the unconscious witch and threw her over my shoulder. I wobbled a bit as I made my way to the front door of the manor. I had to give her credit; she surprised me. That little trick of hers packed quite a punch. Had she been unbound and at full strength, she could have incapacitated me long enough to escape. As it was, I was shaken but none the worse for wear. On the other hand, she seemed to have inflicted quite a bit of damage to herself by the looks of it. The burns on her wrists, beneath the wire I thought to wrap around them, were seared almost to the muscle. She would be in a lot of pain when she woke up. I could heal her, of course, but I didn't care enough to help. She'd been a nuisance from the very beginning, and in her current state, she would pose less of a threat.

I shifted her weight and opened the front door. I was greeted by a human member of the staff who approached with a bland expression. Carrying a body through the foyer was not a rare occurrence.

"Sir, may I be of some assistance?" the man asked.

"No, I've got it. But tell me, where is Alexander?"

"Yes, Sir. He is in his study."

I made a dismissive noise and took my captive to the sitting room. I dumped her onto the sofa and listened, checking her heart rate. It was strong and steady. She would probably be okay for the time being. I looked around for something to rebind her ankles when I heard the wooden pocket door slide back on its tracks. I turned to see Alexander entering the room; his expression was dark, and I swallowed hard.

"That is not Kate," he said flatly, striding into the room. His presence made the space feel smaller. "That's not even a vampire. What have you done now? And, why do I smell burned flesh?"

"Sire," I said, bowing my head. "I have brokered a trade. Kate will willingly give herself over for the release of her friend. You smell the injuries she inflicted on herself trying to escape." I indicated her bound hands.

"She's a witch," Alexander hissed. "Did you not think that her people might have something to say about you kidnapping one of their own?"

I knew I was in danger. I licked my lips and chose my words carefully.

"The only ones who know what I have done are Kate and Marcus. And I doubt the Council will want the witches involved in this any more than we do. I have already made contact with Kate, and she is on her way here. I'm confident the witch will see the benefit of keeping this quiet," I said, watching Alexander to gauge his mood.

"Why on Earth would she do that?" Alexander asked, incredulous.

"They care for one another. They're friends. The witch will trade her silence for Kate's safety," I said, hoping this was true and that this might also keep Alexander from killing Kate out of hand.

"You never cease to disappoint me, James," Alexander said, sounding tired. "I hope you are right about this, but I fear you have created more problems I will have to solve." Alexander let out a long breath. "Oh, my progeny. Sometimes, I think I should slaughter the lot of you and start over." He turned and walked back out of the parlor, leaving me alone with the unconscious witch.

Problems he had to solve? I thought bitterly. When had he ever done anything to help, anything for himself at all? What would he do if he ever followed through on his threat? How would he take care of himself? No, when it came down to it, Alexander needed me, I told myself, but my stomach twisted at the memory of his teeth ripping into my throat.

The witch's breathing quickened. She was awake. One eyelid cracked open, but she didn't move and made no effort to sit up, which irritated me even more. I grabbed her shoulders and pushed her into a sitting position. She screamed, her breath coming in gasps as the muscles in her arms trembled. She was in more pain than I expected.

I settled into a green velvet chair and crossed my legs, waiting for her to regain her composure. She wasn't going anywhere in the state she was in, and I was content to wait. Finally, she opened her eyes.

"You did this to yourself, you realize," I said.

"Fuck you," she spat, her breath still coming quickly. She raised her hands toward her head and winced, then lowered them back to her lap. Her eyes darted around the room. It was lovely, but I doubted she appreciated the upscale European design.

"You aren't thinking of running again, are you?" I asked, refocusing her attention. "I'd just have to hit you over the head again, and frankly, I'm not sure you can take much more."

She pressed her lips into a thin line.

"You shouldn't have to wait long. Kate is on her way, and then you can be on your way too," I said. "She's agreed to come home where she belongs in exchange for sending you back to your people. But I warn you, if there is trouble from the witches over this..." I gestured toward her. "It's Kate who will suffer. I assure you."

The witch chuckled dryly. "Kate mentioned you were nice. At first, you were trying to help her, to protect her from all this. What happened to you? Or are you just a really good liar? Either way, I don't trust you, and neither does Kate."

I looked away from her hard, brown eyes. "You don't have to trust me; you just need to keep your mouth shut. You really don't want to make this any harder on her than it has to be," I said, my voice heavy with regret. Yes, I had regrets, but Kate had taken away my choice. This could have turned out very differently. I sighed.

"You don't have to do this," the witch said, her voice softening to a plaintive tone. The expression on her face was one of pleading instead of disdain. "You could let me go and let Kate go. You took her life; don't take her freedom away. Let her decide what she wants to make of this second life. There's still time."

"You don't understand," I said. "I have no choice. Kate has no choice. Alexander is our sire, and we must follow his orders. It's the only way." I don't know who I was trying to convince, her or myself.

"What about your Council? They seem to think it's up to them to decide what should be done and where Kate should live," she said.

I laughed. How little she understood about the Council and vampires in general. "They won't interfere as long as we handle this ourselves. They just want to maintain peace; having Kate under our roof will achieve that. Once she's here, though, I won't be able to protect her from Alexander if he's displeased. He has a terrible temper," I said, pulling the collar of my shirt aside to show the jagged pink scar running across my throat. Her eyes widened. "No, if the witches create trouble with the Council on Kate's behalf, Alexander will face consequences. But he's proud and hates being lectured by those he considers beneath him. He will be furious, which in turn will cause him to lash out at Kate. Please, for her sake, just go quietly. In time, once she proves her loyalty to Alexander, he'll soften, and she'll have more freedom. Ultimately, it's up to her and you."

I rubbed my face with both hands, trying to scrub away the last few weeks. I was so tired of all this.

"You don't know her very well," the witch said, her tone icy. "She may trade with you. She's a loyal friend to those who earn her friendship. But she will never submit to Alexander. She can't be forced into giving her loyalty."

I sighed once more. "Then she will suffer," I said.

My voice was barely above a whisper, but the witch flinched, and I knew she'd heard me.

34

KATE

The traffic slowed to a crawl as I passed through the city. I almost abandoned the car in favor of running to the manor, but Sara would need a way to get home if she was able to drive, so I gritted my teeth and kept going. After a short while, things picked back up, and I drove into the wealthiest neighborhood I'd ever seen. The houses were all mansions, and I realized the "manor" was actually a manor house.

When I arrived at the address, I tried not to be impressed. The manor was larger than any other house on the street. I drove past the enormous building and parked in front of a neighboring property. After locking the doors, I tucked the keys into the wheel well of the left rear tire, just like we used to when Sara and I shared the car in high school. I smiled at the memory. Sara had always been generous and caring. I thought of the house, the home Sara offered to share with me. I wanted so much for that to be my future. I wanted so much to be able to live that dream.

I paused on the sidewalk and reached for my phone. I composed a message to Marcus, informing him about the trade and confirming that I was going through with it. I asked him to help Sara make things right with the witches if he could. I explained that I didn't want anyone else to get hurt and that this was my decision. I sent the message and then turned off the phone, shoving it back into my pocket. I didn't know what would happen to me after I entered that house and surrendered myself to Alexander. I wanted someone to know where Sara was and what happened in case she couldn't get away.

After several deep breaths, I approached the gate and pressed the call button. I didn't have to wait long. There was an electronic buzzing, and the gate popped open. This was it. There was no going back. Even as sure as I was about what I intended to do, it still gave me pause. I shook off the feeling. My fear was replaced by determination as I made my way up the walk to the front of the house, and I realized the turning point had come the moment James had taken Sara. There was no other path for me now.

The massive wooden front door was banded with black metal and looked like it belonged on the front of a castle rather than a home in the Seattle suburbs, but I had to admit it fit the place nicely. I raised my hand to knock, but it swung open before I got the chance.

Light spilled out of the doorway, and the contrast between the cold grey stone exterior was startling. The rich wood, shining marble, and vibrant colors of the interior should have looked inviting, but instead gave off a sinister glow. I paused, intending to tread slowly, but when the warm air from the inside made its way up my nose, all the hairs on my body stood up. It was Sara's scent but tinged bitter with fear and pain, and mixed with the stomach-clenching smell of charred meat.

I rushed into the house, past the human holding the

door open. My feet skidded on the slick floor as I stopped in the foyer and turned toward the source of Sara's scent.

Glancing into the sitting room, I noticed James first, seated primly in an overstuffed chair. My gaze shifted to the figure on the sofa across from him. It was Sara. I had never seen my friend in such distress. Her complexion was washed out; her eyes unfocused, and the pain she felt was evident on her face. I fortified my internal shields against the emotions in the room. I didn't want to be distracted.

With a roar, I lunged forward.

Before I made it five feet in Sara's direction, however, I was yanked backward. My body went airborne, and then I was falling, unable to stop myself. My back hit the hard marble of the entryway, and the breath whooshed out of my lungs.

I blinked in surprise.

Alexander loomed overhead. Those dove grey eyes from my memory stared down at me, and his mouth was twisted into a vicious smile. "Welcome home, Kate."

35

JAMES

Springing to my feet, I prepared to intercept Kate as she barreled toward the room. At the sight of her, my heart thudded in my chest. My resolve crumbled. I wanted to go to her, to hold her in my arms, even if it was just to keep her from reaching the witch. I didn't see Alexander until Kate was flat on her back. She hadn't even made it across the threshold of the sitting room. I froze, waiting to see what our sire would do.

I didn't dare approach her now, nor did I try to intervene. It would only provoke Alexander more. I stood frozen, barely breathing. However, I did shoot a glance at the witch. I hoped the look I leveled in her direction would keep her quiet and still. She met my eyes and swallowed hard, turning back to Alexander and Kate. She didn't look like she could get up if she tried. Feeling satisfied that she posed no threat and wouldn't be going anywhere, I returned my attention to what was happening in the foyer.

Then, I spotted the new one—I think his name was Thomas, or Timothy, or maybe it was Trever or something. He was at the bottom of the stairs on the far side of Kate and

Alexander. He watched, too, but the look in his eyes was hungry. I wondered if it was blood or the violence he craved. He truly was a good match for our sire.

Alexander stood over Kate. She lay there, staring up at him, gasping and struggling to take enough air into her lungs to speak. The expression on Alexander's face was calm, his voice steady and devoid of emotion as he welcomed her home, but I knew that voice. Alexander was never more dangerous than when he adopted this light, mocking tone. He was playing with her. I started to move forward without thinking, but Alexander's fierce glare halted me. My sire's gaze drilled into me, holding me in place. It was louder than any spoken command. I was not to interfere. I bowed my head and lowered my eyes back to Kate.

She propped herself up on her elbows and took a deep breath. "This isn't my home, but I'm here now. Let Sara go," she said boldly, glaring up at Alexander, her face etched with a scowl.

I quaked inside. She needed to stay down, lower her eyes, and soften her tone. This could still work out if she could just manage a moment of humility. Why would she continue to make this harder than it had to be? It felt like she went out of her way to be difficult and make things worse for both of us.

"You ungrateful bitch. How dare you speak to me that way?" Alexander said, his voice now harsh. In a blur, he lunged forward and grasped Kate by the throat, pulling her off the floor and holding her inches from his snarling face. Her feet dangled, and her hands wrapped around the vise grip holding her aloft.

I watched Alexander closely and saw the moment he

inhaled her scent. His expression shifted from rage to confusion.

He brought his face closer as she struggled against his grasp. "There is that scent again. What is it?" he asked, in a voice that sounded like a purr. "I can still smell my blood in you, but I can smell yours now, too. And it smells delicious. I can see why James would want to keep you for himself." He lifted her higher and opened his mouth wide. It looked like he was going for the base of her neck.

From the sofa, the witch let out a yell of alarm. The sound made Alexander pause. He turned his head away from Kate and looked toward the witch, whose face was filled with pleading and worry.

Alexander shook his head. His brows furrowed. He glanced back at Kate. "She's worried about you. It seems she does care for you. How strange," he said, and some of his sudden fixation on her seemed to drain away as he contemplated this discovery. "Don't go anywhere, my dear," he whispered in her ear.

Without warning, Alexander dropped Kate to the cold marble. I felt the air move and was forced backward as Alexander sped forward, placing himself between the witch and me. I put my hands up, ready to ward off a blow, but Alexander wasn't there for me. He faced the witch.

I moved slowly to the side so I could see her face. She had been staring at Kate, who lay crumpled on the floor, clutching her throat and gasping for air. Alexander moved too quickly for even a witch to see. Now, she stared up into Alexander's face, her eyes wide with shock, and the fresh scent of fear floated in the air.

I glanced back at Kate, genuinely hoping she would stay still, and noticed movement behind her. The blond vampire crept closer. His focus was on Alexander and the witch, but I didn't trust him. He was too new, too young, to turn my back on. I edged further into the sitting room, searching for a spot where I could keep an eye on everything.

Alexander peered down at the terrified witch. "Hers is a better response," he said. He crouched lower, bringing himself closer to the witch's face, his expression unreadable. "You, a witch, are concerned for our little Kate? You care about what happens to her, even though she is one of us? A vampire."

The witch looked like she was about to pass out. Her body was tense, and her hands, still bound, were held out painfully in front of her. She seemed to struggle to keep them as still as possible. I suspected she fought the urge to call upon her magic to defend herself. After a moment, she nodded to Alexander. "Of course. She's my best friend," she said in a remarkably calm and steady voice.

"Absolutely fascinating," Alexander said, pulling his lips back into what might have passed as a smile, revealing his elongated fangs. The witch swallowed hard but remained motionless.

Alexander glanced down at the wire binding her injured wrists. "I assume from the bindings and the burned skin that her power has been effectively neutralized," he said.

"Yes, Sire," I replied.

Alexander reached out, clamping a hand down on the witch's shoulder, causing her to wince painfully. Kate hissed from the doorway, the sound bringing Alexander's head around in her direction. "Keep those teeth to yourself, sweet Kate. I could break her, heal her, and break her again just to listen to the screams if I so wished. And there is nothing you can do about it. The sooner you realize this, the better it will be for you both," he said.

Alexander took back up his falsely calm demeanor. His

hand remained on the witch, but he didn't move to harm her. He studied her like some strange new species of insect caught in his web. "I'll let you go, eventually. But for now, you could be very useful for getting our Kate to behave. Yes, I think you will remain with us for the time being to help Kate settle in and remember to be on her best behavior."

"That wasn't the deal," Kate spat. "People will come for her. I texted someone who works for the Council. He knows where she is."

"Ah, yes, the Council. Don't count on them to save you," he said to the witch. "I'm sure they will inquire, eventually, but as a member myself, I know how they operate. I'm not concerned. Besides, it'll be easier this way, less messy." He turned back to Kate as she got to her feet. "I could force you physically to submit. It's effective but painful; just ask James," he said with a grin. "But I think this is better, less scarring."

Kate flashed her gaze in my direction, and her eyes dipped to the open collar of my shirt. I knew she could see the marks our sire left in my flesh. I studied her face, hoping to see some concern or regret. But whatever I saw in her eyes vanished in an instant, and her gaze turned cold. She looked away from me. I could tell it didn't matter if she stayed in this House or not, whether Alexander claimed her for himself or not; I had lost her.

36

KATE

A disgusted noise escaped my lips as I tore my gaze away from James. I'd held onto a glimmer of hope that he might help me, that he might still do the right thing. But one look at Sara told me all I needed to know. He stood silently in the corner, watching my friend suffer. He'd caused so much pain, taken so much. I expected to feel rage when I saw him again, but all I felt was sadness. He was a pitiful creature, and it had little to do with the scar on his neck. I promised myself that no matter how this turned out, I would not become him.

I refocused on Alexander. I now understood who I was dealing with. I knew that he meant what he said. He would torture Sara to get what he wanted. And he wanted me. How had my life turned into this? I took a ragged breath. "That's not necessary. You don't have to keep her here," I said quietly. "I'll do what you say. You don't need her. I won't fight you." I could hear the defeat in my voice. All my previous bravery fled. My only concern now was getting Sara out of there and to safety.

"Hmm. Maybe," Alexander pressed his lips together and

leveled his stare at me. Measuring. His eyes were dilated, and he looked hungry. "Perhaps I don't need her after all. Let's test that theory, shall we?"

In less time than it took to blink, Alexander stood in front of me again. His sudden appearance made me try to step backward, but before I could, he had me in his grasp once more. This time, his arms were locked around me in an embrace, pulling me against the full length of his body. Inwardly, I recoiled.

With the physical contact, I was unable to shut out Alexander's emotions. No matter how hard I pushed, I couldn't manage to create that space between us. Just like our bodies, his emotions were pressed against me, with nowhere to go.

And I felt it all. All his anger. All his frustration. All his desire.

Although everything in me wanted to struggle to break free, I remembered Sara and what this show of power, of domination, was all about. I closed my eyes and forced myself to remain still as he lowered his face to the crook of my neck. Even when I felt his fangs rake against my skin, I held still. The moment before he struck, I thought of the pink scar at the base of James's throat, and my whole body stiffened.

Alexander's fangs sank deep, and I let out a small cry. There was no tearing, though. This was not a mauling. I heard him moan as he drew on my neck, and I wondered if I would have preferred brutality. This was painful, yes, but it also felt like a violation. I clenched my jaw and opened my eyes, meeting James's gaze over the top of Alexander's shoulder. I let my stare burn into him as Alexander sucked greedily at my throat. James shifted uncomfortably, looking like he wanted to do something, but he didn't move. After a short time, he dropped his gaze to the floor and crossed his arms. There would be no help from him.

I wasn't sure how much more I could endure. Alexander didn't seem to be stopping, and I began to feel lightheaded. For the first time, I wondered if I could actually be killed this way. Could he drain me to death? I didn't want to find out. I started to panic. Regardless of what I said, I wouldn't let myself be killed without a fight. It was clear that if I wanted to get out of this, I would have to do it myself.

The prospect of death stirred something deep within me. Despite the blood Alexander was taking and the spots swimming in my vision, I felt a new power building from inside. I flexed my muscles against Alexander's hold. His arms were still locked around me like iron bands. He was so very strong. Something in the back of my mind whispered that I was stronger. But it wasn't my muscles that were going to get me out of this.

I allowed myself to focus on the place where Alexander and I connected. Not my throat, not the pressure of our two bodies, but the spot inside me, deep within my mind, where I could still sense his blind pleasure in what he did. I concentrated on that point until the rest of the world faded away, leaving only me and Alexander in my mind.

I drew in a deep breath, and as a scream ripped from my throat, I pushed all my revulsion, all my sorrow and frustration, all my fear down the connection between the two of us.

I felt a great wave ripple through me and crash into the older vampire. His fangs tore away from my throat, and he threw himself backward, smashing into a table next to the open front door. He lay stunned amid the splintered wood and broken pottery, staring at me with a look of utter shock on his face.

"Fascinating," he whispered, and I shoved at him again

with resolution and dread. He flinched but gave me a small smile.

I wasn't sure how long it would keep him at bay, but I knew in that moment that I had the upper hand and wouldn't let him hurt me or Sara again.

I glanced at Sara, who still sat wide-eyed on the sofa in the parlor. Movement from Alexander's direction caused me to turn my head again, but it wasn't Alexander who'd drawn my attention. Framed by the open front door stood Marcus, looking as surprised as everyone else.

37

———

JAMES

Stepping forward, I tried to see what became of Alexander. Somehow, Kate managed to throw the five-hundred-year-old vampire off of her. I'd never seen anything like it, especially from one as young as Kate. As the front door came into view, I noticed that Alexander wasn't alone. Marcus stood just inside, taking in the scene. At the sight of Marcus, I halted my approach.

"I see I'm just in time," Marcus said.

Alexander jerked his head toward the front door, noticing Marcus for the first time. He sprang to his feet, brushed off his trousers, and tugged his shirt sleeves, trying to put himself in order. "Marcus. How nice to see you," Alexander said, smooth as ever, projecting complete calm and control I was sure he didn't feel. "I was just sorting a few things out with my new progeny. While I appreciate visitors, I assure you that this is House business and none of your concern."

This was the Alexander I knew and feared. I edged back toward the sitting room, trying not to draw the attention of the two older vampires. I didn't want to get in the middle of whatever Marcus came here to say.

My eyes flicked over as the newest member of the House, Thomas, charged forward. After all the conflict, the appearance of another older vampire seemed too much for him. It wasn't entirely unexpected. Marcus evidently noticed Thomas as well, for he thrust out an arm, sending the young vampire flying backward to skid across the floor to land motionless in a heap at the base of the staircase.

"Is this how you greet guests, Alexander?" Marcus asked, completely unruffled.

Alexander bared his fangs. This was a direct challenge in his own territory.

Then, Marcus spotted the witch.

As he took her in, his expression shifted from smug to completely blank, as if a mask slid down over his features, concealing them from view. The hair on the back of my neck stood up, and I stepped farther away, increasing the distance between me and the witch.

Alexander must have noticed the expression on Marcus's face, too, because he didn't push his protest any further. Instead, he waved a hand toward the unconscious Thomas. "Ugh, ignore him. He's still a bit of a hothead," Alexander drawled lazily, but I could see the rage still dancing in his eyes.

Marcus blinked and turned back, glancing between Alexander and Kate. "No. I believe I arrived just in time to help settle things between the two of you," he said. "And I don't mean to correct you in your own home, but this *is* a concern of mine." He reached down and pulled a sheaf of papers from the satchel he wore across one shoulder. "I'm here to inform you that the Council has accepted Kate's petition for emancipation. She is now a ward of the Council until she applies to a new House for membership and is accepted. She is to be placed in my custody. Immediately," Marcus added, holding the papers out toward Alexander.

"Why was I not made aware of this...petition?" Alexander asked between clenched teeth.

"As you know, it is protocol to exclude Council members from decisions regarding their own Houses. It didn't require your vote or knowledge," Marcus replied.

The muscles in Alexander's jaw flexed as he looked down at the papers he held. Kate, on the other hand, appeared completely surprised by the news. I suspected that Marcus submitted the petition on her behalf. It was clever, I had to admit. But I knew it wouldn't sit well with Alexander and would spell disaster for me personally. I didn't doubt that with Kate out of his reach, I would be the one to bear the brunt of Alexander's rage at the embarrassment and at being denied what he thought was rightfully his.

There was something very unusual about Kate. The little demonstration before Marcus arrived proved this, as did her captivating scent and taste. No. Alexander wouldn't happily let her go, but what choice did he have?

I backed even farther away from the foyer, deeper into the sitting room. I moved slowly, trying to make as little noise as possible. My legs hit a chair, and I turned. The witch's dark eyes stared up at me from the sofa. I breathed out heavily and was glad that looks could, in fact, not kill. I waited for her to say something. To call out and draw attention to my escape. She remained silent, however, as I turned toward the door leading to the hall and into the kitchen.

As soon as I cleared the room, I moved quickly and ducked into the side hall. Two large red hounds blocked my path. They both raised their lips at the sight of me, and a low rumble filled the hallway. *I don't have time for this,* I thought. I lunged, fangs bared, hands curved into claws. The two dogs lowered to their bellies and scooted back. The growls transformed into high-pitched whines as they licked their lips and tucked their heads down in submission. I straightened and walked past them into the kitchen, exiting through a side door into the garden.

I didn't have time to go to my room and get my things. I would retrieve what I needed from my apartment up north and disappear. I wouldn't stick around to see how Alexander would handle the situation. No longer would I be beholden to my mercurial and vengeful sire. I wouldn't bear the brunt of Alexander's failures any longer. If Kate could escape, so could I. But I wouldn't wait for the bureaucracy to sort things out for me. I didn't have a Marcus to assist me or smooth things over. No, I was on my own. I would put so much distance between myself and my sire that Alexander couldn't reach me if he wanted to. Not that he would care; he had Thomas now, after all.

I'd hoped to make this flight with Kate by my side. The dream was so vivid and beautiful. I wished I could go back and change how things turned out. I would have been more careful. I would have guarded my tongue; I would have lied more convincingly. I was still angry that she couldn't understand everything I'd done for her. I'd saved her, no matter how she saw it. But in the end, she saved me, too. I doubted I would have ever had the courage to leave if we'd never met. I had been miserable for a long time. No longer. I would make my own choices from now on. I would do what was best for me. I would be free.

38

KATE

S hock was not the correct expression, I reminded myself, and snapped my teeth together, closing my gaping mouth as I listened to what Marcus was telling Alexander. As I stood there swaying, I realized my mouth wasn't the only part of my body I struggled with. After the release of energy, I felt drained, and not just from the blood Alexander stole. My muscles were weak, and my knees trembled. Marcus had indeed arrived just in time. The power I felt moments ago disappeared, and I wasn't sure I could summon enough energy to walk, let alone fend off another attack. Standing was the best I could do for the moment, and I concentrated on staying upright as I stared at Alexander. His brows dipped even lower while he scanned the documents he'd been given.

I glanced toward the sitting room. Sara was alone and still bound. James had disappeared, and I wasn't going to miss the chance to reach my friend. I managed to make it over to the sofa without falling and without causing a stir in the foyer. The blond vampire was still out cold, and Alexander was now debating the finer points of the Council's decision. From the volume and tone coming from that direction, I doubted he would be finished anytime soon.

Cautiously, I lowered myself to the sofa next to Sara, not wanting to cause her any more pain. "Oh God, Sara. I'm so sorry," I said, reaching for the wire wrapped around my friend's badly burned wrists. The slightest touch made Sara suck in air through her teeth, and I stopped. Seeing her like this tore at my heart. I didn't want to hurt her, but I couldn't leave her like this either. With a thought, I bit into my finger as I'd seen James do at the Tap House and brought the bloody tip to the worst of Sara's burns.

"Oh, that feels much better," Sara said, sounding as exhausted as I felt.

The other burns were just as bad, and I had to bite my finger over and over again as it healed faster than I could spread the blood onto Sara's seared flesh. Finally, the wounds were closed. Sara's shoulders sagged in relief, and I was able to untwist the wire, letting the bloody mess drop to the plush cream-colored carpet. I hoped it would leave a terrible stain.

Once she was free, Sara wrapped her arms around me, and the two of us held each other. The comfort of knowing Sara was all right was almost enough to override the fear of the risks we still faced. We weren't in the clear yet. I didn't have the energy to try to flee, and I doubted I would be of much use if it came to a fight. I just hoped that Marcus would win the argument that was still going on in the next room.

Too soon, the voices from the foyer cut off, and I pulled away from Sara. I glanced over to see both Alexander and Marcus standing in the doorway, watching us. Marcus's face was blank and gave nothing away, but the look on Alexander's could not be mistaken for anything other than disgust.

I didn't need my abilities to tell me that Alexander was unhappy with the way things were going.

"And, I'll be taking the witch with me. I'm sure I've got the paperwork for it here somewhere," Marcus said, reaching for his satchel.

"I care not," Alexander said, his voice sounding bored, but I was wary. Alexander didn't seem like someone who would lose interest so easily. I tried to reach out to gauge his true feelings, but I was too tired. No matter how he felt about letting Sara go, she would be safe at least.

I held my breath. The outcome of the negotiations was still a mystery—whether I'd be allowed to leave with Marcus or left behind. Staying would be dangerous, especially now, when I was too weak and depleted to defend myself against Alexander. In the short term, I wouldn't stand a chance. But if I survived, I'd make him sorry. I *would* get free. The way Alexander looked at me as I stared him down made one thing clear: he knew it, too. No—if I were left behind, I doubted he'd let me live long enough to recover.

"Well, are you two ready?" Marcus asked.

My heart leaped. It had worked—we were leaving together. For a moment, I almost couldn't believe what I'd heard. But Marcus waited, his expression expectant. I surged to my feet, too fast. The room tilted, vision dimming at the edges. One hand shot out to steady myself, but my knees buckled, and I nearly collapsed back onto the couch.

"You need some help?" Marcus asked, raising his eyebrows but keeping his tone level.

"No, I'm fine," I said. Marcus's reaction urged me to pull it together, and I would. I could do this. I took a deep breath, and my vision steadied. "Help Sara, would you? I think she could use it."

Marcus helped Sara to her feet, slipping an arm under

her shoulders and easily supporting her as they made their way to the open front door. I followed behind them, placing my feet carefully and standing tall. Determination pushed me forward. I would leave under my own power. At least, that was the plan. It was a toss-up whether I'd make it to the door, let alone down the front steps. But if I could help it, I wouldn't show weakness in front of Alexander. I wasn't sure why this was important, but something inside told me if I faltered, he would attack. The thought gave me renewed strength, and I straightened my spine further.

Alexander's cold stare trailed me as I passed him. "This is not over," he hissed in a low growl.

Instead of replying, I just nodded and continued out the door.

The chill of the night air felt cool and refreshing in my lungs, helping to clear my head. Marcus and Sara were waiting for me in the middle of the drive. I walked down the steps, pleased that my legs remained steady under me.

I flicked a glance back toward the house before joining the others.

Alexander stood alone in the middle of the destruction he'd wrought. His barely contained rage was evident, but he remained still.

Still and alone.

39

KATE

The ground felt loose under my feet as I stepped up beside Marcus. I placed my hand on the vampire's shoulder to steady myself. No doubt Alexander was still watching, and I didn't want to fall.

Marcus glanced at my hand, noticing its bloody fingertips. His nostrils flared, and his jaw tightened, but he nodded. "You can lean more heavily on me," he said softly enough that I knew Alexander wouldn't be able to hear.

I did as he suggested, letting more of my weight rest on his shoulder. The three of us exited the property by the open side gate. And that's when I spotted the giant wolf.

It was near the end of the block, standing near Marcus's car. Its body was massive, almost twice the size of any dog I'd ever seen. Its brown and black fur stood up on its shoulders as it paced back and forth. It was silent, but I could sense its anxiety and pent-up energy from half a block away, even as tired as I was.

"I couldn't convince him to stay away, but I did get him to wait out here, downwind," Marcus said.

"Silas," I said. It wasn't a question—there was no one else it could be.

As the wolf noticed us, it began to shiver all over and collapsed onto its forelegs. The shaking got worse as we approached, and by the time we made it to within a few yards, the wolf was gone. In its place was Silas in his human form, still shaking. He took a moment to rise to his feet, and then he came towards us. He didn't stop until his arms wrapped around Sara, and he held her off the ground in his strong embrace.

Marcus and I waited for him to put Sara back down so we could all get gone, but they didn't move.

"Hmm," Marcus cleared his throat. "Maybe we could do this in the car?"

"And, maybe find him some clothes or something?" I added, trying to avoid getting an eyeful of the shifter.

Marcus snorted. "I think I have a blanket in the trunk," he said, walking around the pair to get to his car.

Silas finally set Sara down, gratefully accepted the blanket Marcus offered, and settled himself and Sara in the back of Marcus's car. I took the front seat, and we pulled away from the curb, driving into the night and leaving behind Alexander and the horrors of the past hour.

I kept glancing at the side mirror to see if we were being followed, but Marcus assured me Alexander wouldn't bother, not himself anyway. But where had James gone? I hoped it wasn't to head us off. I didn't take a relaxed breath until we were back on the highway, headed for home—my new home.

As we drove north, Marcus explained what he'd been up to since we parted, and before.

"The petition for emancipation was a long shot," he explained. "I didn't want to get your hopes up. And I wasn't sure you would thank me for putting you directly in the hands of the Council, but it seemed like a good alternative if negotiations failed. When James moved against a member of the witch community, I had my lawyer friend—your lawyer—expedite it with a few phone calls. I turned around to meet you at home, but was surprised to find the house empty," he said, raising an eyebrow in my direction.

"Yeah, sorry. You got my message?" I asked.

"Yes, I got your message, eventually. When I couldn't find you, I reached out to Silas." Marcus paused and looked in the rearview mirror at Sara. "I hope you don't mind. I thought I might need backup, and he was the first to answer my call. Plus, I knew he'd be interested in helping me get you back alive."

I turned in my seat to see what Sara would say. She purposely didn't tell Silas what she was up to.

"No. I don't mind. I should have told him in the first place," Sara said. She looked up at Silas, who had a protective arm around her.

He looked down at her with such love and tenderness, it squeezed my heart to see it. "It's okay," Silas said in a soft voice. "You are here and safe. That's all that matters right now." He kissed the top of Sara's head, and I saw her snuggle deeper into his shoulder.

I turned back around as Marcus began to speak again.

"He showed up in wolf form and drooled all over my seats on the way down," he said with mock sternness. He looked back into the mirror and smiled at the two. "Anyway. You heard what I told Alexander. You're now under the protection and direct authority of the Council," he said. "I'm sorry, but it couldn't be helped."

"What does that mean?" I asked.

"Well, firstly, it means neither Alexander nor James can

touch you without severe consequences. It also means that you answer to the Council for now," he said, pausing and shifting in his seat. I managed to get my walls back in place after the encounter with Alexander, and was too tired to lower them at the moment. So I didn't know exactly what Marcus felt, but he looked nervous, and it made my stomach clench. What wasn't he saying?

"And...?" I prompted.

"And they want you to move onto Council property." He quickly held up a hand as I began to protest. "There is a way for you to stay in your own home, at least for now."

I waited for him to continue, but he was taking a long time to reach the punchline. How bad could it be?

"Okay. Are you going to tell me?" I asked.

"I would have to move in to keep an eye on you," Marcus said in a rush.

I blew out a breath. "Yeah, that's fine with me. Sara?" I asked, turning in my seat.

Sara gave a thumbs up, but I saw Silas's brows draw together in concern. That could be a problem at some point, but it was up to Sara and me.

"Yup, it's cool with Sara," I said, choosing to ignore Silas' reaction. "Were you worried we would say no?"

"Well, I wouldn't blame either of you if you had a problem with a vampire moving in, given your experiences so far with our community. Both of you," he said.

"Well, you're not like the other vampires I've met. Besides, I'm a vampire too, you know?" I said.

"Yeah, I suppose so," he said, glancing sideways at me and shifting in his seat again. "By the way, I might have bluffed back there when I said I had authorization to take Sara." He winced at the admission. "If you guys could keep that to yourselves, I'd appreciate it. I don't think Alexander will follow up on it, but I don't want my bosses to find out that I lied to Alexander to get her away."

"Of course," I said, impressed that Marcus would take the risk to help my friend. It meant a lot.

The conversation faded, and the silence lingered as we drove. Everyone was exhausted and had been through a great deal over the past few hours. It was a lot to process.

Although no one spoke and we were safely away, Marcus seemed to be growing increasingly uncomfortable. Finally, he spoke up. "We need to talk about what was going on when I arrived," he said. "Specifically, how Alexander ended up on his ass."

I didn't answer right away, unsure what to say. My ability, gift, or whatever it was, was growing and changing. I didn't know how I did what I did. It made me feel vulnerable to talk about. And there was more. There was something about my blood. Both James and Alexander mentioned it. They thought I was different for some reason. Perhaps the two things were connected.

"I'm not sure, to be honest," I finally said. "He bit me on the throat. I thought he would kill me, and I reacted."

Marcus swallowed. "Hmm, he took a lot of blood then?" he asked.

"Yeah, that's why I had trouble walking. I don't know if it would have killed me, but I started to panic." I looked out the window.

"Kate, this is important," he said, gripping the steering wheel tightly. "When I arrived, Alexander was still at your throat, and the smell of your blood," he paused and swallowed again, like he was having trouble. "It was all around. You did something to get Alexander off of you. You pushed him back somehow, didn't you?"

I took a deep breath but didn't answer.

"It's why you asked me about magic? Special abilities?" he asked softly.

I turned from the window and glanced back at Sara. She was listening to the conversation. Silas's eyes were open, his head resting against Sara's, but he didn't look at me. She met my eye and nodded.

I resettled in my seat and sighed. "Yeah. I did," I admitted. "I can feel other people's emotions. I've always been able to, even before I was turned. It's been getting more intense since then."

Marcus glanced at me, his eyes wide, but he nodded for me to go on.

"When I thought Alexander wouldn't stop, that he would kill me, I sort of, I don't know, shoved at him."

"I don't understand," Marcus said. "Physically? Or..."

"No. I pushed emotion back at him. Made him want to get away from me. Made him afraid and disgusted," I said.

Marcus kept his eyes on the road but nodded again. "Good. Yeah. Kate?"

"Yeah?" I said.

"I'm going to need you to send some of that my way," he said. It was then that I noticed how rigidly he sat and how tense his body was. The muscles in his jaw clenched and unclenched.

"What, now?" I said. "Are you...okay?"

"You are drenched in your own blood, Kate, and it's making me hungry," he said around a set of elongated fangs.

I looked at my bloody fingertips, the ones I'd bitten and re-bitten to heal Sara. There were only a few drops.

"Your shirt, Kate," Sara said from the backseat.

I glance down at my sweater, pulling the neck away from my body to get a better look. He was right; it was soaked through.

"That blond vampire didn't try to attack me," Marcus said, bringing my head up. "He tried to get to you, your blood. Your blood has a very unique scent. One I've never smelled on a human, let alone on a vampire. It's...very tempting."

"Oh. I—" I began.

"Kate, if you wouldn't mind," Marcus interrupted. "I'm trying hard here not to pull over and bite you myself."

I flinched at the tone in his voice. I immediately dropped my defenses and was overwhelmed by his desire and frustration. "Oh yeah, yeah, I'm sorry," I said. Finding the connection wasn't difficult, but I was so tired. I wasn't sure I had the energy for what I needed to do. Slowly, I breathed in and out, concentrating. Shoving at him like I had Alexander wasn't an option. I didn't want him to try to escape; I just needed him not to want to attack me. My tongue swept across dry lips as I honed in on the emotions I wanted to project: calm, control, disinterest. Then I pushed.

I felt the change immediately. The pulsing of his emotions dampened and settled. His craving was replaced with stillness. I glanced over and saw his body relax as he took a deep breath.

"Thank you, Kate," he sighed. "How long can you keep that up?" he asked.

"I'm not sure. I'm worn out," I admitted.

"You need to feed," he said. "Do you still have plenty of blood back at your house?"

"Yeah," I said. "There's enough."

"Good. And, Kate," he said. "If I were you, I'd keep your abilities to yourself. I'm glad you shared that with me. And I might need your help occasionally since we'll be living in the same house. But no other vampire should know what I know."

"Okay, but Alexander knows, won't he tell others?" I asked.

"I doubt Alexander is going to be eager to tell the story of what happened tonight, but we will cross that bridge when we come to it," he said. "If others find out that you're different, they will try to get to you, to use you."

I didn't answer, just stared out the window. I was too tired to worry about it just yet. The streetlights made pools of warm light along the side of the road, and I watched them flash by, letting my mind drift.

We rode the rest of the way in silence. At some point, Sara fell asleep while Silas kept his eyes open and alert. I thought he would probably have trouble relaxing in a car with two vampires. I realized that I wasn't bothered by his scent anymore. Somewhere in the back of my mind, he'd become part of our group. He was devoted to protecting Sara, which made him like family. Considering how the two of us reacted to each other when we'd first met, my feelings were a surprise, to say the least. I wondered if he would ever feel the same way about me, and I hoped that he would.

Dawn was still far off, but I felt my eyes closing and let myself drift into a light sleep as we made our way home. Home, I thought with a smile on my lips. I was safe, and I was going home.

40

SARA

We were turning up the drive to the new house when I awoke. Silas's arm was still wrapped around me, holding me to his chest—his bare chest. I stopped that thought in its tracks. A car full of supernatural creatures was not the best place to think about the wide expanse of muscle my head rested on. I would certainly be thinking about it later, however.

I looked up, and Silas was awake. He gazed down at me with his yellow eyes, and I was reminded of how he appeared in his wolf form. Knowing he transformed into a wolf and seeing it were two different things. That was the first time I'd seen him that way, and it was thrilling.

He smiled at me and squeezed my arm where his hand rested. "How are you doing?" he asked.

"I have a headache, but I'm surprisingly okay. You?"

"Me?" he asked. "I'm not the one who was held hostage and tortured by vampires."

"No," I chuckled. "I guess that's true. It was all a lot, though, for all of us, wasn't it?" I asked.

"Yeah. It was a lot," he said, his smile slipping. He took a deep breath and tightened his hold on me.

Marcus parked the car by the front steps, and we got out and made our way inside.

Kate didn't look so good. The loss of blood and the use of her abilities had gotten to her. Marcus helped her up the steps and into the kitchen, where he settled her into a chair before going to get her something to eat. I'd never been so glad to see the neatly stacked bags of blood at the bottom of our fridge.

I took a seat opposite Kate. As I tried to decide if I had enough energy to make something hot to eat, I felt a tap on my shoulder.

"I'll just...be right back," Silas said, indicating the blanket he held wrapped around his waist.

I nodded and gave him a small smile, and turned away before he could notice me blushing.

Marcus brought over half a dozen bags, set them in front of Kate, and sat down beside her.

"Did you want some?" Kate asked Marcus.

He shook his head. "No, I'm good. You eat up."

Kate started to suck down the packets of blood. It should have grossed me out, but it didn't. I'd been so afraid for Kate back at Alexander's. I was relieved that my friend would be okay; it didn't matter what she needed to drink to recover. It had all become so very normal so quickly.

Silas came back into the kitchen a few minutes later, completely dressed from head to toe, including a pair of work boots much too large for anyone who currently lived in the house.

Kate stopped drinking and stared. "Did you just run home or did you have clothes stashed away here?" she asked, her brow furrowed.

"I have clothing stashed in many places," he said with a broad smile. "It's a shifter thing. It's convenient."

I covered my mouth, stifling a laugh at the look on Kate's face.

Silas took the last of the kitchen chairs and turned to Marcus. "I can fix up a room downstairs for you," he said.

I was surprised at his offer, not that he would do it, but that he would make the offer directly to Marcus. I knew the vampires made him nervous, and I'd assumed he would've asked me privately. I suspected that Marcus earned a measure of trust by reaching out to Silas to help get me back.

"Yeah, that would be great. Thank you, Silas," Marcus said.

"There's a large storeroom in the basement. We can set up a cot in there for now," I said.

Marcus nodded. "That's all I need."

"We can do better than that," Silas replied. He turned to me and lowered his voice. "It's late, and I wondered if it would be okay if I stayed here tonight? I can take the couch—"

"Yes," I said before he got the words out. I knew I was being a bit overeager, perhaps, but I didn't want him to leave. I reached over and put my hand on his. "Please stay."

He smiled warmly, and my breath caught in my throat. I looked away but couldn't keep a returning smile off my lips.

Kate cleared her throat. "Okay, well," she said, rising from the table. "I'm tired. I'm heading to bed. I'll see you tomorrow evening. Silas, maybe I'll see you around?" She gave him a wink and tossed her empty bags in the trash before leaving.

Marcus wished Kate good sleep, but stayed behind.

"Sara, may I check your wounds before I go to bed?" he asked.

I looked at my wrists. "There is nothing to see, really. Kate healed me before we left," I said, pushing an arm towards Marcus.

He grasped my hand and examined the skin around my wrist. It was perfectly smooth and unblemished. There was still some grime there that I didn't want to think about, but the skin itself was undamaged.

"Kate said you were burned?" he asked.

I nodded. "Yeah, it was deep. I nearly passed out from the pain."

Marcus scowled down but released my hand. "Well, good. Any other injuries?"

"The back of my head is still sore," I said, and gingerly touched the tender spot that had been struck repeatedly.

Marcus stood up and walked over. I bent my head down, and Marcus gently parted my hair. I noticed Silas stiffen while Marcus attended to the small cut on the back of my head. I couldn't tell if it was from seeing the injury or from Marcus's fangs as he pricked his finger.

"How's that?" Marcus asked.

"It's better, but my head still throbs."

"Silas, you might want to keep an eye on her today. She could have a concussion."

Silas nodded. I wasn't sure if Marcus actually suspected a concussion or if he was trying to give us an excuse to spend the day together. Either way, I knew Silas wouldn't go anywhere, and that was just fine with me.

Silas and I followed Marcus downstairs and helped him arrange a place to sleep in the storage room before we said goodnight and headed back to the main floor. Silas leaned over and kissed the top of my head, then started to walk toward the living room, but I grabbed his hand. He stopped and turned back.

I gazed up at him. He was tired, and I knew he'd been worried about me. Despite not knowing each other all that well, I felt closer to him than almost anyone in my life. He was a steady presence for me in a life that was becoming increasingly turbulent. I couldn't help but look at the well-developed muscles of his chest and remember resting my head against him. The feel of him, the smell of him. I wanted more.

"Stay with me, upstairs?" I asked.

He looked at me from under his long, dark lashes, and although there was affection in that stare, there was also regret.

"I... I want to, but I shouldn't," he said, holding my gaze, pleading silently for me to understand.

I smiled at him and nodded. "I'm going to get some sleep. Wait for me?" I asked.

He pulled my hand, which still clutched his, to his mouth and pressed a soft kiss to the backs of my fingers.

"Forever," he said, before turning and walking away.

41

KATE

The next evening, I awoke in bed feeling better—more than better, I felt great. I looked at the clock on my phone and was surprised to see it was still very early. According to Google, the sun wouldn't set for another hour. I stared at my phone, confused. I had never woken up this early before; I didn't even know it was possible. At least I had the good sense to check before heading upstairs.

I decided to take a long bath while I waited. I was grateful for the ensuite. I knew the shutters were down in the lounge and the hall door would be closed, but it still made me uncomfortable to think about leaving my room before the sun was safely over the horizon.

When I went upstairs over an hour later, Marcus was already up and out on the porch. I sat beside him on the steps, and soon Sara came out to join us. She was dressed in a parka, hat, and gloves, which contrasted with the thin clothing Marcus and I were wearing. I marveled at how quickly I'd grown used to my new normal.

"What are you guys talking about?" Sara asked.

"What to do now," I said. "I'm grateful to be free of Alexander and James, but I don't know what comes next. I asked Marcus about jobs at the Council, but that doesn't seem like a good fit for me. I don't know," I sighed.

"You don't have to work for the Council. You could always apply to a different House," Marcus said. "Your... condition might complicate that, however."

"You think?" I said in a sarcastic tone. "I don't want to be eaten by my new housemates. Or have to keep my guard up all the time."

Marcus winced.

"Sorry," I said. "I wasn't thinking. At least now I know I can protect myself."

"You shouldn't have to," Marcus huffed out.

"Well, I don't want you to move out," Sara said. "I like living together. Plus, I would be lonely in this big house all by myself."

"Have you talked to your mom or aunt yet?" I asked.

Sara heaved a great sigh. *I was afraid of that.* "Yeah," she said. "Silas convinced me I needed to talk to them and tell them about what happened. And he was right. But it meant admitting to them that I'd been keeping things from them again. Let's just say they were less than pleased."

I lowered my gaze. I hated to think of the two of them being upset. They had done so much for me. I needed to talk to them, too. I hoped we would have that conversation soon, before it was decided what would happen to me, when I would have less control over where I went and who I talked to.

"Hey," Sara said. "It's not that bad. Yes, they're pissed, at me for not telling them about the meeting with James, and you for not calling them as soon as you knew I was missing, but they still love us. Both of us, Kate."

I took her hand and squeezed it. In turn, she leaned her head against my shoulder.

We all lapsed into silence, staring at the moon and stars overhead. It was beautiful—thousands upon thousands of points of light framed by the circle of dark pines.

Finally, Marcus broke the silence. "I think I may have an idea," he said. And we listened quietly as he laid out the plan.

Over the next few weeks, Marcus became part of the group. He was easy to get along with, and having an ally in the employee of the Vampire Council was convenient. Because of him, we managed to gather the little information we had. Even Silas had warmed up to him.

Silas spent over a week preparing a room for Marcus downstairs. He still needed to finish the attached bathroom, but it was far more comfortable than a storage closet. We all wanted Marcus to feel at home. He'd earned our trust and our friendship. And he seemed to feel the same about us.

Sara was working late in the shop off the main house one evening while I sat in the corner sketching. Drawing made me happy and kept my mind off all that happened over the last few months. Silas was there, too, helping Sara label the online orders for the next morning's mail drop. I noticed he was here almost every evening when I emerged from the basement. It was nice to see him, and Sara needed the help. Sara admitted things hadn't progressed as far as she would have liked with the two of them, but I was sure it was just a matter of time.

Since Sara's kidnapping, I had only seen her mom and aunt a few times. Things were no longer tense between us. I apologized, and they assured me I was forgiven. But things hadn't returned to how they were before. It was now mostly Sara alone working at the shop, her mom and aunt preferring to handle the production side of things. Maybe it was their way of letting Sara go, letting her grow up.

Silas approached Sara with a stack of completed envelopes. "Any more for me?" he asked.

She looked up from the boxes she assembled. "No, I think that's it. If you want, you could help me with these?"

He smiled, took a pile of boxes, and sat on the stool beside her. In a low voice, he asked, "Any word of James?"

Sara glanced at me, and I quickly looked down at my sketchbook. She knew I could hear them, but I wanted to give them the illusion of privacy.

"No," Sara said. "The last Marcus heard, he just disappeared. Alexander is trying to keep it quiet, but James handled all the business and communication for the House, and his absence has not gone unnoticed."

"Maybe Alexander killed him," Silas said.

His comment made me think. It was possible. He was, after all, the cause of most of what happened, and we knew Alexander was prone to violence. Marcus had the same thought and dug deeper, but as far as anyone knew, James was still alive, just gone.

I told them about James's plan for us to escape Alexander, and I suspected he'd followed through on his plans alone. However, this didn't mean that we dismissed him as a threat. We remained vigilant for any danger, whether it came from him, Alexander, or whoever Alexander might send to create trouble. So far, we had been left alone. I hoped that would last.

A noise outside interrupted my thoughts. I lifted my head and listened in the direction of the main road.

"Who's coming?" Sara asked.

"I have no idea," I replied.

At that moment, Marcus entered the shop through the door that linked it to the house. "It's your lawyer," he said with a grin on his face.

42

KATE

S ara and Silas remained behind the counter while Marcus and I went to welcome the lawyer. When I opened the shop door and looked outside, I saw a bright orange Jeep with the top down pull into the lot and park.

The man who got out looked nothing like I expected. He was tall, well over six feet, and thin, with long blond hair that fell past his shoulders. Instead of a suit, he sported cargo shorts, a three-ring T-shirt, and a worn pair of old canvas sneakers. He looked like he just stepped off a beach in California. The only thing that seemed vaguely "lawyerly" was the large white envelope tucked under one arm.

Marcus went out, greeted the man with a quick embrace, and then led him to where I waited. He seemed uncharacteristically cheery, and my stomach instantly filled with butterflies.

"Kate, this is Felix. Felix, Kate," Marcus said.

Felix gave me a wide, fangy smile and held out a hand. I shook it gratefully. "Thank you for everything you've done to help," I said. This was our first meeting, but according to Marcus, we owed a lot to this particular vampire.

"Don't thank me yet," he said, giving me a wink before letting go and entering the shop.

Confused, I glanced at Marcus, hoping he would explain. He just smiled and followed Felix inside. The lawyer clearly came with good news, but his response had me on edge. I shook my head and turned to go back in.

Introductions had already been made, and all eyes rose to me as I closed the door, and I made my way around the tables of witchy wares to where everyone gathered. Felix had placed the oversized envelope on the counter in front of him, and it drew my eye.

"Felix called on his way over," Marcus said. "The plan worked. The Council agreed and signed off on everything."

"They did?" I asked, glancing up.

"Have a look," Felix said, pushing the envelope in my direction.

It was made of thick paper and looked expensive. It was something custom-made, not the sort of thing you would pick up at your local box store. I opened the flap at the top and drew out the documents inside. I turned them over and blinked down at what was in my hands. I furrowed my brow. "But this isn't right," I said. "I don't understand."

I looked up at Marcus, who just grinned at me. "No, it's right," he said.

"But, it can't... I can't... I mean..." I looked back down at the paper.

It was a charter for the establishment of a new House, just as we'd discussed. But it was the name of the House that rattled me so badly.

Written across the top of the charter were the words:

The House of Ward

Listed as head of the household was my name.

Kathrine Diane Ward

"But, I thought *you* would be the head of the House?" I said to Marcus. "I've been a vampire for all of ten minutes. How could the Council possibly agree to give me my own House?"

He shook his head. "It was not without difficulty and a lot of debate. No one as young as you has ever been granted a charter before. Felix here pulled a lot of strings, but he and I both agreed that this is your show. I'll sign on as a member, but this is your House. Not mine," he said, grinning at my distress. "Anybody got a pen?" he asked.

I watched in disbelief as Sara handed him a pen, and Marcus motioned for the papers. I handed them over, and he flipped through the pages until he came to the right one. Felix helpfully pointed to the space at the bottom reserved for member signatures.

We all shuffled closer to watch. This seemed like a big moment and not just for the vampires.

I glanced at Sara, who was just as interested as the rest of us. "We didn't really talk about it, but would it be okay if we lived here? Could we make this the location of our new House, at least for now?"

I knew I sounded timid, not at all like a House leader should. But the truth was, I was terrified. I was terrified of taking this on, of what it would mean for me and Marcus, but also terrified that it would change things between Sara and me. I had been offered a home here with her, and I didn't want to give that up. I wanted things to continue as they had these past weeks. I wanted us to still be a family. I was terrified that Sara would say no.

"I have one condition," Sara said, and she, too, looked worried but determined. "I want to be part of your House. I want my name on the charter, too."

I blinked again. "Is that even possible?" I asked. I glanced at Marcus and then at Felix. I figured if anyone would know, it would be the lawyer.

Felix smiled. "You know," he said. "Marcus asked me a very similar question. I went through all the regulations regarding House members, and nothing in the wording specifies that House members must be vampires. Isn't that interesting? I guess no one would have thought to include non-vampires as members. Until now." He quirked a blond eyebrow at me and then tilted his head in Sara's direction. I nodded and glanced at my best friend, who stared back wide-eyed.

"Sara, I would be honored if you would be part of my House," I said.

Sara took the pen from Felix and walked around the counter. Marcus moved out of the way, and Sara bent over the charter and signed her name right below Marcus's. She stood up and smiled at me.

I could feel the tears sliding down my face, but I didn't care. "What will your mom and aunt say?" I asked, sniffling.

"It doesn't matter," Sara replied, her voice steady and strong. "I need to make choices for myself. I'll handle the fallout, but I want this, and I'm not a child anymore. It's my choice, and I choose us." She turned to Silas, who had come out from behind the counter to stand beside her. She reached out, took his hand, and turned back to face me.

I looked over at my friends standing in front of me: Sara, Marcus, and even Silas. Maybe one day he would be more than just Sara's boyfriend, and I would be happy to have him as part of the House too. At that thought, I felt my world click into place. I was still scared. I still had a lot of unanswered questions, and I still doubted whether I had what it would take to lead a House. But I knew I wasn't alone. This was my family. My House

The House of Ward

Please take a moment to leave an honest review. It really helps me, as an independent author, reach more readers like you. And thank you for reading Book 1 in the House of Ward series!

Leave a Review Here.

Don't let the adventure end here!

Order book 2, **Bonded by Friendship and Fate,** now.

For a preview and access to exclusive bonus chapters, join
my newsletter and become a member of
The House of Abbott.

ACKNOWLEDGMENTS

No book is written alone, and *Founded on Blood and Magic* is no exception. I am deeply grateful to the incredible people (and one determined dog) who helped bring this story to life.

To my dedicated Alpha Reader—thank you for being the first to see the raw heart of this novel and for encouraging me to keep going when the path felt uncertain. Your insight and belief in the story made all the difference.

To my wonderful Beta Readers—your thoughtful feedback, sharp eyes, and generous time helped shape this book into what it was meant to be. Thank you for your honesty, your enthusiasm, and your patience.

To my loving husband—your love, support, and endless cups of most excellent coffee kept me grounded and inspired to push on when the going got tough.

To my two wonderful children—your creativity and affection remind me every day why dreams matter. I hope you always follow your own magic.

And finally, to my quirky border collie—thank you for herding me to my desk each morning, rain or shine. I couldn't have written this without your punctuality and your tail-wagging encouragement.

With all my heart, thank you.

A.R. Abbott

ABOUT THE AUTHOR

A.R. Abbott is an emerging author of contemporary paranormal fantasy. She's also a designer, illustrator, and lover of all things supernatural. Currently based in Northern Virginia, she has spent her adulthood moving around the world with her diplomat husband while raising two amazing children. Her passion for vampire lore, stories of witchcraft, and the complexities of power and relationships has always been at the heart of her storytelling. Her debut novel, *Founded on Blood and Magic,* is the first book in *The House of Ward* series.

Join the House at arabbott.com

A.R. Abbott can also be found on:

facebook.com/A.R.AbbottAuthor

instagram.com/a.r.abbott

bsky.app/profile/arabbott.bsky.social

9 781967 520022